PRAISE FOR YEAR'S BEST HARDCORE HORROR

"…glutted with graphic scenes of torture, dismemberment, evisceration, and pornographic
sex." (Vol. 2)

—Publishers Weekly

"Not for the faint of heart or weak of stomach,
the 19 stories in this new best-of annual anthology feature episodes of graphic gore and
violence—including torture, dismemberment,
self-mutilation, and home abortion—that are
designed to push buttons as well as boundar-
ies—strictly for hardcore horror fans." (Vol. 1)

—Publishers Weekly

ALSO BY RANDY CHANDLER

EDITOR:
Stiff Things: The Splatterporn Anthology
Red Room Magazine
Year's Best Hardcore Horror

NOVELS AND COLLECTIONS:
Stolen Roads
Bad Juju
Daemon of the Dark Wood
Devils, Death & Dark Wonders
Dime Detective
Duet for the Devil (with t. winter-damon)
Hellz Bellz
Angel Steel

EDITED BY CHERYL MULLENAX

Stiff Things: The Splatterporn Anthology
Red Room Magazine
Year's Best Hardcore Horror
Vile Things: Extreme Deviations of Horror
Sick Things: Extreme Creature Anthology
The Death Panel: Murder, Mayhem and Madness
Necro Files: Two Decades of Extreme Horror
Deadcore: 4 Hardcore Zombie Novellas
Deadlines: Horror and Dark Fiction

YEAR'S BEST
HARDCORE
HORROR
VOLUME 5: GOING GLOBAL

EDITORS:

RANDY CHANDLER
CHERYL MULLENAX

Red Room Press

WWW.REDROOMPRESS.COM

First Red Room Press Trade Paperback Edition
May 2020

Red Room Press is an imprint of Comet Press

ISBN: 978-1-936964-14-7

Visit Red Room Press on the web at:
www.redroompress.com
facebook.com/redroompress
twitter.com/redroombooks

Copyrights Continued on page 280

RED ROOM PRESS

WWW.REDROOMPRESS.COM

Diabolically dedicated to all the hardcore and extreme publishers, editors, and authors.

TABLE OF CONTENTS

GOING
GLOBAL

INTRODUCTION BY
RANDY CHANDLER AND
CHERYL MULLENAX

2019. The year certainly made its mark on the world—and more than its share of scars. It also made for a bounty of good horror stories of the extreme kind, the best of which the tales herein serve to illustrate.

2019 was the year YBHH went global. Not by design but because the stories inside just happened to have been written by authors hailing from various parts of the globe. From Australia by way of South Africa, to Italy, Scotland, Norway, Taiwan, North America and India—the common denominator being that their tales come from darkest regions of imagination.

Kicking things off in fine feminist fashion, Hailey Piper flips the script in "Feast for Small Pieces" to show us things from the perspective of the *femme fatale* herself. If she *is* a wicked seductress, maybe she has good reason.

Kristopher Triana carves out his return to our pages with "Goddess of Gallows" from Necro's irreverent *The Big Book of Blasphemy*. With his trademark hardcore style, Kris pulls no punches and won't leave you hanging—but Ixtab the Mayan goddess whose name translates as "hangwoman" might have other ideas.

"Late Night Incident At The White Trash Motel" ponders what would happen if the director of a film similar to *Get Out* was kidnapped by white nationalists. Duane Bradley has it all worked out in his "black" redneck noir comedy.

From one of our favorite anthologies of the year, *The New Flesh: A Literary Tribute to David Cronenberg,* comes Gwendolyn Kiste's "A New Mother's Guide To Raising An Abomination." In true Cronenbergian spirit, she offers advice you won't find in any self-help articles. Seth Brundle would surely get it.

From perhaps the unlikeliest anthology of the year, *Tales From The Crust,* cooked up by David James Keaton and Max Booth III, we serve up "Upper Crust" by Michael Paul Gonzalez. Turns out the guys really deliver the goods with all the tasty horror toppings. The trick will be forgetting what you read here the next time you order pizza.

Annie Neugebauer also makes a return to our pages with "Redless." Annie describes this one as "nutso and fun" and we think you'll agree (if you have a hankering for hardcore gore and juicy storytelling).

Bram Stoker Award-winning author Tim Waggoner is back with "A Touch of Madness," Tim's disturbing take on the fear of insanity from *The Pulp Horror Book of Phobias*. When the consummate horror writer plumbs these pulp depths, you know you're in for a shuddering treat. Don't be surprised if this one wins Tim another prize.

When Joseph Bouthiette Jr. recommends stories to us, we always pay close attention because he has never steered us wrong. As editor of *Honey & Sulphur,* he turns out some of the best fiction and poetry available anywhere. Joanna Koch's "Paradisum Voluptatis" is an ekphrasis of Hieronymus Bosch's "The Garden of Earthly Delights." It's absolutely one of the best stories we read this year and we thank Joseph and Joanna for the privilege of reprinting it here.

Sean Patrick Hazlett pays tribute to Thomas Ligotti in his examination of the *root of all evil* in corporate corruption with "Radix Malorum," an eerie tale haunted by smiling flesh balloons.

Also from the Cronenberg tribute anthology is Leo X. Robertson's "Lackers." A journalist investigates a strange new community who celebrate their physical imperfections in this twisted orgy of body horror.

Rajiv Moté guides a return trip to Bosch's Garden of Earthly Delights—but what could possibly be delightful in a landscape of monsters, torture, and mayhem? See for yourself in "Why Do Birds Suddenly Appear?"

Syon Das's "Darjeeling" takes us along with a group of teenage scouts to the Himalayan town to spend a night at the Banerjee

Estate, a place with a haunted history of brutal murder. But the housekeeper has been keeping a terrible secret in the years since the slaughter occurred.

In "MRSA Me" Alicia Hilton tells this chilling story from the point of view of Methicillin-resistant Staphylococcus aureus, a bacterium that causes infections in different parts of the body and for which there is no sure cure. As Alicia's tale so vividly demonstrates, the unseen threats are the most terrifying.

In "What Did You Do To The Children" David L. Tamarin gives us an unhealthy dose of torture porn with a decidedly demented twist. Anyone easily triggered should probably skip this one.

Next comes Matthew V. Brockmeyer's "Have A Heart." Some tales tug at your heartstrings, but this one may rip it right out of your chest. This is a deeply disturbing story of a small child in hopeless jeopardy. If you thought Stephen King's "Gerald's Game" was unnerving, be warned: this tale is much more so.

D.A. Xiaolin Spires takes us on a tour of the tallest building in the world: Taipei 101. If you've never seen this magnificent building in Taiwan, we suggest you find images of it online so you can truly picture the full body-horror effect. This story is from Sarah Read's *Gorgon: Stories of Emergence,* a wonderful compendium of new myths of transformation. Highly recommended.

Alessandro Manzetti's "Kirti" gives us a rickshaw ride to a *rendezvous* with an enticing Calcutta prostitute named Kirti. We wouldn't say her john's bitten off more than he can chew but things certainly don't go according to his lusty plan.

From Melbourne, Australia, Deb Sheldon delivers the ultra-violent historical tale "The Tea and Sugar Train." Trust us, this is in no way a tea party. There are bloodthirsty monsters in the harsh desert lands of the Outback and the pregnant protagonist has to fight for her life.

Also from Down Under, Ben Pienaar introduces "Stargirl,"

a psychopathic musician who attempts to create a new kind of music using the sounds of suffering. She starts by torturing small animals but doesn't stop there. As her fame spreads round the world, the effect of her strange sound begins to manifest in disturbing ways. With no end in sight.

Scáth Beorh wraps things up with *Queer Weather: A Poetic Tablua Rasa*. This mind-bending poem could be a love/hate letter to God, or something else entirely. Take it as you will. It's a fitting coda to this year's cursed tome. For now we'll wrap this up so you can get on to the tales. As Scáth says in his poem:

"Embrace these misty monsters now
they are your brothers, sisters."

—Randy Chandler & Cheryl Mullenax

FEAST FOR SMALL PIECES

HAILEY PIPER

From *The Bronzeville Bee*
Editor: Sandra Ruttan

Never underestimate the seductive power of a woman who's minding her own business.

"There's just something about her," they say. I see myself splashed across a pulp magazine cover, a distraught man in the background. The tagline reads, "He met a woman he Could. Not. Resist." As if that's my problem.

These writers don't realize it's me they've placed in their stories. I'd hoped to escape them when I left England, but their tide is unending. They scarce remember passing me on the street, only the fire I've lit in their minds, hearts, and other places. Later they sit with their notebooks or keyboards, tapping out the story of how a man's peaceful life was shattered when he met me in some chance romance.

Sometimes I'm cast as a vampire. Other times I'm the half-human spawn of an elder god. I might be Eve. Never the same, but always me.

Half of these fictional sisters show no interest in men, while others drown in men's wishes. She dressed that way that night knowing she'd rock his world. Her genetics must've known she'd meet him someday and grew her bones and flesh to suit him. We're all so subtly loud in men's eyes.

Feast on a true story.

I visit a grocer to buy tomatoes, plump ones. A man approaches. Were he to write about me, it would be my fault, but the pen is in my hand today. Whether I wear a hoodie two sizes too big with baggy jeans that hide my figure or a skirt that barely passes my waist, it does not matter. I am buying tomatoes.

"Hey, pretty lady. Doing anything tonight?" He shuffles behind me, impatient. "What, you have a boyfriend?"

It's never the same. A compliment, an insult, requests for my name, marital status, smiles, evening plans, swept to sea on tides of apathy.

"If you're single, why not go out with me?"

"Because I don't want to."

Here comes the outrage. Some don't need to be spurned first. Even seeing a woman they like reminds them of their frailty, how their blood is dragged as the moon drags the tide. I don't know them inside, but I've seen what comes out. I'm more fortunate than most. For the woman across the street, this is the moment he beats her or runs her down with his car, anything to destroy her.

His angry words breathe down my neck, all names I've heard before.

I turn, the first time I set eyes on him. "You will leave."

A writer would have slunk away to jot me down as beldam or succubus. A painter might color me an untouchable mother. To a musician, a ballad would pretend we were lovers. They dream of joining me as I dream of leaving them. We live in a world where my fantasy is to buy groceries unmolested.

But this man is no creator. There is no art to him, only crude craving by the responsibility in his pants that I never knew was mine. He would destroy me.

I abandon my shopping today, tomatoes in their basket. "Follow," I say. A stupid part of his brain might believe he's going to get his way.

Killing him would be kind. He would die believing himself like those pulp heroes, a tragic figure who lays his fate at my feet. When they persist, I give them purpose. These men wish I was a vampire, a cosmic demon, a witch. They wish for a clean death.

My workshop is a wooden shed behind my cozy house. By the rustic shingles, sweet green grass, pleasant canary yellow paint, you could never tell what I do there. I keep it insulated, the walls soundproofed. It stinks with heavenly residue. No matter how many airings out I try through its open wooden double doors, the smell remains.

The persistent men never notice. I lead this one inside, where on a wooden workbench I keep my tools shaped from fallen stars, across from the four-poster bed. It's soft, comfortable; its guests will spend a great deal of time on it. I order him to strip and then lie down. He's too eager to tear his clothing away and stretch across the crimson sheets.

That isn't the only stripping I need.

Doors closed, I dig my fingers into the workshop wall and tear aside a curtain that blocks this world from the shining heaven few ever notice. In that place, flesh is scarce and sanctified. Even his. Its cosmic perfection pours into his body, makes him ready to be given purpose. My fingers begin the work.

"Lie still," I tell him. His fearful eyes dart this way and that, but he won't get up. It is enough to work with.

There are worthy causes everywhere you look. Here, a woman's vertebrae rub together, causing her daily pain. There, another's skin is missing after a house fire. Blood, hair, eyes, intestines, bones. When I've placed a persistent man in my workshop, I strip what he has, cleanse it in unearthly light, and use it to mend the hurt I see around me. His pieces live on in these healed women, aware. They are pieces put to better purpose than serving him.

A month passes. He is only bone and fragments of skin and muscle. Still aware, still staring from the bed. I need not tell him to lie still anymore; he has no choice. In my neighborhood, a girl falls from a tree and snaps her leg. It could heal with a fracture line, but I make it good as new. Another woman cannot move on after her mother's untimely death. She doesn't know, as I offer her coffee, that it's laced with the strength to find purpose again. She thanks me for the coffee, not the gift from the persistent man.

Everything he was becomes forfeit, even his time, even his will. I waste nothing.

The work finished, I eat what little is left of him. It is only fair after he's put me off supper for weeks. He lives briefly in my digestive track before those remnants, too, are stripped away, become me.

Eventually the women and girls he's helped will grow new cells in their livers and skin, replacing his pieces. He'll fade from the world little by little while the good he's done persists.

Hand that fate to the pulp hero, to the writers, painters, musicians, let them blame me for finding that some men are greater as the division of their parts. I do not shatter lives. They shatter themselves against me, panes of glass thrown at an immovable rock, long weatherworn by rain, eroded slick by frothing waves.

And the tide is unending.

AUTHOR'S STORY NOTE

There was a day at a subway station where a man would not leave another woman alone. That happens a lot, but this was worse than I'd seen or experienced before. She explained a dozen times in so many words that she wasn't interested, and yet he still wouldn't let up. I wanted to speak up, but I didn't want his attention either. The moment stuck.

Much later, I happened to read, between different magazines and anthologies, three stories in a row where the protagonist was a glum man who destroys his own life in pursuit of a supernatural femme fatale, yet the narratives put her in the wrong. By the end of the last, I was bristling same as that day at the subway station. The woman at the station and the femme fatale stood alive as one individual in my mind. She needed to speak.

GODDESS OF GALLOWS

KRISTOPHER TRIANA

From *The Big Book of Blasphemy*
Editors: Regina Garza Mitchell & David G. Barnett
Necro Publications

deal? Probably an overdose of painkillers while in a Jacuzzi."

Pete rolled his eyes. "Seems a bit blasé. How about being fired out of a cannon?"

John put his drink on the bar. "I'm talking realistically."

"What about jumping off Mount Everest?"

"Nah. That mountain is covered in shit."

"What?"

"It's true. So many people have left their feces behind you can't even melt the snow to drink. It's too contaminated."

"Jesus," Pete chuckled. "Alright, so how about dying doing something you love?"

Now it was John's turn to roll his eyes. "I don't believe in love. Not after Carol."

Pete had always lent his ear to John when he lamented over his divorce, but they'd already been over that topic this evening. He ignored John's lead and pressed on.

"There are still things to enjoy. Why not go out doing one of them?"

"Suicide by cop could be fun. Go out like I'm in the old west, gunned down by the law."

Pete shook his head. "You really don't know how to have a good time, man. Have a threesome and then get the women to shoot you instead."

"Didn't I say *realistic suicide*? I've never had a threesome. I haven't even been laid in, like, seven months."

"That's 'cause you make zero effort."

John signaled the bartender for another. "You're one to talk. You forget where we met?"

Pete smiled only with his eyes, a true victim of depression, the kind he'd endured before this recent change. It had led him to the support group, a coffee-guzzling gaggle of miserable and mentally ill introverts, one of which had been John.

21

"Yeah," Pete said. "But the difference between us is you still go to those meetings."

"And *you* still talk about suicide. Now you just do it when you get drunk with me."

"Well, I've chosen hanging as my ideal suicide. It's classic, even poetic. And when it comes to getting laid—"

The bartender slid over John's fourth drink and went back to fussing with dishrags. John did not sip from it. He was waiting for Pete to continue.

"So . . . what about getting laid?" John asked.

Pete raised his eyebrows. "You wouldn't believe me."

"Tell me anyway. Fantasies are all I've got."

"Let's just say I've been having good nights. Good days too."

John leaned in, hungry. "Oh yeah? What's a good day for you?"

Pete put his hand on John's shoulder and the intimacy of it, even between two heterosexual male friends, made John's heart swell. He'd been missing the touch of others more than he realized.

"What makes my days so good," Pete said, "is that they're nothing like what my good days used to be. Until recently, for me a good day was when I could sleep in instead of going to work, followed by me lying in bed reading mindless articles on my phone. *Whatever happened to Emilio Estevez*; shit like that. If I didn't need to take a morning dump I may never have left bed at all. I'd take my pills, apply my Rogaine, and eat junk food while watching TV in the dark until it was late enough for me to feel comfortable drinking."

John nodded, unfazed. Too many elements of Pete's story were personally familiar to shock him. Depression was funny like that. It drained not just your mind but also your body, causing it to react in stereotypical ways.

"Sounds like my weekends," John said, "except I start drinking the moment I get up."

He finished his Jack and Coke as if to prove it. His alcoholism was not only obvious, but visible. He had the bloated face and pink skin of all hard-drinking men in their forties. In time his nose would glow with busted capillaries, his eyes going permanently bleary, the sorrow behind them numbed by an elixir that was eating his insides. What little hope was left in John was fading like the last light of day before the darkness swallows everything, leaving only a cold, dead moon to illuminate the pain on his face.

But Pete seemed to think he could save him.

"What are you doing tomorrow night?" Pete asked.

* * *

John hated going out. He was haunted by the notion that anywhere he went might be the last place he ever did. Death's unpredictability followed him around like a starving dog. Easily exhausted by the presence of others, he restricted his social life to occasional, one-on-one outings with a friend. Unless he was going to work he stayed in, especially after the sun went down. *Too old*, he always thought, *too tired*. But Pete had made some very interesting promises. John doubted this party would deliver on them but, after the spectacular failure of his brief experiment with online dating, John saw this as a chance to mingle with the opposite sex, something he rarely had access to. And if the women were as friendly as Pete said they were, it might be worth sacrificing just another night of Netflix and bourbon.

The building was a brick shaft with windows that emitted no light. It reminded John of an old-fashioned firehouse, only timeworn, raw. North of dilapidated, south of rustic.

"You look like shit," Pete said.

He was standing on the curb in slacks and a button-up shirt, the kind John only wore for work. His thin hair was freshly cut, teeth somehow brighter even in the golden light of the streetlamp. John was wearing his most comfortable jeans with the holes in the knees and the gray hoodie with the permanent coffee stain, his typical Saturday attire. He hadn't shaved, hadn't even brushed his hair.

"Didn't know this was some gala event," he said. "You were pretty vague."

"I told you there'd be women. You could at least try not to look like you just got beaten up."

"Nah. I'm through polishing this turd. You get close enough to a woman and eventually she's gonna see who you really are. Best to be honest from the start. That's why all that Tinder crap doesn't work. People use pictures from ten years and thirty pounds ago, then wonder why you're disappointed when you see them in person. *This* is who I am."

He pulled a wrinkled cigarette from his pocket—no pack—and lit it up.

"This is who you *are*," Pete said, "but what about *who you want to be?*"

John blew smoke. "I don't know who that is."

"That's about to change."

"Christ, Pete, this isn't going to be some deal where we're going to end up selling steak knives is it?"

Pete smirked and put his hand on John's shoulder. "Now that would be something to really be depressed about."

＊　＊　＊

The interior was a vast improvement over the exterior of the building. Practical furniture. Soft light glinting off jewelry and wine glasses. Black curtains at the rear of the open ballroom. Ambient piano music cluttered by jovial conversation. Tailored suits and tight dresses with no backs. The crowd looked not rich, but elegant, as if they were at a wedding or award ceremony for some corporation. There were a few other people in jeans, but they were pressed and had none of the paint and grass stains John's had. A few wore simple t-shirts. Many had tattoos and facial piercings. The deeper John moved into the crowd, the more eclectic it seemed. Mostly Whites and Latinos, but some Blacks and Asians. Almost everyone was drinking. When John spotted a young woman smoking, he lit up too, grateful to be able to relieve some anxiety. He kept beside Pete, who was weaving through the others like a football player going for the end zone. He was a different man than the one John had met at the support group. His face was bright. Ten years seemed to have fled from it.

"Some party," John said, but Pete either didn't hear him or was too focused on getting wherever they were going.

They kept on. People were looking at them. No, not at them—at John. Women met his gaze then looked him up and down as he passed by. Some men did the same and John averted his eyes. He was tempted to talk to a redhead who wet her lips as she stared at him like he was a dessert cart, but was too worried about losing sight of the only person he knew here. They rose up to an area slightly elevated over the rest of the floor and Pete stopped before a large man with a shaved head. He wore black lipstick that matched his neck tattoo, a black bar that ran completely around his neck.

"This is John," Pete said.

He shook the man's meaty hand.

"Galveston," the man introduced himself. He turned back to Pete. "She went to the back with a newcomer, but that was maybe forty minutes ago. Shouldn't be much longer."

They stood there in a silence that only seemed awkward for John. When a woman came by with a tray of drinks, he snatched one that looked like whiskey. It was smooth, pure; a big change from the rotgut he was used to. A hallway lit by black lights glowed behind Galveston. Even above the music, the sound of a door opening echoed down the hall, and two shapes emerged, one thin, one round. Their skin was an alien purple in the light, the skinny one moving out of the shadows to reveal himself as a man, a Joker smile spackled onto his young face. He drifted into the crowd below. The larger shape's hips moved in feminine manner, the body a swollen hourglass. Dark hair. Gold dress and matching bracelets. A beautiful face on a plus-size body.

"Hello, Pete," the woman said.

Pete's smiled shined, a child flying his first kite. He took the woman's hand, kissed it. John actually scratched his head at this formal, outdated gesture.

"Ix," Pete said. "You are more lovely every time I see you."

Gag, John thought. *And what the hell kind of name is* Ix?

"This is my friend, John."

Ix's eyes fell upon him. They were painted in an Egyptian manner. Cleopatra, a Sphinx.

"This is your guest of choice?" she asked Pete, to which he nodded. "He certainly looks in need."

John crossed his arms, unsure if he should be offended. When Ix extended her hand to be kissed, he reluctantly did so. She pointed somewhere behind him and John turned to look. A petite blonde woman was smiling at him from behind the rim of a wine glass. A blue choker necklace emphasized her large eyes.

Ix leaned in to him. "Do you want her?"

"What?"

"Do you want to sleep with Angelica?"

He looked back to Ix. She was closer now, huge. "Sleep with?"

"Yes. Unless you're interested in someone else."

John's face soured. Now he understood. "Listen, um, I don't think I can afford—"

"This is not a whorehouse, John. This is a gateway. There will be no payment other than your own body."

John turned back to Angelica, his lips going tight. She was one of those women so attractive it pains you to look at her. And she was coming toward him, this mirror of Taylor Swift, this Naomi Watts impersonator.

"I'd be crazy not to want to sleep with her," he said.

Ix put her hands on his shoulders. She smelled of stale perfume but it failed to cover the odor of the sex she'd just had.

"Well then," she said. "There's no sense in going mad, now is there?"

* * *

All he wanted was water. In his everyday life he never touched the stuff, but his everyday life didn't include fluid-draining sex with a beautiful woman. John felt withered. The sheets stuck to him as he sat up, moving Angelica's pale arm from off his abdomen. She turned over, snoozing. He thought about waking her up with a surprise insertion, but his dry throat told him it had to wait. He clumsily put on his clothes and shuffled into the hall of black lights in search of the drink-tray woman, finding Galveston first. The big man took him by surprise with a bro-hug, smacking his back as they embraced.

"Welcome, brother."

"Um, thanks."

"You're just in time. The ceremony is about to begin."

"Ceremony?"

But he could already hear the crowd.

"Come on," said Galveston. "You don't wanna miss this."

The big man kept his arm around John's shoulder, a father leading his son into a baseball stadium for the first time. They exited into the main room where the others were gathered. John tensed at the sight. He'd never seen so many naked people in one place. It was like some intense, embarrassing dream, especially when he spotted Pete in the throng, his boney ass bare to this gathering of nudists. A new tattoo that matched Galveston's had swelled his skin pink, a black bar that ran around his neck like a preacher's collar. Pete did not notice him in return. He was too busy shouting the same unsettling words as the others.

"Ixtab!" they cried, clapping. "Praise Ixtab!"

John's throat went dry. Galveston began to strip and when John stepped away from him a slender arm wrapped around his neck, squeezing gently. He recognized Angelica's scent just as her tongue went into his ear canal. When he sighed she clenched his neck tighter. Too tight. Nude now, Galveston joined the crowd just as it began to change shape, as if a line were forming for half of them while the others stepped to the sidelines. The rear wall was still hidden behind curtains, and before them was a long-backed chair, a purple throne with gold onions on the top. He excused himself, pulled out of Angelica's hold and moved up the platform that overlooked the main floor.

Ix was seated in the chair atop a pedestal, her plump, naked body slouched in the seat, a young man between her legs, his face in her crotch. Her huge breasts flopped to each side of the chair, a man holding one, a woman holding other, both slurping milk from the engorged nipples. All three of these worshippers had nooses around their necks, the ends of the ropes held by others who watched on. John stepped back, hoping to find a shadow to hide in. Maybe there was an emergency exit somewhere. He checked his pocket for his phone, knowing damn well it must be gone. So were his wallet and keys. He turned his head to the black hallway he'd come out of. Angelica was gone too. She must have joined the others in their cabalistic hailing of Ix.

He made slow steps backward. That's when Pete spotted him. As his friend trotted toward the platform, genitals flapping, John's feet froze instead of running as they'd been told to do. Pete hugged him even harder than Galveston had.

"Welcome to the fold, my friend!"

John slid out of his embrace. "What the fuck, Pete?"

"Huh?"

"What is this?"

Pete smiled with farm boy innocence. "Can't you see?"

"I see a cult."

"No, no, no. This isn't a cult—"

"The hell it isn't."

"This is the answer, brother."

"What's the goddamn question?"

"All the questions, John. This is it. The solution!"

"What is? Random sex or lapping at that fat cow?"

Pete's jaw went hard. "I know this is a surprise you need to adjust to, so I'll pretend you didn't blaspheme about the goddess."

"Ix isn't a goddess. Do you even hear yourself?"

"Ixtab. The indigenous Mayan goddess, from the time of the Spanish conquest of Yucatán."

John sighed. "Jesus, Pete . . ."

"Jesus was a false prophet. She's the real thing."

"I want my keys and phone back—"

"Brother, listen to me. She's not just any goddess."

"—and my wallet."

Pete grabbed John's head, forcing him to look him in the eye. Pete's were large like Angelica's, dilated and bloodshot, screaming with a crazed, new life.

"John, she's the ancient goddess of suicide by hanging."

*　*　*

More than half the crowd was on the floor.

It was a writhing mass of flesh. Sweaty limbs. Pumping hips. The wet, slapping sound of fucking. The ones that weren't part of the orgy on the floor were having sex standing or kneeling. And there were nooses everywhere. Rope, leggings, wire—a gallery of autoerotic asphyxiation. There were leashes that ended in a series of collars so one master could choke three people at once. John felt as if he were witnessing a porn film with an all-rabid cast. Galveston was on his knees, taking turns sucking off two different men while another choked him with a leather belt. Three others were penetrating Angelica in every orifice at once while she pinched their throats with choke chains. She clenched them in her fists like the reins of horses she intended to break. And the line to give Ix head and suckle at her mighty tits was an endless train of bodies, a black mass of sexual mania.

"I'm your idol," she moaned above the noise of the ground.

Pete took John's arm. Being the stronger of the two, he managed to haul John into the throng of sweating perverts. All John could do was try to reason with him.

"Look, Pete. It's cool if this is your thing, but I don't think this is right for me."

"You haven't even begun to understand what this is really all about. Didn't you enjoy Angelica?"

"Yeah, of course, but this whole—"

"Free love is just the beginning. You've been looking for the right escape, for something to show you the way out of the pain of being alive. Ixtab isn't some empty promise politician. She isn't a god that goes unseen, who doesn't answer prayers because he's too busy letting children be raped in his own place of worship. She doesn't promote bigotry or encourage terrorist attacks. She's not a demanding goddess, she's a merciful one. That's why she always lactates, even though she hasn't given birth. She's a psychopomp, an angel that guides us from this world to the next."

"This is psycho. That's for sure."

Pete took John to the line and the others waiting stepped aside, welcoming the newcomer to cut ahead.

"Sex is freeing," Pete said. "It liberates us from regretting what we could have done in our time here and prepares us for what we've wanted all along. That's why a woman out of your league just slept with you. It was a way of setting you free from yourself."

Ix saw them approaching and shooed away the worshippers that licked at her body. Close up and in better lighting, John noticed the scar that ran completely around her neck. She spread her legs, her shaved sex glistening, and squeezed her pillowy breasts together, making the nipples ooze.

"Eat this pussy, for it is my body," she moaned. "Drink this breast milk, for I am the mother."

John resisted the urge to wince at this sickening communion. All eyes were on him now. He swallowed hard, crippled by the staggering peer pressure of a hundred lunatics. He turned to Pete in one last hope of finding his old friend behind those wild eyes. Instead he saw only madness.

John knelt before the goddess.

He drank of her.

*　*　*

Being nude made him feel even more helpless.

He was drenched in sweat, his dick pink and swollen from having just fucked Ix upon her altar, the cult cheering him on. He'd been coaxed into doing so. It was part of the initiation for all newcomers. She pulled him in deep when he ejaculated, and when he was finally released two women crawled across the floor to Ix. The older one held a bible. The women positioned themselves between Ix's thighs and when the older woman opened the bible the young one ripped two pages from it and curled them into thin tubes. Each woman put one to their lips, moved in toward Ix's sopping pussy, and slurped John's semen out of it with their biblical straws.

This triggered an even stranger orgy. People were breaking out costumes.

Ix rose from her throne and raised her hands.

"I am your idol," she proclaimed. "Let no other gods stand before me!"

From behind the curtains at the back of the ballroom, a shape moved into the crowd. There was wide applause as the man came through, carrying a crucifix on his back. A crown of thorns ripped into his bloody head and pinned down his long hair. A pair of vinyl-clad dominatrix women followed behind him, breasts exposed, faces concealed behind gimp masks. They cracked their whips, separating the flesh of his back.

To John's left came the sound of someone speaking in a foreign tongue. He turned to see a man dressed as Muhammad on his knees reading from the Quran while masturbating men formed a circle around him, showering him with ropes of semen. One of these masturbators had the image of Muhammad tattooed on one buttock, the ass hair shaved into the prophet's beard.

An orgy of blasphemy erupted. Crucifixes were used as dildos. Joseph sucked off Jesus while Mary was gang sodomized by wise men. A Star of David was used as a cock ring. A man took a dump on the floor, ripped the Quran from Muhammad's hands and wiped his ass with it before throwing it back at him. Muhammad laughed with bright joy. Each of the mock deities seemed in a state of euphoria, even the lashed-until-bloody Jesus.

John closed his eyes against the grotesquery. The insides of his eyelids made complex patterns of light and when he opened them again the light remained as mild hallucinations. He felt short of breath. Had his drinks been spiked? Had everyone's?

"Sacrilegious masochism only further proves our devotion to Ixtab," Pete explained. "We must cleanse ourselves of other gods."

"Look, I'm not offended. I'm agnostic. But I can do without the shitting on the floor."

"Some of it's disgusting, I admit, but no false idols can fill our hearts. Not in our moment of glory. There's word we've been found out, that the police or FBI are on to us. There's no time to waste."

Ix bounced across the sweaty bodies on the floor. A sheer, purple gown covered her without concealing anything.

"My sons," she said. "The sons of suicide."

John shivered despite the room's overwhelming body heat.

"You've brought us a worthy new member, Pete. He drips with a sorrow only I can heal."

John stammered. "Listen, um . . . I um . . ."

She put a finger to his lips. "Shhh. Hush now."

Her finger slid down his chin and found his throat. It ran across, the nail nearly sharp enough to shave his stubble.

"You have an elegant neck for a man. Did you know that?" She put her finger to the damaged flesh of her own throat. "Almost a shame to tattoo yours. Mine was never that pristine. It was altered upon my birth; my most recent reincarnation, that is. The umbilical chord strangled me as I was forced out of my mother." She titled her head back to give John a better look. "I was born dead but was resuscitated—*resurrected*."

Pete bowed his head. "Praise her."

"There's no escaping our past lives," Ix said, "and there's no escaping our fate."

Tears brewed in John's eyes but he was uncertain of their origin. He felt suddenly weightless, adrift. Pete put his arm around him.

"The ideal suicide, brother," he said. "Just like we always talked about. What could be better than doing it together, as part of one large group? Think of the bold statement it makes! Our deaths will be remembered. And we're only a single batch. The family keeps growing and moving. The Goddess of Gallows will guide new members from this world to the next. One mass suicide after another until our numbers topple the measly nine hundred of Jonestown."

There was a ruckus from the crowd. Ix turned away.

"Excuse me, my sons. It is time for the baptism."

She moved through the people on the floor, their hands jutting up to caress her thighs as she passed.

"Baptism?" John asked.

"I'm so excited. I was baptized, but I haven't seen a fresh one yet. It must be beautiful."

"A fresh one? Man, I don't like the sound of this. Please, we've got to get out here. This isn't the answer. You need help."

Pete's face pinched. "*I* need help? Didn't you remind me just yesterday where we met? A goddamn depression support group! It was like AA for suicide ideation. And you still go there, John. You still want to kill yourself."

"That may be, but I'd want it to be on my own terms. You force me to stay here and it's not suicide, it's murder."

Pete looked away. "Come on, man. Don't put that on me."

"It's fucking murder. I thought we were friends."

"We are! I love you like a brother. That's why you're here. They trusted me to pick one person to be a new member. *One*! And I picked you. You were the only person I knew who has dealt with the same hopelessness, the same pain as I have. But now I know all of these other people here, people just like us. There's no race here, no social status. No one's richer or poorer than the other. In suicide, we're all equal."

John nodded. "You know what? I'm okay with these people doing whatever they want. It's no skin off my ass if they want to choke each other to death while jerking off in the face of Jesus. But when it comes to my life and the life of my friend, I have to—"

A loud, musical note cut him off, like a single hit of a gong or someone pressing down on a pipe organ. John couldn't see the source of it. His vision blurred when he moved too quickly, making him woozy. But what he did see was all that mattered. The blood left his face, turning him albino white.

"No . . ."

Ix's chair had been replaced by a different kind of altar, a podium with a slab at the top the size of a cutting board. Beside it was a table, a silver bowl on top of it already half filled with blood. Standing over it was a man opening a vein in his forearm. He bled into the goblet of gore, those in line behind him stretching their necks to watch. But this wasn't what weighed down John's chest. What was on the podium's slab caused him to stop breathing.

The baby squirmed upon the board but did not cry, unaware of the madness of those who had placed her there. She wore a sheer, purple gown—a miniature of Ix's. A nude man stood at the podium, patting the fine hair on the infant's skull, and beside him was a woman holding his other hand. Long hair hid half of her face but the part John could see was calm to the point of serenity. Though much thinner than Ix, the woman's breasts were also engorged with milk.

The parents, John realized.

Ix appeared behind them like a wraith. Upon her head was a huge Mayan headdress, a crown of wood, cloth and brightly colored feathers. Jewels dazzled the engravings of jaguars upon her forehead. Her bracelets jingled.

"All praise Ixtab!" someone shouted.

The cult followed. "All hail Ixtab!"

John feared a weapon, but her hands were empty. *They did say* baptism, he thought, *not* sacrifice. He looked at the bowl of blood. The gatherers had been contributing to it three at a time. It was close to overflowing.

You have to do something.

He looked to Pete again. His friend was wide-eyed, but his expression was one of joy, not terror. He was gone now. No point looking to him for help. John stepped back but Pete was too engrossed in the ritual to notice. John moved through the crowd, shivering every time his flesh grazed someone else's. He felt filthy, diseased, as if the insanity all around him was transmitted via bodily pathogens. Still celebrating their new member, the others applauded his approach and gave him passage to the altar. He was close enough now to make a grab for the baby. The others would probably beat him to death before he could make it halfway to the exit. The woman with the drink tray appeared beside him, her nude body like a centerfold's. Instead of beverages there was a single, small length of rope curled upon her tray, a noose at the end just big enough to fit around the throat of . . .

"Take it," the woman said.

John could neither blink nor breathe.

"John, my son," Ix said, "take this noose. This baby is my new, true body. Just as I die tonight, so I will be reborn, entering the next life the same as I entered this one—doused in the blood of those who loved me . . . and strangled by them."

The infant's mother took the baby in her arms.

"Don't!" John cried, but the mother ignored him and dipped the infant in the wet gore. Now the child began to cry. "That's the blood of countless people. Any one of them could be carrying a disease!"

"There is only one true disease," Ix said. "The disease of existence, the result of which is endless suffering."

"Please, don't choke the baby. Let her experience life for herself. Don't make the ultimate choice for her."

Ix raised her hands. "There is no true choice. There is only one way."

The curtains behind her came all the way open.

Hidden behind them was a row of gallows, a wooden platform with five poles with which to hang people, trap doors where they would stand. It looked like something out of the old west, a morbid relic of public executions. Completing the picture, a muscly man with a protruding gut stood at the lever, a black mask concealing his face. And a neck filled each noose. Three men and two women stood upon the platform, nude and smiling, the ropes around their throats.

"Kill me," they chanted. "Praise the Goddess of Gallows."

John gasped as the lever was pulled. The trap doors opened with a deafening crack. He looked away, his stomach turning over. As the bodies swung, the crowd gazed up at the fresh corpses in glowing admiration, and John saw their distraction as an opportunity, the best and only one he could hope for.

He darted toward the baby.

The mother turned her head, seeing his intention, and pulled the child to her chest.

"I'm ready to do it now," he lied. "Seeing these people hang changed my mind. It's . . . it's so beautiful."

The mother eyed him, her mouth curling downward.

Ix looked back at John. "Take her. It is time for me to be delivered."

As the dead were freed from their killing ropes, Ix stepped up the platform, her weight bowing the wood. As the noose went around her neck, she nodded once at John, unflinching, unblinking. The mother stretched out her arms to offer him the blood-slicked baby. He scooped it up, took the little noose and fit it around the screaming infant's neck.

Run, he thought.

But there was nowhere to run to. Lunatics surrounded him, covered in cum and blood, nooses of varying materials around their necks. Some were being garroted by their lovers. Some were doing it to themselves, the muscles in their arms going taut as their faces bulged purple.

There was another loud crack and their goddess fell through the trapdoor. The crowd gasped in awe, and then there was another snapping sound as the hanging pole gave out, unable to sustain Ix's weight. She hit the ground below with a thud, causing her devoted followers to rush the stage to assist her, to show how much they cared, to gain any iota of additional love from their idol. Even the baby's parents turned their backs on it to dive into the stampede.

As the final members climbed up to the stage, John saw Pete at the front of them. He was crying. So were many others. But there was only so much time.

John ran toward the front doors. He didn't bother getting dressed. He didn't even bother undoing the baby's noose. He just ran, his every nerve gone electric. Some yelled from the stage. Others called his name. He ignored them as he reached the front door, pulled the handle and swung it wide, the crisp, clean air of the night hitting him before the lights did. They were red and white, swirling and flashing, dizzying him in his drugged state. Cars lined the street, blocking the way out as shadowed men rushed out of them.

"Show me your hands!" someone yelled.

Disoriented, John held out the bloody, screaming infant. The rope swung from its neck, dripping.

"Jesus Christ!" someone shouted. "He's got a baby!"

Two men in dark clothes flanked John on either side, one holding a gun on him while the other reached out as if waiting to catch a football.

"Give me the child," the man said.

The crowd behind John caught up to him. Sweaty hands reached for his limbs, nooses swinging for his neck. He lunged forward to escape and though he tried to clutch the child close to him the man who'd flanked him snatched it away, calling John a sick son of a bitch. John grabbed for it again just before seeing the man's badge.

The other officer fired three shots, but one was all it took.

AUTHOR'S STORY NOTE

"Goddess of Gallows" was written for *The Big Book of Blasphemy*, an anthology I was invited to by Necro Publications. It's about two friends, John and Pete, who both suffer from crippling depression. But Pete has found a new lust for life through a clandestine group. When Pete takes John to one of their private parties, he is introduced to an eccentric woman named Ixtab. John quickly realizes something is terribly wrong, but it may be too late for him to leave alive. The story was inspired by the indigenous Mayan goddess of suicide (a goddess whose existence has been debated by scholars). I also figured the other contributing authors would go after Christianity with their blasphemous tales, so I made it a point to insult as many religions as possible. As an atheist, I had fun with that.

LATE NIGHT INCIDENT AT THE WHITE TRASH MOTEL

DUANE BRADLEY

From *Deep Fried Horror*
Editor: Becky Narron
Deadman's Tome

Getting your ass whupped by a redneck is bad enough for a regular person, but when you're famous, it's worse.

When you're a stand-up comic turned actor-slash-director, when you've worked with big names and made a dozen films, when you've won awards and graced magazine covers and been linked to some of the most glamorous women in the world, losing a fight to someone named Zeke is about as humiliating as it gets.

In my defense, my mind was on other things. The African-American Film Critics Association and the Black Film Critics Circle had just showered me with awards for my movie *Neighborhood Threat*, a body swap horror picture where rich white folks transferred their souls into the bodies of poor black folks to give themselves a shot at immortality. Everyone thought I was Making A Statement and wanted to reward my good intentions, so who was I to tell them my movie was basically *The Mephisto Waltz* with a racial twist?

The critics quit kissing my ass shortly after midnight and I was searching for my car keys when Zeke jumped me in the parking lot. I've been in my share of fights (on film anyway) but nobody had hit me in the head for at least six months so when Zeke appeared I wasn't ready. That's my statement and I'm sticking to it.

If you've never woken up in the back of an El Camino with nothing except a spare tire and some moldy newspapers for company, I don't recommend it. Especially if you're coming to terms with having your ass handed to you by a fella with prison tattoos and missing teeth. I also do not recommend giving in to self-pity and going on a crying jag while covered in mildewing copies of the *Dallas Times Herald*.

This wasn't rock bottom, by the way. I didn't know it yet, but this was just the next rung down on a ladder that descended straight into Beelzebub's living room.

It's amazing how a long ride in a dirty trunk can alter your perspective. In the space of a few hours, I went from kidding myself that I was going to break some heads the moment they popped the trunk to admitting that there were probably several other guys besides Zeke and they all had shooters while I didn't. I didn't know where they were taking me or what the hell Zeke had in mind, but it probably didn't involve a nice meal and a mariachi band.

The car groaned to a halt. The driver set the brake, killed the engine and for the first time I heard Zeke's voice.

"When does it get light around here?"

"When the sun comes up," someone said.

"No fucking shit, Dick Tracy. You got an ETA on that?"

"Couple hours yet. Why?"

"It's a full moon tonight. I don't like being out in the sticks when it's a full moon."

Doors slammed. The trunk popped open.

Two shotguns filled the space, and behind the shotguns were two goons with tattoos and ripped t-shirts, central casting's idea of how a redneck might look. Behind the goons stood Zeke, not armed as far as I could see but clearly enjoying himself. A smug grin was smeared across his face like lipstick.

"*Hola*, Rudy," Zeke said. He pronounced it *hole-arr*. "Fellas, say howdy to Rudy Ray Washington. Back home in Cal-eye-for-nah-ay, he's the hottest ticket in town right now. Out there, he can name his price and do just about anything he wants. Hell, I bet he even gets to tell white people what to do. Give it up for Rudy, boys."

The goons clearly weren't fans. They stared straight ahead, shotguns raised, saying nothing.

"Don't mind if we take up some of your valuable time do you, Rudy? I mean, you're not working at the moment, are you?"

"Have your people call my people," I said.

"Ho ho, he's funny. He's lying in my trunk with guns in his

face and he's funny. Let's get him on his feet and see how funny he really is."

The goons reached inside and brought me out. We were in an empty tarmacadam lot, it was dark and there was a bad smell on the air, the kind you associate with a motel that rents rooms by the hour.

I staggered across the macadam to the room and thought about shouting for help, decided it probably wasn't such a good idea. These guys likely knew the motel owner, who I doubted was on the side of the angels.

Drawing the curtains, Zeke pulled the couch into the middle of the room and pushed me onto it.

"Okay," he said. "Cards on the table. From now on, your ass belongs to me. Got the deed right here, see? It says do what I say or I'm gonna shove my foot so far north that Rudy Jr is gonna feel it."

"I don't know you," I said, "but I'll tell you this much. Today, you got lucky. Any other day, I could whup a grizzly bear in a fair fight."

"That right?"

"I've got witnesses."

"Well, goddamn, I never would've thought. This is really messing up your head, isn't it? Getting clobbered by a white boy, I mean."

"Stranger things have happened."

"Like what?"

"Your mother fucked your father."

Zeke absorbed this.

"My mother was a saint," he said. "Mention her again and I'll kill you."

"Your mother was an asshole. She took a dump, dressed it in rags and named it you."

"What was that now?"

"Why don't you just say your piece and leave me at the nearest bus stop? I've got better things to do, and you've got a probation meeting in a few hours."

Zeke actually chuckled at that.

"Yeah, I heard you were funny," he said. "Heard your movies are a real hoot. I wouldn't know, I don't watch black propaganda films."

"Prefer *Barney The Purple Dinosaur*, huh?"

"It's easier to sit through. None of that shit white liberals want to hear, like how we should allow the races to mix. They think you do that, you're gonna end up in a utopia. Doesn't work like that. Once you mix the races, you're counting down to white genocide."

"I'm more of a *The Banana Splits* guy myself."

"You people don't find white civilization comfortable, that's your problem. Every time we tell you to follow the rules, you howl about being oppressed. We say walk down the sidewalk, not down the middle of the street, you scream oppression. We say stick to our standards of punctuality, you complain about victimization."

I didn't say anything. I had an image of seven-year-old Zeke sitting a test and giving up after five minutes because math was hard and drawing pictures was fun. He'd gone through school like that and when as an adult he realized he'd never earn decent money, somebody told him it was the fault of minorities and Zeke believed it.

"Victims, my ass," Zeke said. "You can't even follow our age of consent laws."

"There's a point to this, right?"

"Oh there's a point alright, *amigo*. There is definitely a point. I know how you all love to portray whites as lazy and stupid, but that's not the truth. We're smart. We're educated. We've been working on . . . hey, Charlie, what's that word again?"

"Regenerate," Goon #1 said.

"Regenerate, right. We've got a serum that attacks a body's bad cells and *regenerates* them as good cells. When you inject it into a black fella, it turns him into a white fella."

I stared at Zeke. He didn't look like he was kidding.

"We'll be the first people to try it out," he said. "It's gonna make us famous."

"No doubt about that."

"And rich."

"Unlikely."

"What do you think?"

I glanced back at Zeke. He still wasn't kidding.

I looked at the goons. They weren't kidding either.

"I think you're full of shit," I said.

"That's what I thought you'd say." He nodded to the goons. "Time for a demo."

Four arms pinned me to the couch. Zeke fished a hypo out of his pocket and held it up for me to see.

"You might feel a little prick," he said.

"You say that to all the guys."

"C'mon, it won't hurt a bit." He thought for a moment and said, "Well, maybe just a bit."

The goons held my arms from behind but my legs were free so when Zeke was close enough I lashed out. I got him a good one between the legs and as he bent double he tried to administer the injection while falling forward.

It didn't work.

Zeke was aiming for my neck but one of the goons had an arm there and Zeke's aim was off. When the needle broke skin on the goon's upper arm, the guy screamed like a girl, jumped backwards and, losing his footing, fell flat on his ass.

He hit the floor, *whump*, and instead of groaning and starting to get up he began screaming and lashing out. He pulled out the needle and sent it flying across the room.

Zeke said "Charlie?" a few times but Charlie wasn't home, he was coughing and spluttering and about ready to go into convulsions. With his eyes squeezed shut and his mouth open wide enough to reveal a full set of yellow gnashers, Ol' Charlie sure looked like he'd seen better days.

Curled into a fetal position with his head moving back and forth, he might've been a dog dreaming about chasing rabbits. This went on a while longer, then the spasms became twitches and eventually stopped. Charlie lay very still and looked very dead.

Zeke watched all this with folded arms and a disappointed expression. I didn't know the exact relationship between him and Charlie, but Zeke looked like he was mentally composing some bullshit excuse to Charlie's next of kin.

Goon #2, whose name turned out to be Marvin, knelt over Charlie and felt for a pulse.

"Well?" Zeke said.

"You want the good news first?"

"What's the good news?"

"He didn't shit his pants."

"What's the bad news?"

"He's fucking dead."

Zeke was quiet for a spell. He started pacing.

Eventually, he looked at me and said, "This is your fault."

"That's right, blame the other guy," I said. "That always works for you. What the hell was in that needle, anyway?"

"Weren't nothing bad," Zeke said. "Was supposed to scare you, is all."

"What was it?"

"Tap water."

"Sure it wasn't holy water?"

"Huh?"

"There must've been an air bubble. Have you ever given an

injection before?"

"Do I look like I have a degree in fucking medicine?"

"No," I said. "You look like a white trash dumbass whose stupid bullshit just killed a man."

Zeke soured.

"What we gonna do?" Marvin said.

"I'm not the brains here," I said, "but I vote we get the fuck out of Dodge."

"Copy that. How about it, Zeke?"

Zeke nodded.

"Motion carried," Marvin said.

There was a knock on the door.

"Aw shit," Zeke said. "I forgot about Grover."

"Who's Grover?" I said.

"Charlie's brother," Marvin said.

I looked at him.

"It was gonna be part of the gag," he said. "We'd shoot you up with water, then Grover'd come in dressed as a cop. The joke was, he'd escort you out of here, and just as you started to think you'd got away he'd beat your black ass and dump you by the side of the road."

"Ha ha," I said.

Another knock on the door.

A voice said, "Police."

Marvin looked to Zeke for support, which was like asking him to explain string theory. Zeke sighed, shook his head and gave his best *fucked if I know* shrug. I suspected that he used the shrug often.

Turning to me, Marvin said, "Give me a hand."

"To do what?"

"We're gonna put Charlie on the couch."

"Why?"

"So it looks like he ain't dead."

"I don't think that's going to work."

"Got any better ideas?"

I didn't say anything. While Marvin grabbed Charlie under the arms, I took his legs and we moved him into a corner of the couch, laying him with his arms spread out and his head on a cushion. Charlie still looked very dead but as Marvin noted, at least he hadn't shit his pants.

A kick sent the door wide and Grover stepped in, carrying a shotgun and looking like he meant business. Real cops didn't carry twelve-gauges on routine calls, but I wasn't explaining that to a guy who looked like he could swallow nails and shit you a tool box.

Grover was tall and built like a wrestler whose steroid intake should be closely monitored. His arms were thick with muscles and made the shotgun look like a peashooter. The uniform was more or less the right size, but it suited him the way a waistcoat suits a gorilla. He didn't make a very convincing cop unless the cop in question liked to scalp cheerleaders and wear their ears on a chain around his neck.

Having made his big entrance, Grover walked to the center of the room and, giving us his best Randy Savage stare, said, "Police."

"No fuckin' shit," Marvin said.

"Simmer down, redneck. Seems you boys are enjoying yourselves a little too loudly for your neighbors. Want to tell me what's going on?"

Marvin shrugged. He was standing about a foot away from the couch, trying to block Grover's view of Charlie while simultaneously giving Zeke a look that said *Distract him, dumbass*.

Zeke took the hint about as subtly as I thought he would. He grunted, and started rubbing his chin while he thought of something to say.

"Uh," he said. He was quiet for a spell, then added, "Guess we were loud, huh?"

Grover nodded.

"You want us to keep it down?"

Grover nodded.

"Not a prob, Bob. Not a prob."

Zeke nodded back, and when Grover realized that was it for his contribution, he turned to me and said, "What about you, Peggy Sue? You're a troublemaker if ever I saw one."

"I was just leaving," I said.

"Sure you were."

"Zeke's giving me a ride," I said. "I've got things to do, and he's got a meeting in a few hours."

Grover looked at Zeke but Zeke avoided his gaze. Marvin did the same. When he turned back to me, Grover shrugged and spread his hands.

"I could give you a ride," he said.

"Yeah," Zeke said, his face lighting up. "You get him out of here."

"You boys sure you don't mind?" Grover said. "It's not gonna inconvenience you, is it?"

"Aw hell, no. Does he look like a friend of ours? Goddamn gatecrasher thought he could mooch off us all night."

I made a run for the door but Zeke stuck his leg out and I tripped and fell and landed in front of Grover. Grover reached down, roughly brought me to my feet, then stared at me for five seconds that felt more like five minutes. To say I wasn't expecting what happened next is a major understatement.

Charlie emitted a low groan and fell forward, scaring the shit out of Marvin, who squealed and jumped backwards. He hit the other end of the couch, fell ass over teakettle and when he hit the floor, the shotgun discharged.

Charlie's head disappeared in a red mist.

What was left of him rolled off the couch onto the hardwood floor and suddenly Grover forgot about being a cop. He shot

Marvin in the chest. Marvin flew across the room, bounced off the wall and lay tangled in a bloody heap. Grover wasn't finished with him yet, though. He apparently believed that unless you stomped on a guy's skull and urinated on his corpse, you were letting him off lightly.

Grover was tucking his equipment back in his boxers when Zeke saw an opportunity and took it.

Grabbing the twelve-gauge, Zeke hit Grover in the face several times. One, two, three and down he went. While Zeke racked the shotgun, Grover grabbed his foot so Zeke hit him again. This went on for a while, Grover keeping hold of Zeke while Zeke hit and kicked him, until eventually Grover pulled him down to the floor. I watched them wrestle a while and then ran outside.

Grover had arrived in a Pontiac Aztek, proving beyond doubt that he wasn't a real cop. I removed some shotgun cartridges and hunting knives from the seat and had the engine running when Grover burst through the doorway and looked around. That was the last thing I saw before I drove away.

I drove south. I had no direction in mind, I just wanted to put as much distance between myself and the motel as I could. I had no idea where I was so I looked out for road signs, Grover having failed to install a GPS system.

I'd covered less than two miles when the knocking began.

It might've been going on for some time, but I didn't become aware of it until I started to catch my breath and relax behind the wheel. A thump followed by a muffled groan. I didn't have to think too hard to realize what it was.

I pulled over to the shoulder and popped the trunk, knowing what I'd find.

Staring down at a black man with a gag across his mouth and his arms tied behind his back, I said, "Welcome to the party, brother."

AUTHOR'S STORY NOTE:

It's a simple premise: what would happen if the director of a film similar to *Get Out* (but not too similar—legal reasons) was kidnapped by white nationalists? Would they congratulate him on his Oscar win? Or would they tie him up, torture him and use him as the guinea pig for an experimental serum that turns black skin into white skin?

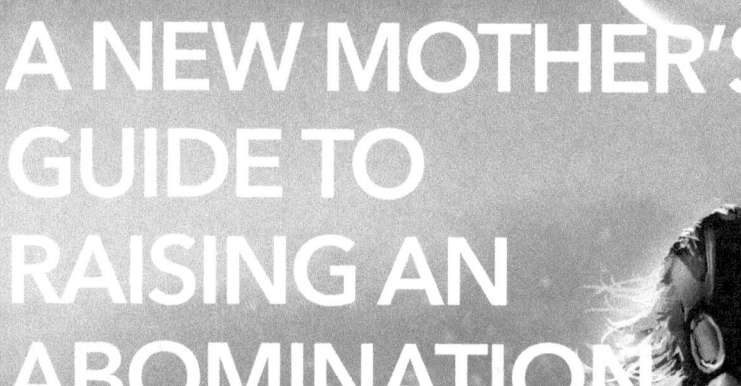

A NEW MOTHER'S GUIDE TO RAISING AN ABOMINATION

GWENDOLYN KISTE

From *The New Flesh: A Literary Tribute to David Cronenberg*
Editors: Sam Richard & Brendan Vidito
Weirdpunk Books

Your new bundle of joy is almost here. Keep track of the days, because this will be the most exciting time of your life.

It starts with the wings of houseflies. Dozens of them, scattered everywhere in your home. On the cutting board in the kitchen, stuck to the bathroom wallpaper, resting neatly on your pillow as if placed there by a gentle hand.

There are no bodies or legs or bulging eyeballs. Only the disembodied wings, delicate as tiny swatches of wedding lace.

"We'll call an exterminator," your husband says, and sweeps them into the trash.

You clasp your hands in front of you and nod, but when the next wings appear, you make sure he never sees them. Tucked away in the secret compartment of your vintage jewelry box, you keep the wings safe. They're your secret, these strange treasures left in the house just for you.

At night, when your husband is sleeping, you examine them in the glow of the nightlight. How beautiful they are.

As though in agreement, the thing that lives in your belly kicks and coos. You pretend not to feel it, pretend not to know what it means, but it's already been three weeks since you've first felt the stirring within you. That longing you can't define, an unease you can't shake.

You shouldn't be so afraid. This pregnancy was planned, right down to the day, with red circles drawn on the calendar, and your basal temperature taken each morning. This was what you wanted. That's what you keep telling yourself. You wonder if it's still true.

"I'm pregnant," you finally tell your husband the next morning, and he smiles and claps his hands and twirls you around like you're a maudlin couple in a dated rom-com whose happy ending you never did believe.

Another wing waits for you next to the coffeemaker. You slip it into your pocket, never letting your husband see. You won't let anyone see what you really are.

Prepare a bag for the hospital. A comb, a camera, a crucifix. You can never be sure exactly what you might need.

The thing in your belly escapes the womb an hour before midnight.

It all goes according to plan at first. Your water breaks, and your husband rushes you to the community hospital, just like the two of you have been practicing for months.

"I can't believe it's time," he says, and you nod and tighten your hands into fists.

The two of you are the perfect couple. Everyone says so. It's easy enough to think, with you beaming in all the wedding pictures, your bright smile never quite cracking around the edges. You wear happiness like a disguise.

But tonight, you can't hide. When you won't dilate, the doctors open you up, their pale scrubs drenched in red, their metal implements tearing your flesh.

"Something's wrong," someone says, and you try to speak, try to find out what's happening to you and your baby, but in the din of the surgical suite, your voice evaporates like mist.

As streams of frothy liquid pour from you like a fountain, the doctors grab clippers and sutures and a two-bladed speculum. No one asks how you're doing. They probably figure they don't need to. You're still screaming, so that means you're still alive, and as far as the doctor and the nurses and your husband are concerned, that's good enough. They're more worried about the thing that's inside you.

"What is it?" a physician's assistant asks, but no one answers. A strange flutter within you, like an irregular heartbeat, and everyone in the room edges closer.

Your husband gapes at the place between your legs. He no

longer sees you. Right now, all he can see is what you've created.

"Why does its skin look like that?" His eyes go gray and distant and scared. "And why is it making that noise?"

He's not the only one bothered. A couple of nurses clap their hands over their ears, and the anesthesiologist weeps quietly next to a table of gleaming forceps. You don't know why it troubles them so much. It sounds like the sweetest lullaby to you.

That's the only comfort you have. The operating table slick with red, you wonder how you can lose so much blood without losing consciousness. You also wonder in the hours and days to come, what else you'll lose.

A final tearing of your flesh and an emphatic snip-snip of a tangled umbilical cord, and you're officially a mother. Through filmy eyes, you gaze at the infant, draped in downy scales, with a pair of lacy wings dripping with colorless afterbirth.

"It's a girl," the doctor says, his voice splitting in two, and as your head lulls back and the room tilts around you, you've never been more afraid.

The early weeks of your baby's life might be challenging. Remember: this is normal. Everything is normal.

Two days after you bring your daughter home from the hospital, the dead things start arriving at your doorstep.

A pile of mice with their tails tied in slimy bows.

Rats with twisted faces and intestines drooping from their bloated bellies.

Red-wing blackbirds, their silky feathers plucked out and placed in the shape of fairy rings around them.

And those are only the ones you can identify. Some of the things are no more than splintered bone or matted fur.

For the first week, you're convinced someone is killing them. A deranged neighbor perhaps, or a member of a new religion that's formed for the occasion of worshipping your strange daughter. But no, that's not it. These animals are just giving up and dying on their own. They're too tired to be bothered with living anymore, especially in a world like this. A world that's produced a baby more unknown than human.

You almost envy the dead things for that, how simple it is for them to escape. You wish you could get out so easily.

Your husband does his best not to notice. On his way out the door to work, briefcase in hand, he steps over the garden variety of rot that's waiting there next to the morning paper.

"See you tonight," he says.

You wave goodbye and watch him leave. It's your job to clean up the mess. You might not have done anything wrong—or at least not done it on purpose—but everybody knows that when a monster is born, the mother is the one punished for it. You cradled the creature in your womb, after all. Really, you should have known better.

After the oozing decay is deposited in the neighbor's trashcan—a sparrow this time, or what was left of it anyhow—you bundle up your daughter in a onesie that doesn't fit around her scales and wings, and you take her to her first checkup across town.

At the clinic, you cradle her in your lap and try to read a magazine article about a reality star you never heard of. The other mothers inch away from you, clutching their babies tighter.

"They say it's happening all over," the nurses whisper to each other behind the front desk, but when you look up at them, they stop speaking and just blink back at you. Of course, you don't need them to explain. You've seen the nightly news.

All over. Girls like your daughter are being born across the country, maybe even around the world. Birthing monsters must be the latest trend, like helicopter parenting.

In the doorway, someone calls your name, and you walk across the waiting room, past all those wide-eyed mothers with their wingless newborns wrapped in little pastel blankets.

Alone in a narrow, bleach-stinking room, you wait for the results of another blood test.

"Inconclusive," the nurses tell you. "Again."

"I'm sorry," you say and hope your contrition is enough. The doctors had agreed to let you take your daughter home after a week in quarantine showed no obvious contagion, but that doesn't mean you get to keep her. You have to prove to them they can trust you. Otherwise, it's off to a lab where they can study her. *Fix* her.

"Next week, we'll try again," they say. "Don't be late."

As you exit the way you came in, your daughter flutters in your arms, and you grasp her tighter, your hands smoothing her back. The front door isn't even closed behind you before the other mothers and the nurses start to speculate about her, their whispers like thorns in your back. You'd think they'd be hoarse from the gossip by now.

You fix pot roast that night, your husband's favorite, but he doesn't speak all through dinner, not even to ask you to pass the salt or to find out how the checkup went. You don't say anything either. You just push your green beans around the plate with the bent tines of your fork and pretend you're someone else.

Nearby, in her high chair, your daughter parts her gray lips and emits that strange noise, her own lullaby in a key she invented. Your skin buzzes pleasantly, and you almost sing along with her, but then your husband stares up at her, fear churning behind his eyes, and you think better of it.

The two of you were the perfect couple. Everyone said so. But he was expecting what all men like him expect: a happy wife, a normal daughter. He never signed on for this.

After dark, you lock the nursery door, sealing in your progeny as though her bedroom is a coffin. Not that you ever really escape. All night, you dream of her—what she is, what she'll become—the waking nightmare of your life seeping in at every edge. The way her claws will grow and thicken and rend flesh. Her throaty laugh when she'll fly over those doctors and neighbors and complete strangers who gape and gossip and never understand.

Even when you bolt awake, sweat drenching your body, you can still hear their screams.

With your husband asleep next to you, you crawl from your bed and open your jewelry box. There are so many lacy wings inside that they overflow onto the dresser and cascade to the floor.

Breathing deep, you remind yourself that your daughter hasn't done those terrible things yet, and you can't blame her for what hasn't happened. She's still so small. It will be years before you'll have to worry.

You're also wrong.

Dealing with the needs of an infant is difficult, but as every parent soon learns, they grow up too fast. You'll miss these days, so treasure them while they last.

She blossoms overnight, far quicker than an ordinary child, but then nobody ever dared to say your daughter was ordinary.

You rouse one morning to discover a cocoon plastered to her bedroom walls. Your husband grabs a shovel from the garage to scrape it away, not caring that your daughter is still inside, but you get upstairs first.

"Leave her alone," you whisper, your body blocking the doorway to the nursery. "Besides, removing it might only make it worse."

Not that you can fathom how anything could be worse than this.

When she emerges that evening before supper, you almost can't recognize her. She's outgrown her skin, sloughing off the past, her bones twisting and contorting and stretching anew. In hours, she's grown what should have taken her five years. She still looks otherworldly, those wings of hers broadening, her skin thick like plated armor. But somewhere behind the eyes, she looks a little like you too.

Your husband doesn't say this, doesn't accuse you, at least not aloud. The way he won't look at you or touch you any longer is more than accusation enough.

The doctors, as always, are of no help. They can't tell you why your daughter sprouted up overnight. They can't tell you anything. You tell yourself that's okay. You're starting to get used to the not knowing. It's almost comforting.

It's summer now, with barbeques and Fourth of July sparklers and colorful swimsuits you don't wear anymore. At a backyard soirée where your family is invited as the spectacle of the day, your daughter moves quicker than the eye. Here and there and back again, her gaze the color of motor oil.

"Have you thought about other options?" one of the mothers says, as they all gather around you at the picnic table, so close they nearly smother you.

"Options?" You stare at their plastered-on smiles. "Like what?"

They don't answer. Instead, they let the truth settle heavier on you than the summer humidity.

Let the doctors fix her. Let the doctors *have* her.

It would be for the best, their pitying gazes insist.

Your chest constricts, and you search for your husband, for an ally, but even when you spot him, standing with the other fathers around the Weber grill, you realize you're more alone than ever. He stares back at you, everything about him gone cold. Maybe he asked these mothers to talk to you. Maybe considering "other options" is what he wants too.

Your teeth clench, holding in a sob, and you glance away from him, only to see her there across the yard, sequestered from the other children. All alone, your daughter twirls in circles, the grass turning to ash at her feet, her thin wings catching the air and nearly lifting her off the ground. She babbles her ethereal nonsense, while overhead, a starling exhales its death knell and plummets into the punchbowl.

A mother screams, and then another, and a father too, but not you. You just smile at your daughter. You envy her a little too.

That evening back at home, after the lights are out, you creep down the hall and crack open the nursery door. Tonight, you won't hold her back. If your daughter wants to flutter about on her own, then who are you to argue?

You nestle in bed, a gulf of crumpled sheets separating you and your husband, and for the first time since you became a mother, you sleep a dreamless sleep.

No matter how hard you try or how many books you read, not everyone will agree with your parenting style, so prepare yourself for constructive criticism.

The television flicks on at all times of day, the talking heads on the screen with their daily messages of doom. As the number of strange daughters born across the country ticks higher, dead things keep appearing everywhere. They're in your house too. No longer content on the doorstep, the rot makes its way inside now, oozing on the carpet. Knotted tails of animals you can't name. Feathers riddled with mites. Fly wings like confetti scattered across the carpet.

"We can't live like this," your husband says, his jaw clenched.

That night, you awaken to a cold bed and a scuffle down the hall. You stumble to the nursery. There he is, his rough hands grasped around her throat, his knuckles white and tightening around her, even as she only grins back at him.

You stand frozen in the doorway, not even breathing. A good mother would scream, would run toward them, would pry him away from the child any way that she could. A good mother would also underestimate her own daughter, believing every little girl needs to be rescued.

Fortunately, you're not a very good mother.

"Have fun, baby," you say, and close the door behind you, just as she raises up those claws, and your husband starts to scream.

In the morning, there's no proof he was ever there. Not a drop of blood or a clump of hair or even a bone shard brushed away into the corner like dust. You taught your daughter to put away her toys when she's finished with them, and she listens to her mother.

"He went out for cigarettes and never came back," you say when the sheriff comes looking for him, and then you say nothing else. They can't prove it was her, and you certainly won't be the one to turn her over to the police. But your word alone won't satisfy them.

"We know what she did," the other mothers hiss in your ear, as you stand in line at the grocery checkout.

With a steady hand, you place your items on the conveyor belt. A pound of ground beef.

"You can't pretend forever."

Three cans of chicken liver pate.

"We'll stop her one way or another."

A jar of split pig's feet.

"We know what she is. We know what you've created."

Your brown paper bags in hand, you turn away from them and rush off to the parking lot where your daughter waits for you in the car, her long fingers tapping an arcane message on the glass. A message you're convinced somebody somewhere can hear. Perhaps many somebodies.

Through the front window of the store, the other mothers watch you go. They think you're afraid, and maybe you are a little, but more than anything, you drive off quickly because you want to hide the grin that won't leave your lips.

Sometimes, your new family will outgrow your old home. At that time, relocating might be the only reasonable option.

You leave in the middle of the night, abandoning what little remains of your life.

"Where will we go?" your daughter asks in a humming voice only you can decipher.

"I'm not sure," you say, but that's all right. She already knows the way.

"Keep going," she whispers, gazing out the car window. "Until the highway ends."

You follow her directions until you find it. A compound tucked away in a desolate forest, right at the end of a county highway, like she said.

A man is waiting at the front door of a derelict lodge, as though he's been expecting you. You swear you've seen him before, on a trashy daytime talk show or a late-night infomercial, his hair slicked back. But then again, all New Age masters with silver tongues and dollar signs glinting in their eyes look the same.

"Welcome," he says, and that's when you realize you're not alone here. Peeking out of all the windows and behind the trees are the mothers like you along with their daughters, the ones you've heard the world whisper about.

Before you can stop her, your daughter rushes to the other girls, and instantly, they join as one, a clique of the unknown, dozens of them, almost too many to count in the dark. Together for the first time, they grasp each other's long hands and take flight. It's a dizzying display, all of them in the air, darting back and forth, their colorless bodies smearing across the sky. When they land, their feet burn a perimeter around the property, the trees twisting in grotesque shapes overhead, branches turning to ash in the girls' presence.

The lawn glistens beneath you, and at first, you think it's fresh dew. Then the moonlight shifts, and you see that the shimmer is from thousands of disembodied fly wings.

"You'll be safe here," the man says, and you wonder what he knows of the word, but you don't argue. You're just glad your daughter is not so alone.

Still, you know why he's happy to take you in. It's because he thinks he's running the show. Men like him always think they're in control. They're so often wrong.

"I can lead you to glory," he says and tries to bend all the daughters under his rule. He does his best to straighten their wings and tell them where to fly, when to sleep, how to summon the dead things to them. They shrug him off, uninterested in cowing to the cult he's desperate to craft in his own honor.

"This isn't the way, girls," he tells them, but they don't listen, not now that they have each other.

So he does the only thing he can think of. He betrays them. He summons everyone he can—their former doctors and the sheriffs and the neighbors always at the ready with a torch and a grudge. The world's been looking for them, and he knows it.

As figures bear down on the house, their voices close enough to prickle your skin, you awaken your daughter in her bed.

"We have to run again, baby," you whisper, but she beams back at you.

"No, we don't," she says, and it finally occurs to you that this was always part of the plan. Everyone in one place, all of those who thought the girls should be fixed, exiled, suffocated. Here on your daughters' terms, now that they're together and strong and ready.

The invaders assemble on the lawn, and the girls meet them there, your would-be leader at the forefront.

"You had your chance to listen to me," he says to your

daughters, but one of the mothers shakes her head and draws the blinds. None of you wants to hear another word from him. Gathered in a circle in the living room, you spend the rest of the evening playing different card games. Rummy and War and Patience. You win three hands.

Outside, there's a symphony of chaos and pleas and the cracking of bone, but with the shadowy outlines of your daughters buzzing merrily past the blood-streaked windows, you just smile.

It's become so easy to ignore the screams.

Sometimes, all the advice in the world won't help. Sometimes, you have to let your child figure it out for herself.

In the morning, it's quiet on the compound, and you discover the phones have gone dead. Of course, you don't mind. There's no one left out in the world you want to talk to.

As the other mothers murmur in their sleep, you go outside with your coffee. There are no bones on the lawn. No people either. There will never be new people arriving here again. The girls make sure of it. You wonder if the town you left behind is still there, or if on your daughter's command, it's decayed away into nothing, the same as all the trees past the perimeter. While annihilation is a nice thought, they're probably still out there, those other mothers with their wingless children, wandering the grocery store aisles, their eyes vacant, never seeing anything. Certainly not seeing you.

But they're no matter now. This is where you belong, a place no one will ever go hungry, not so long as the dead things keep appearing on your doorstep. Rabbits with their throats torn out. Deer that skin themselves. The scent of rot no longer bothers you. Maybe you've grown accustomed to it, or maybe it's grown accustomed to you.

Smiling, you kneel in the grass and scoop up a handful of

housefly wings. Then with your daughter fluttering past, giggling, you let the wings cascade back to the earth, falling one by one from your palm, like withered rose petals.

As the sun sneaks up through the ashen trees, you listen to your daughter, and all the other daughters too, singing their strange lullabies to the sky. And at last, when you're ready, you part your lips and join in, the final voice in a chorus that rumbles through the earth and turns the universe to dust.

AUTHOR'S STORY NOTE:

"A New Mother's Guide to Raising an Abomination" was first published as part of *The New Flesh: A Literary Tribute to David Cronenberg*. I've always loved Cronenberg's unique take on body horror, and I wanted to pay homage to that aspect of his work in this story. I was also eager to explore the body horror from a female perspective. The story's wraparound, with its "helpful" suggestions for new mothers, is my way of having a little fun with all those self-help articles that can actually be rather detrimental in their advice. Rather than listening to that generic wisdom, the mother in this story has to learn how to face the world in her own way, especially when it comes to her monstrous little girl. All things considered, I think she does all right in the end.

UPPER CRUST

MICHAEL PAUL GONZALEZ

From *Tales From The Crust*
Editors: David James Keaton & Max Booth III
Perpetual Motion Machine Publishing

B ack in college, I ran in some good circles. Not the best. I always wanted to be in the best. *Now*, I'm in the—I was looking for a fraternity, because you know it's *who* you know that gets you ahead in the world. I wanted to know the important people. Only the best. My father, when he sent me off to Wharton, he told me, I don't give a shit what you learn or what your grades are. I care who you meet. *That's* where the important lessons are. Know *who* to know, and *what* you know becomes second place.

One night, I'm at a rush party for Delta Kappa Epsilon. Lot of good people in that—Gerald Ford, the Bush Family, you see where I'm going—but this is obviously before any of them were president. I'm at this party looking at a goddamn oil painting of my great grandfather, he pledged so many years—but even legacies have to earn their spot. Out of nowhere, I feel something slide into my pocket. I look down, and there's this hand—silk glove, red silk, sexy as hell and—good party when someone's reaching into your pants before you've finished your first drink, right?

I turn, and there's this woman behind me, just *painted* into this silk dress. Everything red. Hugging every—I mean everything, the curves and her nipples—she just smiles at me, extends her hand, and says, "Ursula Dupree." Just like that. So I kiss her hand, and she flicks a finger toward my pocket, turns, and walks away.

In my pocket there's a little engraved business card. Gold. Sharp as a razor. Still got it here somewhere. You can see the stains from our meal on the—we'll get to that.

TANNER STEED—YOU ARE CALLED

SEPTEMBER 14, 1964

10PM

FULCRUM

ANWEALD · FEOH · WEALDAN

FOLLOW YOUR GAZELLE

Gazelles! That's what they called them . . . anyway. And you've seen the Fulcrum logo on my desk. That's usually covered by the first dollar I ever "made," nobody gets to see—but I have to show it to you tonight. And you've seen it, so now you have to—my father sent me there to meet people. Fucking is meeting, right? You don't pass up opportunities.

So, I followed her to this big ballroom, and everyone's eating dinner. We sit, she says, "Don't eat, you'll be eating later tonight," and she slides a finger up her thigh and gives this little shudder, and I'm—well, you get the idea. But she eats! Seven courses. Clam chowder, oysters Rockefeller, escargot, poi and sashimi, mustard potatoes, lamb with mint sauce and jelly, and a pineapple upside-down cake for dessert. I remember all seven, it comes back later. I'm just supposed to watch her eat? But the way she did it was—she could do things with that mouth, and—so we're talking, small talk, and then the last course comes, the waiter sets this little silver dish down, lifts the lid, and nothing's there.

Ursula stands up, and I swear, I don't know how they cut this dress, but it slides open across her thighs, and there, eye level, *pow*, her pussy, right in my face. Just a long enough flash that I can see how neatly trimmed, and she says, "Dinner was delight-ful. Are you ready for dessert?"

You're thinking what I'm thinking, right? She walks away. Up this spiral staircase in the corner of the room. There's these two guys standing right at the top of the stairs, like big stones—these were, one of them was probably Samoan, I mean huge—and the guy just looks at me and says, "Card." Just, *card*.

And the other guy has his hand out, gentle on my shoulder, but like a granite—so I give them the card, right? I pull it out from on top of my money clip. Back then I was like you, stupid, thinking that power came with showing wealth—anyway, showed them the little card she gave me, and they melt. Big, soft teddy bears. They step aside, backs to the wall, but like I said, big guys, so I still have to squeeze between, and then this door slides open a few feet away.

Maybe she's a prostitute, right? That's what I'm thinking, these were her bodyguards, they saw the money, they thought I—anyway, I step inside, thinking it's a bedroom, but it's an elevator. The door closes. She's not there. Small elevator. Red lights. And I can't even feel it moving, I'm just waiting for five minutes to move and—the doors open, and I'm on another floor. Basement. Way down. Didn't know it at the time.

I step into this waiting room. Two benches, one along each wall, look like they were from a museum. Like they'd been there since the 1700s, and that's because *they were*. Immaculate condition because people only sat on them once every four years. That's how lucky I was to—anyway, one wall, four ladies sitting. Four silk dresses. Red, purple, blue, and green. Other wall. Three guys. Not even college guys like me. One of them was my age, the other two were older and—they don't matter.

I stood by them. Here's a little secret. If everyone's sitting, you stand. If everyone's standing, you sit.

The walls are covered, floor to ceiling in these small oil paintings, little two-foot-tall portraits of men, great men. Didn't know it at the time. That's another secret—most of the truly powerful men, you never know their names, because there are positions. Roles. Some people are behind the scenes, some people, like me, are destined for the stage. So. We're just looking at these ladies, and they're not talking, just sitting there looking as hot as—and then these two big double doors open.

And the ladies stand, and this is where it gets good. This guy, this little butler, comes out wheeling a cart. On top of the cart, four leather collars, each attached to a chain. Without a word, the ladies stand up, unzip their dresses, and slide them off. You've never seen anything like—I mean, they all had underwear on, same color scheme, red—I guess Ursula had just put them on—and blue, green, purple, somehow that was even sexier than if they'd been naked—each one puts on a collar, walks over to us, hands us the leash. The butler gestures us through the big doors.

Inside, there's a—I'm not supposed to talk about the room, but you're going to see it soon enough, so I'm not really spoiling anything—like a courtroom fucked a brothel. Best way I can— there's a big, tall judge's stand. Big podium, three chairs way up high. On one side, a jury box. Sits twelve people. On the other wall, nothing. Well, almost nothing. Two little iron loops that I didn't notice when we—I'll get to that.

In the middle of the room, where the lawyers would normally go—a small table, like we're here to play poker. I don't know what the hell's going on, I just know I have Ursula's hot blonde ass on a chain. I'm up for anything. The butler claps, and the ladies lead us to a chair. High-backed, satin cushions, and the cushions match our ladies' clothes. My chair's red, guy next to me is blue, the—you get it. You understand. The ladies pull out the chairs, we sit, and they stand just behind us.

The butler claps again and says, "Judges." Two more doors open. Twelve guys in robes file into the jury booth. Then the butler rings this little bell. And it gets quiet. A door opens behind the podium, three men walk in, and they have full hoods on. Can't see their faces. They sit up high. The Triumvirate. You'd know their names. You've read about them in history books. They have done great things—that's a history you only get to learn if you pass tonight.

They sit, and I figure this is it, we're being hazed into the fraternity, right? Couldn't be more wrong. The Triumvirate, as one, they raise gavels and tap three times. The one in the middle says, "Dinner is served."

The butler leaves and comes back, with—get this—a pizza. A fuckin' pizza margherita. The most boring—cheese, tomato slices, some marinara. Smelled good, but I mean, *this* is what you dragged us down to—and nobody else reaches for a piece, so I don't either. I don't know where this is going.

"Gentlemen," the butler says. "This is the gathering of the Fulcrum. You've been carefully selected to begin the process of advancement to an echelon of society known to your fathers and their fathers. Every four years, we open our chambers around the world so that men can prove themselves worthy of joining the ranks of the Fulcrum. Is the Triumvirate prepared?"

The guys behind the podium gavel in turn. They go in order, left to right, saying Secundus, Primus, Tertius.

And Primus bangs his—god I wish I was allowed to tell you his name, you'd die, you wouldn't believe—anyway, he bangs the thing and gives us this speech.

"We are the playwrights of society. We control the stagecraft of the world. This is not an honor, it is the highest achievement a man can strive for. In the Fulcrum, there are no individuals. Behind these doors, we are many. In the world, we are one. If one of us succeeds, it is shared victory. If one of us is slighted, we are all wounded. This is your opportunity to join us. *Sacrifice* is a word greatly misunderstood. *Power* is a word greatly misused. *Fortune* is a word whose meaning few people truly grasp. Tonight, you will sacrifice. You will understand what is required to obtain fortune. With fortune comes power, responsibility, money, and no need to sacrifice again. To show your willingness to move to the next phase, you must break bread together. *La Festa dei Burattinai.* Will you take a bite of the food before you to show you are willing?"

That's all they wanted? I check the competition. They each grab a slice. Me? I do it big time. Slide a knife under a piece, guide it up to my plate with my fork. Cut a slice, the right size, not too big. I pick the guy across the table, the first to grab a slice. Unbroken eye contact while I chew. I look at the next guy, same thing, keep chewing until he looks away. I swallowed before I had a chance to look at the third guy, but he got the idea. It wasn't the best pizza I've ever—and then, after one bite, the butler whisks it all away and another guy brings in a different pizza. This one has sausage. Hot peppers. Like really hot, the ghost kind, we don't know from—and then the Primus says, "The world presents resistance. Can you push through hesitation, work through discomfort, withstand the heat of the forge?"

This time, maybe they're on to me, they're really testing my resolve, because all the cutlery goes away. I have to pick up the slice with my bare hands like these other chimps. We take a bite, and it's hot, really fuckin'—I mean, we need water, and we're laughing at this point, because we can see this coming. Spicy food, gross food, whatever, we're pledging, getting hazed. Same drill again, one bite, butler goes out, new guy comes in with a new pizza. This one is covered in black crickets and live earthworms.

"The world is rife with poor, simple creatures. The mechanisms of society are infested. You must consume them. Their bodies exist to nourish and sustain you."

And here, of course—I mean, fried crickets, yeah, that's disgusting, but live worms? But then again, it's fraternity life, right? So one of us, not me, I'm not ashamed to admit, goes first, big bite, and then we all dive in. Not as disgusting as I thought. Tastes like dirt. Cold and soft, though. Like a dead lady's lips. I figure once they stopped squirming it would be—but they never really stopped. I could feel them moving in my stomach for—probably a lesson in there somewhere.

"People are the salt of the earth. Though it may turn your stomach to mingle with them, you can, and must. Farm them, nourish them, consume them." Right as the Primus says this, the butler's back in with another pizza, plain tomato and cheese. Big slices. And behind him, another guy's pushing a cart with small cardboard boxes.

We hear this scratching. Pecking. *Peeping.* Our ladies open the boxes and pull out these fuzzy chicks. Little baby chickens. Without a hitch, they take the chicks, and *krick-krick-krick-krick*, break their tiny legs. They set them on a slice, and these little birds are . . . not fluttering, vibrating. The wings are moving so fast and their eyes squint from the pain and—and the primus says, "Sacrifices will always need to be made. Vermin and pets alike. You consume them all, those you revile and those you adore. Increase their suffering or end it, but the suffering is not the matter. Our nourishment is. The door awaits."

We stare at each other. Hazing is one thing, but this was . . . and Ursula leans down and whispers—and I can still feel her juicy lips brushing my ear when I think of this, gives me goose-bumps—she says, "Do it. For me." I don't know what the other ladies were saying, and I didn't care, because this time I was first. If only one of us was going to win this game, it had to be me. I rolled the little bird up in the pizza slice, cradled it with the head pointing at my mouth, because I figure, you break the neck and then—and it was a clean bite, I have strong jaws thank god, and it was . . . it didn't taste like I thought. Crunched like . . . and the beak just felt like an unpopped popcorn kernel, if it was stuck in a cottonball soaked in blood, and . . . I saw the other guys going for it too. And the butler, thank god, tells us, "You may spit."

The ladies give us a chalice, and we spit out the mess, and just stare at each other. It was the act, not the eating, you understand? Ursula gestured to me. I had this little piece of gristle and a tiny feather stuck to my lip.

The Primus says, "The game begins. Woman. The ultimate tool of resistance and persuasion. Her fortitude is incomparable. Her service to you is irreplaceable. Her greed will push you to greatness. Her guile will bring down those who would seek to hurt you. Uncontrolled, her fury will consume you. Choose your tools wisely."

The butler brings out the next pizza. A plain ham and cheese.

Each woman rotates to the next man at the table. Now I've got blue next to me. They plant their hands on the table and snort. I mean, big, phlegmy . . . and they start spitting on the pizza. Just greaser after greaser. Big, green shiny . . . coating the whole thing. Then they fold their arms and stare at us.

After the birds, this seemed like nothing to me, so I grabbed a slice and took a bite. I mean, I had plans to bury my tongue in Ursula's asshole, what's a little spit? We all take a bite. The women rotate again. They put our slices on the floor. The butler gives them sneakers. Each one announces where they walked from to get there. "I took the train from Shitburgh to blah blah blah," you get the idea. They made it clear, these shoes had been through spook neighborhoods, or immigrant shitholes, whatever piss-stained, dog-shit-encrusted sidewalk you could think of. And they stood on the slice. Really smeared their foot in there. Then, without lifting the shoe up, they took it off, carefully slid a hand underneath, flip it, and served the piece to us, like the shoe was a plate.

This one made me hesitate. You know me and germs. Eventually the other guys ate, so I had to.

The Primus says, "Four courses: The women will weed out the weak. They will serve until two remain. This will comprise the end of the second chapter. If all four pledges remain, the women are deemed to have failed. Fortune does not accept failure."

A new pizza comes in. Cheese only, nothing else.

The Primus says, "Sauce."

And two of the ladies squat over it and piss all over the—soaked it—and this was where things got weird.

The Primus says, "Toppings."

You know how sick a woman can—the lady in blue says, "I'm menstruating." Drew out the word like it's supposed to scare us. Reaches into her underwear and pulls out this fat, brown piece of cotton.

The butler comes over with a silver tray and she sets it down, gets out a scalpel, and carefully cuts it into little pepperoni slices, putting them on the pizza. She says, "Who wants a fresh one?"

I figured if I got it while it was still warm, I could—and you know, it tasted—have you ever had a bloody nose? Sort of like that. I meant the cotton was . . . it wasn't easy to chew. But thank god, the butler clapped again and we were allowed to spit that into the chalice too. So far, we're all in.

Ursula though, what a bitch, brings out this small plastic box with a picture of her dog on it. And she says, "This is Mopsie. She's a purebred Pomeranian." I hated that dog, by the way, so glad when it died. Little worm-infested—always chewed up my—anyway, she opens the box. "Mopsie eats only the finest cuts of meat and pure vegetables. Mopsie made this for all of you."

She takes tongs and sets down one perfect little roll of Mopsie shit on each piece and stares at us. Like little tootsie rolls with rice noodles embedded in—dead worms, you see? And win or lose, eating this means a trip to the doctor's office. You can't succeed without eating a little shit. That's what my father always told me.

It was too much for the guy across from me. He pushes the plate away. The first failure. He starts to curse the Triumvirate, ask them what the hell they thought they were doing, if they knew who he was, who his father was, and in come the Samoans, you know, dragged him out and things got quiet.

The Tertius stands at the podium, and points a finger at the guy's lady. She's dressed in the blue, right? And he says, "NAME?" nice and loud, and I swear I saw a little squirt of piss shoot down her leg. And she says, "Savannah".

"Expendable."

The Samoans are back. One grabs her arms, handcuffs her. The other puts this ball gag in her mouth, and then they chain her neck to the iron loop on the empty wall. Put a big spotlight on her.

"That's a sight," I say. Got the Primus to smile at that. Always try to make friends. Read the room.

"Three remain," the Primus says. "Crimson has proven her breeding. One woman can be a worthy ally and a fierce adversary. A group of women can be insurmountable. Where Crimson leads, the others will follow. Present the next challenge."

And I'm thinking, wow, I got the good one, right? She won, she gets to go again. And the other two women look nervous. Like maybe they're all playing a game too, and Ursula's on the brink of winning their end or something?

"Dinner tonight was splendid," Ursula says. "Seven delicious courses." The butler brings out another pizza, this one just bread. Nothing else on it. But it's deep dish style, right? It looks like a giant bread bowl almost. Our women move back to us and sit in our laps. And even with everything we'd been through, feeling that ass in those silky panties on my—anyway, they sit.

"Our compliments to the chef," Ursula says, and she sticks two fingers down her throat, and everything she ate earlier that night comes back. Chowder, some pineapple cake chunks, the oysters Rockefeller, escargot—whole fuckin' snails, the poi thing, man, the smell of that, and sauce, wine, she stops and pumps her stomach again—like a cat with a hairball—I mean this was Chicago-Style. Just *gallons* sloshing and—I'm just feeling her ass clench every time she retches and watching her ribs expand and lurch as she pours it all out. And it was almost sexy. Almost. I think she's done, but no! The potatoes, more wine, the lamb with mint sauce and jelly like green chunky toothpaste, and all of it's in this perfect cone on the pizza, and then to top it off—how did she do—a perfectly whole pineapple ring from the cake. Like she saved it just, *bam* on top.

And the smell?

The Primus looked at me and said, "You shall begin. The next man to eat may allow his woman to add to the feast. The game continues."

Ursula looks at me, just . . . the other women, they're all over their guys, right? Rubbing thighs, shoulders, nuzzling their ears—I mean, they all got a shot of mouthwash first, but—they look like they're pleading for their lives. Not Ursula. She's got this gaze of steel, just looks at me and says "Do this. You will do this now." Her eyes are wet and wild, like she's somewhere between crying and orgasm, her crotch is like a dripping furnace sitting there on my thigh, and she's just *animal* and I dove in. I can't explain it, and I know she looks a little tough now after all the surgeries, and who cares, you don't worry how the car you sold twenty years ago looks now—I mean, back then, she was *something*. I don't know how to—and I mean, it's just food. That's all I thought. It's all just food.

I swallowed. Tried not to chew. Terrible. It was like chili. The bile made it taste like old sausage—but the other two guys, it took them another five minutes to even start. I thought I won, for the longest time, I thought, this is it, Steed, you win. But then another guy, the guy across from me, chows through a bite. So his woman gets to puke on the pizza too, and now it's down to the third man. That's all they ever wanted us to do, right, just a bite. That's the big thing. The hesitation. They want you to get over the—but the last guy, he couldn't do it. He went to push the plate away, got some of puke on his fingers, and then *he* puked, everywhere. Bam, in come the Samoans, *boom* out he goes.

"NAME," the Secundus, this time, stands up. And the woman, this is the lady in purple, she says, "Posey." And she looks so sad, like a pale little flower. That was the first time I felt sad that night. She's crying right? Because same thing, here comes the Samoans, the handcuffs, then they force a piece of puke pizza into *her* mouth, then the ballgag, and *bam,* chained to the wall.

"The game continues," the Primus says. "When your competitor falls, it is up to you to utilize his assets."

I don't know why it was worse to know a man's puke was part of this soup now, but Ursula did this thing with her palm, like cupping my—you know—and instant, I mean *instant*, like Viagra has nothing on—and so I took a bite. Unbroken eye contact until I swallowed. And the other guy whispered, called me an asshole, and he took a bite too.

It's just me and him. Eyes watering, trying not to lose it. Ursula in red. His woman in green.

The Primus smiles. "Blood and money are the finalists. Names?"

"Ursula," Ursula says.

"Amalie," the lady in green says. Pretty name, I'd never heard it before. Usually you hear AHM-uhlee, but she was AM-alee. Cute girl. Great ass.

"Tanner Steed," I said, offering the other guy my hand. I guess I can tell you, it was Colton Northcutt. Remember him, ran for president a few years ago? Anyway, he goes to shake, and I did this thing, you know my trick, pump twice, and pull them in. Got his whole forearm in that puke pizza. He knew who was in control. You have to break them.

The Primus says, "Loyalty and Ambition will provide *il corso principale*."

The big guys come in, real careful, and take that table out. Didn't spill a drop out of that puke-soup pie. They bring in a new table. White marble, unfinished. That's when I noticed the walls for the first time. Same white marble. Like big tiles, all with these abstract color designs on them. Reds and browns. A year inscribed at the bottom of each one. Little plaque with a name—a woman's name, I would later learn. You see where this is—Ursula in red and Amalie in green sit at the table, staring at each other. The butler sets two empty wine glasses next to a new empty pizza. New pizza, new table. Thin crust. No toppings. No plates. Not even a pan under the pie.

"The gentlemen will pour," the Primus says.

The butler hands us these knives, like little syringes. Or funnels. Like big tubes of . . . and we couldn't figure out what to do with them, but the Samoans come back, and they unchain the two ladies from the wall. Savannah and Posey. Bend them over the table, yank back on their hair, their necks are just hovering above the wine glasses. They're panting through those ballgags, just frothing and moaning and crying. And the veins on their necks jump up and, just coated in sweat, and you know they're in their little underwear, and this whole thing is kind of sexy until the one Samoan holding Savannah looks at me and his eyes go to the weird knife-funnel thing, and he says, "Sir, will you pour?"

He tapped a finger on the vein in her neck.

I looked at Colton across the table. Looked at Amalie and Ursula, but they only had their eyes on each other. I push the needle into the side of Savannah's neck and—have you ever popped champagne on New Year's? You know? Just . . . everywhere! Sprayed everywhere! Everything's red, Ursula and Amalie in their little underwear, just soaked and the Samoan is kind of helping me, right, guiding my hand, keeping the funnel pressed in so that I fill up one wine glass with Savannah.

And Colton, in for a penny, in for a pound. They didn't—and see, this is the thing with power, they didn't even have to explain to us exactly what we were playing for here, it just made sense—so Colton pops Posey's neck, and she—maybe she's dehydrated, she's not a squirter like the other one, and she pours out, one glass, and the Samoans grab the ladies by the nape of the neck, haul them out of the room, like meat. Empty boxes. I thought they were taking them out back to ditch the bodies, but—can you believe it—I actually saw Posey at a function a few years later. She couldn't really look me in the eye. Fucks like a rabbit though, little—anyway—they're gone, right? Now, it's the big deal. Colton and I toast each other and take a sip.

The Triumvirate stands. The butler announces, "The game will conclude!"

The jury stands, and shit, I'd forgotten they were there this whole time. The judges have their hoods off. And they all start saying their names, full names, names you'd know! Cereal companies, newspaper barons, cattlemen, oil magnates, you name it. Fortune. They said their name followed by a woman's name. Not the women they married. Not a woman I'd ever heard of. You'll see in a minute.

"Appetizers have finished. Each woman has hidden a gold ring. The game concludes when an entrée is prepared and served and the ring is found," The Primus says. God I wish I was allowed to tell you his name, it's gonna blow your—anyway.

The butler lays a sword on the table. A real, god-damned ancient . . . I mean not like a big broad—just like a little curved—an Egyptian dagger thing. I'm standing on one side of the table, Colton's on the other. Ursula to my left. Amalie to my right. The big Samoans are holding them with a short leash. All of this in an eyeblink, mind you, I see their stomachs, bare skin, I see the veins in their necks, smell the sweat, and I just get it. Dinner. It's my job to serve.

So I go to grab the sword, and Colton realizes it too, but I'm faster. All he can do is watch. I swing for the fences, just *hi-yah!* right into Amalie's midsection. Cut it wide open in one—like a piñata! But instead of a bunch of little spic kids running around grabbing candy, it's just me and Colton watching Amalie *literally* spill her guts onto the table. And the Samoans help. White glove service. They're just delicately guiding her large intestine out onto the blank pizza pie, piling it like spaghetti, and it's just—you can see what she ate *moving* in there, right? Even after the puking! Still so much food left. Pulsing and squeezing, and they just keep feeding organs out. Liver, kidney, spleen, stomach and this is a *mess* I tell you.

"The ring is presented!" the Tertius shouts. "Claim your prize."

And the ring—they said she hid one, remember? Way down in her intestine, I see this hard little outline, kind of round on one side, flat on the top. She swallowed it this little film canister thing, see? The ring has the seal of—well, you see it here on my finger. I can't tell when Amalie died. Maybe it was fast. Probably. I mean, her head was rolling back and forth, mouth open, eyes like glass. You get disemboweled, you can't really scream. It was like bad opera. Embarrassing. That was the—I can't describe it. I saw her soul leave, and whatever was left was staring at me, and all I thought—and I said this out loud—was, *I deserve this.*

"Will you serve?" the Primus asked.

I took the sword and cut a piece of pizza. I don't know when they led Colton out of the room, but it's just me at the table with Ursula, chewing this other woman's guts. Ursula had to eat too. They all ate. All of the jury, the Triumvirate, they all came down and took a bite, like this is the best buffet they've ever—And they're all applauding us, and Ursula's crying like Miss Fucking America, covered in blood, and shit, and filth, and she takes my hand, and I'm—I mean normally I'd tell them to take this bitch out and give her a bath, but this was a *moment*, you understand?

I took her hand, and I looked her in the eye, and I kissed her. And I swear if the challenge would have gone further, I would have sat her bare ass in that pile of guts on that pizza and fucked her, right there, that's how happy I was. Because I understood everything.

But it didn't come to that. I don't want you to think I *actually*—Anyway. That was my dinner that night. That was my entrée into fortune. The *Festa dei Burattinai.* These days, they make fun of me in the press for eating bland food. Steak and ketchup. Simple things. They have people working at restaurants. They test you. They slip in little pieces of things sometimes. And if you're eating fancy food, you might miss it. I want the flavor to stand out. The sacred organs. Liver. Kidney. Hearts. Guts. It reminds me who I am and what I'm capable of. The flavor of life.

You have to meet the right people. And you have to eat a little shit. I told you it takes guts. Didn't say whose. Your job, your only job tonight, is to come back here with my daughter on your arm. Full, and happy, and content. Fortune favors the bold.

AUTHOR'S STORY NOTE

This story might seem like a thinly veiled allegory about a corrupt, power hungry, egomaniacal real estate tycoon with an insatiable appetite for power and self-aggrandizement. It might seem like an indictment of America's obsession with the hyper-rich and our endless desire to experience high society living. It might be a warning that the rich eat the poor, and their appetite is endless. It might be a call to arms. It might be the epitaph of America.

REDLESS

ANNIE NEUGEBAUER

From *The Binge-Watching Cure II*
Editors: Bill Adler & Sarah Doebereiner
Claren Books

t's the stop sign that finally does it. As I stand at a crosswalk, grimacing at the brilliantly green grass and the softly blue sky and the obnoxiously yellow sun, I look up at the octagon standing above my shoulder, and it's brown.

Brown.

Not faded, either. Not that dull orange or dusty maroon that some stop signs eventually slip into after years of faithful service. No, this sign is distinctly, shiningly brown, as if printed that way.

I cross the street, hurrying toward the next stop sign. It, too, is off-colored. I jog to the next: orange. I sprint to the next: burgundy. I look around, my eye twitching, head aching, and I suddenly see it. The utter lack of my lady. The missing.

How have I failed to notice? For how long?

It's always been my favorite color. It's the boldest, so you can't just douse everything with it. My lady, she's an accent, not a base. She's special. She's the star.

Most people seem to get that, more or less. Sometimes you'll see some color-dumb dope paint a whole living room or go overboard with matching shirt and accessories, but by and large, people know instinctively to use her sparingly. Her matching game is strong, too, so she can't be part of a "motif" or you end up with that overly-styled look. Just a hint—a pop. Let her breathe.

That's almost certainly why it's taken me so long to realize she's missing. I don't know how long, exactly, but I sense it's been weeks—maybe even months.

So many other things were subconsciously explainable. Apples come in green and yellow. The strawberries were under-ripe. My sister got a new phone case. The flowers in the office were white, blush, and lavender. Bookshelves were still an odd assortment of neutral and bright. Blue jays and sparrows still flitted outside. Emergency exits have always erred toward that faded, orangish hue.

Perhaps her absence explains my growing sense of malaise. We never realize how important color is to us until it's gone. I haven't been able to put my finger on why I've had trouble waking up in the mornings, why I feel my patience shortening with every person I talk to—my gaze roaming their outfits—or why the headache behind my left eye has grown from a dull ache to a constant throb that makes my skull pound and my skin twitch. Until now, I couldn't put my finger on what's changed, why I feel bland and angry, why everything seems pointless. I've broken up with my boyfriend, stopped calling back my mom (which hurt) and my sister (which didn't), and started showing up late to work.

I run to the candy store downtown. Every brand of sweets the store sells is quietly missing one shade. The rainbow cacophony of the store is still present, still sharp, even, with neon pink, yellow, and orange, but there's no raspberry to be found. No strawberry. I ask the clerk for cherry gumdrops and he scoops out white. "No, cherry," I correct, and he tells me they're white cherry.

I go home, search my house. I've used her sparingly, but I have always used her. The pillow in the entry chair is faded coral by the sun. The only condiments in my fridge are mustard and ranch. My favorite scarf is nowhere to be found.

It's not right, this world. It's not right without her. If she's no longer here, I don't want to be either.

I go to sleep under my gray comforter, in a cocoon of colorlessness, eyes leaking, head throbbing, and don't come out for days.

Vaguely, I become aware that my cell phone's been ringing for a long time. It blinks with messages. There's also pounding at my door, nearly synchronized with my head. My sisters's hollering through the window. Typical. When I finally drag myself into the living room, I see her peering through the door window, phone pressed to her ear even as she knocks. With a heavy sigh, I unbolt the lock and let her in.

"Are you okay? Where the hell have you been? Why did you lock the door? I've been worried sick. Damn, you look awful. Are you okay?"

I shut the door behind her, shuffling to the center of the room. I lift my hands in a lackluster gesture. "Notice anything?"

She falls silent, looking around. "No?"

"You don't notice anything missing?"

She looks again, searching, but her eyes keep sliding back to me, wary and concerned. I shake my head, stumbling into the kitchen. I stick my face under the faucet and gulp water.

"You don't notice anything at all?"

Suddenly, I know that she knows. I see that she sees it but doesn't care. I glance at her shoes, an uncharacteristic shade of noxious pink. Her nails, mauve. Her lipstick, a gross bluish purple. Boysenberry or some shit—the color of the season—and I know she chose this. Maybe even caused it.

"No," she lies. "What the hell is going on? Your boss said you've missed a whole week."

The knife block sits half a foot from my hand. I imagine all the tomatoes they've sliced. Ripe watermelon and fresh strawberries and raw steaks. I see their black handles and I gently withdraw the largest one. When my sister finally starts screaming, she screams until her wind is gone.

The first spurt eases my headache. The second ceases the twitching of my eye. The third splashes the floor. The fourth the cabinets. On the fifth, I begin dragging my sister through the house, into the main room, where my lady coats the floor, accents the sofa, paints the walls. I aim her at the ceiling, make sure she covers. On and on she goes, and only now do I finally realize that I was wrong about using her sparingly. She's an accent, she's a base, she's the world.

My living room has never looked better.

A TOUCH
OF MADNESS

TIM WAGGONER

From *The Pulp Horror Book of Phobias*
Editor: MJ Sydney
Lycan Valley Press

Kristina Lawson sat at a corner table in a small cafe, coffee sitting in front of her, gloved hands tucked beneath her legs. Folk-pop music played over the cafe's sound system a vain attempt to give the place a relaxing atmosphere, but it was filled with so many people—ordering at the counter, sitting and talking to one another, working behind the counter and operating various whirring, whooshing, or grinding machines—and the air thrummed with tension.

She glanced around at the other customers. A couple sitting at a table, each involved in whatever was displayed on their phone screens instead of looking at each other. A father sitting with his twin daughters—who were five at the most and dressed in superhero outfits complete with capes, one green, one red—sipping juice boxes while their dad drank his coffee. A pair of middle-aged women in blue medical smocks talking over coffee and pastries after a long hospital shift. And a dozen more, including the staff behind the counter. All of them appeared completely normal. Completely *sane*. But she knew better than most that appearances didn't mean shit. Anything could be happening behind their eyes, their thoughts a chaotic maelstrom of wild imperceptions and barely restrained homicidal impulses. Any one of them could be on the verge of succumbing to the lunacy raging inside, and then all hell would break loose. Pam would've told her she was being paranoid, and maybe so. But she'd seen it happen before, and if it had happened once, it could happen again.

She wasn't sure why Pam had asked to have their session in a public place like this instead of her office. No doubt she thought there was a good reason for it, maybe some new type of therapy that she wanted to try, but Kristina wasn't comfortable around people, especially this many. She looked down on the tabletop to avoid meeting anyone's gaze. She flexed her hands, felt them move under her legs, was reassured to know they were still protected. She made no move to touch the coffee in front of her. She didn't want it, didn't really like coffee much. She'd only bought it so she wouldn't look any stranger sitting here than she already did.

Pam rushed into the shop then, blond hair a frizzy mess, make-up slightly askew, as if she'd applied it too fast. She looked around, saw Kristina, smiled, and hurried over to her table.

"Sorry I'm late," she said. "Do you mind if I order something before we get started?"

Kristina *did* mind. She wanted to get whatever this was over as soon as possible. But she shook her head. Pam smiled again then headed to the counter. There was a line, and Kristina watched her stand there for several moments until it was her time to order. She trusted Pam—as much as she trusted anyone, that is. She'd seen a number of therapists over the years, most of whom had treated her as if *she* was the crazy one. Pam had been the first to treat her as if she was a person instead of merely a psychologically fascinating puzzle to be solved, a shattered porcelain doll whose pieces needed to be put back together. She'd been seeing Pam for almost two years, and she couldn't deny they'd made progress together. Two years ago, she never could have come into a place like this by herself, order a drink, sit, and wait for someone. But here she was, and if she wasn't comfortable, so what? She was *here*.

Pam returned to the table carrying a large cup that most likely contained a latte with an extra shot of espresso. During one of their earliest sessions, she'd mentioned it was her favorite drink. She sat down opposite Kristina and took a long sip before setting the cup down on the table. Normally, Pam began their sessions with some chit-chat. *How have you been since we last talked? Anything new going on with you?* But not this time.

"I'm sure you're wondering why I asked you to meet me here today."

Kristina smiled. "The thought had crossed my mind."

"I'd like to try something different today, and I thought this would be a good place for it."

Called it, Kristina thought. "Were you late on purpose in order to give me a chance to handle being by myself?"

Pam took another sip of her latte.

"The thought had crossed my mind," she said, and despite herself, Kristina laughed. "So what was it like?" Pam asked.

"Tolerable. Although if you'd been much later, I'd probably have left."

"Good thing I wasn't any later then, huh?"

Pam's expression grew more serious, became what Kristina thought of as her *doctor face*, and she knew their session was about to start in earnest.

"How are you feeling about the TV show this week?"

Kristina grimaced. "Okay, I guess. The bastards have stopped trying to contact me, so that's a relief."

The producers of a lurid true-crime TV show called *Unnatural Acts* were doing a segment on Kristina's mom. For a month they'd bugged her nonstop, desperate to get an on-camera interview with her, but she'd ignored them and they'd finally decided to go ahead without her participation. She'd had enough media attention over the last decade to last her a lifetime. News reporters who fought to be the one to interview her first. True-crime authors who wanted to write books about what had happened. One was eventually published—*Blood on Campus*—and it had become a modest success. She hated the attention, hated how it always brought the memories of that awful day back full force. For the last ten years she'd hoped people would forget and find a new atrocity to be fascinated by. But it hadn't happened yet, and she was starting to wonder if it ever would.

"That's what I wanted to talk to you about," Pam said, then added. "Kind of."

"Oh, god. Don't tell me the producers hired you to be a consultant."

Pam's eyes widened in surprise, and then she laughed.

"No, and even if they asked me, I'd turn them down. It would violate doctor-patient confidentiality. Plus, it would be a total dick move."

Kristina relaxed. The thought of Pam betraying her like that was too awful to think about.

"So what *do* you want to talk about?" She felt her defenses going up. She didn't like to remember that day, let alone talk about it. But Pam had done a lot to help her, so she'd go along with whatever she wanted to do. To a point.

Pam took another sip of her latte, a long one, as if fortifying herself for what came next.

"We've talked about that day before," she began. "Several times. And during those conversations, I never questioned the truth of what you told me, never disputed the reality of any of it."

Kristina nodded cautiously. She didn't like where this seemed to be going. Her other therapists *had* questioned, had tried to convince her that it hadn't happened, or at least that it hadn't happened the way she remembered. One of the things she liked about Pam is that she'd never done that. But maybe she'd just been waiting for what she thought was the right time to bring up the subject.

"I went to the university yesterday."

An ice-cold hand gripped Kristina's heart, and she began trembling. Pam went on, speaking faster as if hoping to get everything out before she freaked.

"I'd never been there. I went to college in Chicago before my husband and I moved to Ohio. It's a beautiful campus. Lovely old buildings, lots of grass and trees . . . Very different from the downtown campus I attended. The Science Center's not there anymore. They tore it down years ago and planted trees there. They put up a remembrance plaque, too. I think you might find it healing to see it."

Kristina trembled harder now, and her mouth and throat felt dry as desert sand. She didn't want to reply, but if she tried, her words would've likely come out in a hoarse croak.

Pam continued.

"I looked for the fountain, but I couldn't find it at first. I thought maybe it had been torn down, too. But I found it eventually, and it was peaceful and relaxing, just as you described it." She paused, and then added, "I took some pictures with my phone."

Sudden nausea erupted in Kristina's gut, and her vision blurred. She wanted to jump up from her chair and run toward the exit, but she feared that if she tried, she'd pass out before she made it halfway.

"I'd like to show them to you, if that's okay."

She wanted to shake her head violently, but she was unable to move. Taking her silence for assent, Pam removed her phone from her purse, brought a picture up on the screen, and then held it out for Kristina to see. She scrolled through a series of images, and although Kristina wanted to look away, wanted it more than she wanted her next breath, she watched the pictures go by, one after the other.

* * *

Kristina saw the statue on a hot afternoon in late July when she was thirteen years old. She was supposed to be attending the second morning of a weeklong summer science workshop for middle-school kids run by the university, but after her mom dropped her off in front of the Science Center and drove away in her Lexus, she'd decided to wander the campus instead. She *hated* science and never got good grades in it—which was the reason her overachieving parents had insisted on signing her up for the workshop. But as much as she hated science, she hated being told what to do even more. Rules, regulations, do this, don't do that, be a good girl, don't be a bad girl . . . Why couldn't everyone just leave her alone to do *what* she wanted *when* she wanted? Her parents, teachers . . . all her life people had told her what to do, and she was sick of it. The only rules she was interested in following were her own.

Her parents might've enrolled her in the workshop—and paid for it—but they couldn't make her attend if she didn't want to. Yesterday had been so *boring!* All they'd done was make "inventions" out of cardboard, tape, glue, plastic straws, Popsicle sticks and other odds and ends. More arts and crafts than science. Kids stuff. Today she planned to skip out and kick around campus for a couple hours until it was time for Mom to pick her up, and then she'd meet her back in front of the Science Center and feed her some bullshit about what the instructors had the kids do today. Her parents were smart—Mom was a lawyer, Dad a pediatrician—but they were so busy they only ever paid partial attention to what she did. Lying to them was almost embarrassingly easy.

This wasn't her first time at Ash Creek University. Her parents were both alums and had been dragging her to campus concerts, art shows, and theater productions since before she could walk. But in all those visits—dozens of them—she'd never gotten the chance to explore the place. High time she rectified that, she decided. But after a half hour of walking around in the sun and heat, she was not only bored but miserable. She supposed the campus was pretty enough. Red brick buildings, well-landscaped grounds, large trees . . . But there wasn't anything to *do*, and because it was summer, there weren't many people around, which made the place feel empty and lonely. She did like the fact that no one paid any attention to her. The few people she passed—students, professors—didn't so much as glance at her, as if a thirteen-year-old walking around campus by herself was completely normal. It made her feel very grownup.

But she'd been walking nonstop since her mother left, and she was tired and sweaty. And while the campus was pleasant for the most part, there was a lot of construction going on—parking lots being resurfaced, buildings being remodeled—and that meant noise. Machines running, tools striking metal and concrete, people shouting to each other as they worked. She wanted someplace quiet where she could sit in peace for a bit, preferably in the shade. She was on the verge of saying to hell with it and going back to the Science Center and attending the stupid workshop when she saw the red dumpster. It contained odds and ends from campus construction—chunks of broken concrete, lengths of discarded wood. It was in no way remarkable. She'd seen a dozen like it during her self-guided tour of the campus so far. But what *was* remarkable was what lay behind it. She almost missed it, so completely did the dumpster block the view. But there was a tiny sliver of space between the side of the dumpster and an old oak tree, and through it she caught a glimpse of what looked like a fountain. Intrigued, she slipped past the dumpster and found herself standing at the entrance to a—well, she wasn't sure what it was exactly. A place for people to sit, relax, and think, she supposed. A stone fountain sat atop the third level of a dais, a curving half circle of stone wall behind it with an arched open doorway in the middle. Wooden benches rested on either side of the doorway, where people could sit and watch the fountain and listen to the gentle trickle of water. The water bubbled up from the center of a large round stone surface to flow over the edges and into a pool beneath. The water emerged from the edge of the dais in a small waterfall surrounded by large stones placed to look like a natural formation. Trees surrounding the fountain, separating it from the rest of the world, making it seem as if it were a place out of a fairy tale, a secluded, magical setting that only a lucky few ever found.

There was shade here, along with a pleasant breeze, and the sound of the gently rustling tree leaves—combined with the running water—soothed Kristina. She knew where she'd be spending the rest of the time until her mother came to get her.

Then she looked to the left of the fountain and saw the statue. Her parents had both had been raised Catholic, but they weren't religious. Ash Creek University was a private Catholic institution with a reputation for academic excellence, and that was the only reason her parents had come here for their undergraduate degrees. Kristina sometimes wondered if they still considered themselves Catholic, culturally if not spiritually. They took her to Christmas Eve and Easter mass every year—to "broaden her horizons," they said—and on the way home they'd give her a speech about how religion was nothing more than a way to instill moral values in its followers by using metaphor and symbolism, and it wasn't to be taken literally.

Thanks to her "broadened horizons," she recognized the statue as the Virgin Mary, the mother of Jesus. Mary stood atop a granite pedestal, bare feet sticking out from beneath the hem of her robe. She held her hands out before her, fingers steepled as if praying, her hood-covered head bowed. There was no expression on her face. Her eyes were closed and her mouth was little more than a line with only a suggestion of lips. But the detail that stood out the most to Kristina was what looked like a thick reptilian tail protruding from the back of her robe and curling around her left foot. She frowned upon seeing the tail—for that's what it had to be, couldn't be anything else. She was no expert on Catholic theology, but she felt confident that Mary wasn't supposed to have a lizard's tail.

There was something written on the granite base the statue stood on, and she walked over to read it. It was a single word.

PANDEMONIA.

And beneath that, in smaller letters, a quote: *If there is a universal mind, who says it has to be sane?—Charles Fort.*

Was this some kind of weird piece of art or maybe a joke of some kind?

And then the tail twitched. Just the tip, and it happened so fast she wasn't sure she'd really seen it. She looked up at the statue's face and ice-cold fear hit her when she saw its eyes were now open. They weren't the same gray-white as the rest of the statue, though. Instead they were a glossy obsidian, and while she could read nothing within their empty blackness, she could feel the weight of the statue's gaze upon her.

You do well to shun the false god of science, child.

The statue's thin mouth didn't move. Its voice—cold as midnight and dry as ancient bone—echoed in her mind.

Science pretends there is order to existence, that for every question, there is an answer. This is a lie. Existence is random and meaningless, and that is glorious.

The statue bent toward Kristina and stretched it hands toward her. At first she was so terrified she couldn't move, could only stand and watch the stone fingers draw closer. But then her survival instincts kicked in, and she threw off her paralysis and turned to run. But before she could take more than a single step, the stone tail lashed out and encircled her waist, stopping her. She pulled and tugged, but she couldn't break free of the tail's stone coils.

The statue closed its hard fingers around Kristina's right wrist and held her hand steady as its lips parted and a pearl of thick dark liquid emerged. It fell onto the back of her hand and sat there for a moment, burning cold on her skin, before flattening against her flesh and slowly disappearing into her body. She felt no different, but a shudder raced through her just the same.

The soothing rhythm of the fountain ceased, and the sudden silence drew Kristina's attention. She glanced over to see the water had stopped flowing, and instant later blood welled up from the center of the round stone, crimson and thick. It oozed across the surface, overflowing the stone's edges, falling in ropey threads into the pool below, before finally emerging as a red waterfall. She looked into the statue's obsidian eyes, its face only a few inches from her own now.

Go forth and share the gift I have bestowed upon you, my daughter. Free them. Free them all.

* * *

Kristina had no memory of the statue releasing her, no memory of beginning to run. One moment she was standing there, trapped in the statue's embrace, staring into its obsidian eyes, and the next she was running full out, heart pounding, lungs heaving, sweat pouring off her. She had no destination in mind, wasn't capable of anything approaching rational thought at that moment. Her body operated on autopilot, returning her to the place she'd started from: the Science Center. She was relieved to see her mom's Lexus parked in front of the building, and she ran straight to it, only partially aware of the tears streaming down her face. She ran to the driver's side window and began pounding on it to get her mother's attention. It was several moments before she realized the car was empty.

"*There* you are!"

Kristina stopped pounding on the window and looked up to see her mother exiting the Science Building, her face a mask of anger. She continued chiding Kristina as she walked toward her.

"I was in a meeting with a client when the workshop director called to ask me why you weren't present today. I hauled ass down here, grinding my teeth to nubs the whole way. Why can't you, for once in your life, do what you're supposed . . ." She trailed off as she reached Kristina, her expression softening. "Are you okay, honey? Why are you crying? Did something happen?"

Before Kristina could respond, her mom took hold of her hands and gave them a reassuring squeeze. The instant their flesh came in contact, her mother stiffened, and her eyes widened in shock. She began shaking her head, as if trying to deny something only she could see. She paled, an expression of absolute horror coming onto her face, but instead of turning away from the unseen whatever-it-was, she continued looking and slowly her features slackened and her expression became placid. She remained like that for several heartbeats, still holding onto Kristina's hands, and then she spoke in a calm, almost toneless voice.

"Thank you. I understand now." She looked at Kristina, and in the same flat voice said, "I'm going to go tell the director I found you and you're safe. I'll be back in a minute."

She released Kristina's hands, turned, and walked back into the building.

Kristina's tears subsided to a trickle, but she was no longer aware of them. She stared at the glass door that was the entrance to the Science Building, unable to escape the feeling that something was terribly wrong. For a moment she forgot about the statue, or rather she forced herself not to think of it. When Mom got mad—*really* mad—she stayed that way for a while, sometimes hours. Kristina had never seen her calm down so quickly and completely. It was like a switch had been thrown inside her, shutting off all her emotions. It was beyond weird.

And that's when the screaming began. It was muffled, but the sound was unmistakable. It came from somewhere inside the building, and when she looked toward the second floor—where the science workshop was taking place—she saw a smallish, child-sized hand slap the window from the inside. The hand was covered with blood and left a red smear on the glass as it slid away.

Her own paralysis was broken by the sight, and she ran into the building and went up the stairs, taking them two and three at a time. The screams grew louder and fewer the closer she got to the second floor, and they were punctuated by moans of pain. She slowed as she approached the classroom where the workshop was held. She didn't want to go in, didn't what to see whatever waited for her, but she *had* to. Her mother was in there.

The door was open, and by the time she reached it, the sounds had stopped. No more screams, no more moans. Just silence. She stepped inside, not far, only a foot or so. The room was set up the same way as it had been yesterday—ten circular tables with chairs around them, materials for students to use in constructing their projects in the middle. It was more like art class than science, which had been one of the reasons she'd found it so boring. But what she saw now wasn't boring. Far from it.

Bodies were scattered around the classroom, mostly kids her age but there were a couple adults as well. Some lay on the floor in various positions, while others had collapsed into chairs or onto desks. They had sustained numerous cuts and blood was everywhere—on their clothes, on the desks and chairs, on the floor and walls . . . and all the corpses, around twenty in total, appeared to have died the same way, by having their throats cut.

Kristina's mother stood in the middle of the room, holding a pair of box cutters, her clothes, hands, and face covered in blood. She turned to face Kristina and smiled, her teeth a startling patch of white in her otherwise crimson face.

"Thank you for helping me to see how things really are, sweetie. Thank you for setting me free."

She raised both box cutters and pressed the tips of the razors to the small hollow at the base of her neck. And then with a pair of vicious outward swipes, she laid open her throat. Blood fountained from the wound to join that which already covered her. If she felt any pain, her face didn't show it. Her smile widened, and her eyes seemed to almost glow. Kristina didn't know the word *beatific,* but if she had, that's how she would've described her mother's expression.

Her mother stood like that for a time, but eventually the box cutters slipped from her hands and thunked to the floor. A moment later, she joined them, collapsing and staring up at the ceiling with wide, unblinking eyes. Her smile, however, remained in place.

And then it was Kristina's turn to scream.

*   *   *

Kristina saw the fountain, the stone wall behind it, the rocks in front of it, the trees surrounding it—but there was one thing she didn't see on the phone's screen: the statue.

"I checked with the campus groundskeeper's office," Pam said, "and they told me that not only isn't there a statue next to the fountain, there never has been in the university's one hundred and twenty-two year history." She closed the phone's photo app and replaced the device in her purse. "There *was* no statue, Kristina. In your mind, yes, but not in the physical world. It didn't infect you with . . ." She frowned, as if unsure how to put it. "With its madness. And you didn't pass it on to your mother when she grabbed your hands. You aren't responsible for what she did, and you never were."

All of Kristina's therapists had argued that the statue wasn't real, at least not the way she'd perceived it. But none had gone so far as to visit the campus and take pictures, let alone check to see if the statue had ever existed. A part of her that was still thirteen, and maybe always would be, wanted to shout at Pam, accuse her of lying. But the rest of her, the woman she'd become in the last ten years wanted to believe her. What a comfort it would be to believe that her mother had done what she'd done for some other reason than because she'd touched her daughter's hand and come in contact with a contagion that Pandemonia had infected her with.

"I know how to prove that you had nothing to do with what happened," Pam said. "But you'll have to trust me. Do you trust me, Kristina?"

She hesitated, but then she managed a single nod.

"Good. Put your hands on the table."

Kristina stared at her, not quite sure she'd heard correctly.

"You told me that you've worn gloves every day for the last ten years, that you won't even take the right one off to bathe. All because you don't want to risk infecting anyone else."

"Yes." She'd been extremely—no, *obsessively*—careful over the years.

"But if there was no statue, there's no infection to pass on. And that means you can touch someone without anything bad happening. So you can touch me."

Pam put her left hand on the table, palm up.

Katrina looked at Pam's hand, head swimming with vertigo.

"What's more likely to be true? That some . . . *thing* chose you to spread some kind of psychological plague, or that your mind made up that incident so you wouldn't have to believe your mother was responsible for killing all those people?"

Katrina knew which of the choices was the most logical, but that didn't necessarily make it the correct one. Still, she took a deep breath and slid her hands out from under her legs. She wanted to get better, she truly did, and she recognized that this would be a huge step toward making that possible. She removed her left glove—the one that she didn't really need to wear—and placed it on the table. And then, after another moment's hesitation, she removed the right and placed it next to the left. The air felt cold on the exposed skin of her hands, but it felt stimulating, too. Then slowly, fighting every instinct inside her that screamed she shouldn't be doing this, she lowered her right hand onto Pam's, and for the first time since that day, she touched another human being. Pam curled her fingers upward to grasp hers, and tears of joy welled in Kristina's eyes. Pam had been right. The statue *hadn't* been real, it *hadn't* . . .

Pam's eyes glazed over and her features went slack. She pulled her hand away from Kristina's.

"No," Kristina whispered. "No, no, no, no, no!"

Pam didn't respond. Instead, she rose from the table and walked toward the counter. But instead of stopping in front of the register, she continued on, stepping behind the counter where the staff were working. They looked at her for a moment, as if uncertain what to say or do. Then one of them, a skinny twenty-something with a goatee and a man bun, stepped forward to block her way.

"I'm sorry, ma'am, but you're not—"

Pam reached down and from somewhere—Kristina couldn't see from the table—grabbed hold of a knife. It was long and sharp, with a black plastic handle, one of the implements the staff used when preparing sandwiches or slicing bagels. Man Bun started to raise his hands, as if he thought he could ward off Pam by gesture alone. But before he could complete the gesture, Pam swiped the blade across his throat in a single swift motion. Flesh parted, blood spurted, and Man Bun clapped his hands to his throat in a ridiculously ineffective attempt to stop the bleeding.

People started screaming then, and while some stared at Pam, dumbfounded, the majority bolted for the door. Too many tried to go through it at the same time, but the crowd behind them pushed until the jam was broken and everyone could get through.

Pam turned away from the bleeding man, whose mouth kept opening and closing like a fish as he attempted to speak, but all he managed were wet clicking sounds, and then his eyes rolled white and he slumped to the floor. His coworkers gaped at his prone form for a second, but when Pam came out from around the counter and started back toward Kristina, they saw the opportunity to get the hell out of there, and they lost no time in doing so, fleeing into the street after their departed customers.

By the time Pam returned to the table—still gripping the knife, blade slick with blood—the café was empty except for the two of them.

Kristina wanted to look away from Pam's gaze, wanted to close her eyes and wait to feel the knife edge's kiss on her own throat. But she forced herself to meet her therapist's eyes. She half expected to see they had become a glossy obsidian, but they looked the same as they always had, save for the complete and total lack of anything resembling human emotion within them.

"You were given a gift." Pam spoke in a toneless voice that reminded Kristina of the way her mother had spoken before going inside the Science Building. "And you've wasted it."

Moving so swiftly that Kristina hardly saw her move, Pam grabbed hold of her right wrist and pressed her hand to the table.

"Time to return what you've squandered."

She pressed the sharp edge of the knife against the tender skin of Kristina's wrist.

Kristina impressed herself by not feeling afraid. It would be a relief to be rid of Pandemonia's dark gift. And if she bled to death after Pam performed her impromptu amputation, what of it? At least she would've kept her sanity at the end. She gritted her teeth to steel herself for the pain to come and curled her right hand into a fist, the tips of her fingers pressing hard into her palm.

Ten years she had avoided touching herself with her right hand, terrified of what might happen. Now she knew. More, she *understood*.

Pam kept the blade pressed against her skin for another moment, but then she pulled it away and released her grip on Kristina's wrist. Face still expressionless, eyes still dead, she handed the knife to Kristina, and then stood there, waiting. Katrina examined the blade, turning it this way and that to see how the light played across the metal. The barista's blood still clung to the knife, and she brought the blade to her mouth and licked it clean. She cut her own tongue in the process, but she didn't care. The pain was exquisite, and the blood she swallowed—hers mixed with his—tasted sweeter than any wine.

She looked at Pam.

"Thanks for everything," she said, and then rammed the blade into the woman's chest, expertly slipping it between a pair of ribs and into her heart. The non-expression on Pam's face didn't change as she slipped free of the blade and collapsed to the floor, dead. Instead of licking the knife this time, Kristina wiped it on her cheeks, smearing them with Pam's blood.

Many times over the years, she'd tried to imagine what it had been like inside her mother's mind after she'd experienced the dark touch. The closest she could come to was to imagine Mom's skull as a hive filled with angry buzzing bees furiously trying to sting one another to death. She was surprised to discover she hadn't been far off the mark. The sound—one of absolute and total disorder—was magnificent. It was the song of discord and upheaval, of malady and torment, of decay and dissolution, and she couldn't wait to share it with the world.

She heard Pandemonia's voice one last time.

That's my girl.

Kristina tossed the knife onto Pam's lifeless body and started walking toward the door. She flexed the fingers of her right hand, as if limbering them up. She had work to do—*important* work—and she couldn't wait to get started.

AUTHOR'S STORY NOTE

"A Touch of Madness" originally appeared in *The Pulp Horror Book of Phobias* from Lycan Valley Press. For that anthology, authors could choose from a list of phobias, and I chose agateo-phobia, fear of insanity. I thought this would be different from the more familiar phobias other authors might select. (Trying to avoid more obvious ideas is one of my strategies when writing for a theme anthology). Plus, I figured fear of insanity would be less restrictive than something narrower, like fear of chickens. (Although chickens can be pretty damn creepy.) During the time I was mulling over story ideas, I was teaching at a summer writers' workshop at the University of Dayton. While I was wandering around campus during a break, I came across a statue of the Virgin Mary. UD is a private Catholic school, so seeing the statue wasn't a big surprise. What did strike me as odd was that Mary had a large, reptilian tale protruding from the beneath her robe. I stared at this detail, feeling a delicious sense of unreality, but after a moment I realized Mary didn't have a tail. She was standing with one foot on the head of a serpent—Satan, maybe?—and the tail was curled around the back of her feet. I'm not Catholic, so I had no idea if this scene was one out of Christian myth or something the sculptor had dreamed up, and I didn't care. I had the image I needed for my story of insanity, and Pandemonia was born. I first encountered the quote from Charles Fort, which appears on the statue's base—"If there is a universal mind, who says it has to be sane?"—in *The Mothman Prophecies* by John Keel. It's the last line of the book (spoiler alert!). I read the book when I was around twelve or so, and the quote blew my mind. I was so impressed by Fort's question that it became a bedrock theme of much of my fiction. My oldest daughter had attended a week-long summer science camp at UD several years earlier, so I decided to toss that detail into the mix as well. I then threw in copious amounts of blood, stirred well, and the result was "A Touch of Madness."

PARADISUM VOLUPTATIS

JOANNA KOCH

From *Honey & Sulphur*
Editor: Joseph Bouthiette Jr.
Carrion Blue 555

Nate and I stagger out into the sunlight on Colfax. The plateau of concrete and Denver's altitude intensify the glare. I cover my eyes and Nate shields his groin as though the sensory assault is directed between his legs. Of course neither of us have sunglasses.

"Jesus, I'm blind," I tell Nate's hand.

He turns to my voice with a slurred half-smile, acknowledging the sound. I don't expect a response. Nate likes my voice. He never listens to what I say. That's why I'm so into him.

I'm not the type to cheat on my boyfriend and get drunk by two p.m. on a Wednesday. Or any day. Nate and I share some unspoken agreement that the rules don't apply with us. It happened the first time we met. I hated myself, but I needed the magic. Nate probably needed a doctor. Not that I cared. So we keep meeting. Instead of studying for class or cello practice, I curse Denver's pristine sky and try not to face-plant on the sidewalk.

"We need some pot," Nate says. Then he laughs. I don't know what the joke is. "I know a guy on Zuni."

I say, "Man, I used to live on Zuni. They've got pig faces in the grocery store up there."

"Yeah, I know," Nate says. "Come on."

It's a long way to Zuni, so we stop for a fifth or a pint or whatever it is. I can never remember. Nate knows exactly what to say. The guy behind the counter at the liquor store looks Nate up and down and then looks at me like I'm for sale. Nate's a regular. He's there every day. When we leave, Nate says he's going to tell the guy I'm his daughter. "And then next time we go in, we'll make out in front of him. Can you imagine?"

I don't want you to think I'm a bad person. Eric, loosely defined as my boyfriend, views me as an accessory. I'm just part of the outfit he wears for public events when he comes home tired after weeks away on assignment. Affection is out of the question. Sex is hit and run. When I try to talk about our problem, my thoughts deconstruct as they fall out of my mouth. Eric micro-analyzes every word into oblivion. Talking twists it all into my fault, my failings, my lack of experience and unreasonable demands. I offer to leave. He begs me to stay. Eric's made a million promises and then chastised me for speaking up when he didn't keep them. He's used my voice as a weapon against me.

Nate's never listened, never worked, and never promised me shit. Alcohol unites us. Nothing is real, everything is permitted. When intoxication curbs Nate's agility, we get creative. "God, you're nasty," Nate whispers with awe. It doesn't feel like cheating. It feels like a vacation in Interzone.

"Baby, this is so cool," Nate says. Beyond downtown, the rocky path along the viaduct is un-gentrified. Gang tags, shoes without mates and rotting toys mark the trail. A path of broken glass breadcrumbs glitter in the dirt, leading stray children to or from the witch's house: who cares what direction? A path is a path. Nate's always on his way to find something.

A block before Zuni, a white bag blows out of the bushes like a little ghost rising to greet us. It crackles end over end along the gutter to snatch at our feet. The faces behind the dim windows of a cheap retirement home glow, watching us without seeing. They line up like puffballs in a fairy ring unstrung to conform to a linear narrative, forced out of their circle to concede to time. They look the same now as five years ago when I first came to Denver. Featureless from age, pale sentries grow atop stalks rooted in a lifeless medium. I stop. The baby ghost bag yields to us. Nate banishes it with the tip of his black Chelsea boot and pulls me onward.

"See that?" he says. "When you're drunk long enough it's like you're on acid. Then when you get stoned it's like, you know . . . this is going to be great. We've been drunk for what, two days?"

"I'm not drunk," I say. We almost trip over each other laughing.

The guy on Zuni is gone, back to Juarez. Nate talks his way into the house anyway.

"Our shit is better than weed," the new guy says when Nate gets around to asking. I've never bought drugs. I didn't know you had to socialize. The vodka is gone and the house smells like boiling baloney. Damp, too. The men trickling from room to room don't look at me like I'm for sale. They look at me like I'm lunch.

"How much?" Nate asks.

The guy hands him a little Hello Kitty pillbox filled with colorless gunk that looks like lip balm. "Two fifty."

"You're killing me."

"Two twenty-five. Last forever, bruh."

"Serious."

"Two-ten, last chance. Try it out."

"How?"

"Rub it on your ear, wherever. Your lady gonna freak, see."

Nate puts a dab on his finger, rubs his ear, and holds the gunk out to me. I shake my head. Nate puts his pinky in the gunk and says, "Come on, baby. I want you to get stoned with me." He brushes the back of his hand across my cheek. At moments like this, Nate is almost loving, almost tender. Nate's finger slides into my ear and I taste oak in the back of my mouth, like the finish on a fine red.

I feel the oak in my teeth. Music comes out of them. The men's voices slow down and grow deep like the undulating bass line of a soul song. High, windy tones splash through the open window. It's traffic, urging me to accede.

The pores in my skin exalt as if each one has an independent breath. They hyperventilate, an echoing chorus high on oxygen. The sound of Nate's screaming slices through the music. He's unbuttoned my shirt and then fallen back in panic. The other men shush him. I see they wear masks. I follow their stares to my chest and seek my reflection in the black screen of a dead television. In place of my breasts, a symmetrical set of enormous ears opens like the wings of a butterfly.

My voice silences Nate's squeal. My voice grinds like the tires on the asphalt outside from a whisper to a roar. Then all is quiet. A man with a shit-eating grin approaches me and says, "Check this out." He sinks to his knees and blows across my chest. The ears tingle. I gasp.

His mask covers only the top right quadrant of his face. His tongue protrudes like a reptile. He flicks his tongue across my left lobe and exhales into the aural canal. Fine cilia play a symphony within. He circles, breathing deliberately and barely touching the ear until the music melts into liquid and spills out. His head swerves and he sinks his teeth into the lobe.

His neck is exposed. Heats cut through the center of my chest. A knife springs forth between the ears and slashes his dirty throat, dousing my torso in his blood, warm and wet.

"Holy fuck," Nate says.

The other men gibber and scurry. I grab the Hello Kitty pillbox Nate's dropped. I smear the gunk across the flat edge of the knife and enjoy the blade quivering in ecstatic response. This is what an erection feels like, I guess. I pull the knife from between the ears on my chest and sink it into my right eye. Colors explode. Many-faceted insects fly like diamonds from my eye in an army of knives that plunge into the fleeing and fortifying men. My eye sits on the tip of every blade, buried in their hearts, their lungs, their guts. My eyes stay alive inside them for centuries, watching them rot. Their bodies feed roots reaching into the future and the past, roots of the fungal mind-web living inside the earth.

Half-blind, I recognize the pox behind their masks. She came from the stars eons ago and inoculated our unborn planet. Creation spread like a contagion, a disease breeding many imposters and known by many names. Before the sixteenth century, physicians agreed all illness sprang from a single source. The pedigree of infection traced the disease of life to one fertile spore. Miasma poisoned the air, effluvium spread her symptoms. She was afforded proper worship until she bared her naked face at the close of the fourteenth century. Syphilis masqueraded through medieval Europe, and one hundred years of case histories quantified the Divine Pox: the smallest minds of the millennium replaced a deity with a diagnosis.

Her ancient roots grow through my multitude of eyes and the dead men on the ground and the wet floor of the house on Zuni Street. Where Nate cowers, a white oak spawns multiple trunks that erupt like sudden mushrooms in the damp house. Their gnarled arms communicate simultaneous narratives interlocking through hidden tree rings. History and the future connect within them like a chain linked from end to end in a circle. The clasp holds the chain together inside our warm flesh as a warning bell peals into the present day from fifteenth century Europe: once we map the New World, Eden is impossible.

Before 1490, the fungal arms of white oak bloomed on all corners of the planet from shared roots like mad, insistent corals. Her trunks were felled, planed, and sized, made ready to receive the pigment and prayer of craftsmen and artists. Layers of animal skin glue and gesso failed to obscure the living message carried in her veins. Medieval altarpieces hewn of her provenance intoxicated congregations by their mere presence. As time aged and desiccated the panels, curators harvested her sap as a sacramental balm, further depleting her potency. In the modern age, only the boldest heresy retains a trace.

The silence of the Inquisition on this matter proves their complicity with the argument embedded in the wood: a tree grows within a forest underneath the ground, an ancient fungal infection, a mind that mutates men into fruiting bodies of her will. "You are liars or fools who say I traveled to the Old World on the ships of Columbus or Cortez. I am endemic wherever there is life. Man is my vessel, and through him I will repopulate the stars. I am in the earth, but I am not of the earth."

"Baby," Nate says, scuffling through the carnage. "Babe, I can't understand you but I think we have to go."

Nate's voice again is gentle, tender, almost loving. But I don't need him to understand. I need him to hear. I need him to hurt me. I need him to hurt. I need him to come with me and stumble onto the sidewalk or into the abyss or out of this allegory and throw wide open the flat panels pinning us like a forgotten butterfly collection to the surface of things. I need him to help me come out from behind the glass.

"As above, so below," I decree. Nate pauses in his rush to escape the chaos. He peers at me in his shy way with his slurred smile. He's always been shy, started drinking young to manage his anxiety. Kept drinking to drown his father's voice calling him a fag because he liked art and fixed his sister's hair. Nate wanted to make his world more beautiful and ended up making it a slum. I met him when his life was done, when his stories were over-told and his clever ideas recycled, when his daughter refused to see him again and his ex-wives milked him dry. When I met him, Nate had nothing to offer me. I took it.

Nate holds my wrist and dips his finger in the little tub of gunk. He paints it onto my upper lip, dips again, and works on the lower with careful strokes until he's satisfied with the effect. His grip around my wrist leaves the watermark of his fingertips in my skin. His shy glance asks me if I recognize him: the hero playing the vagabond. I try to remain inscrutable. He kisses me. We drink the melting substance smashed between our lips with the seven tongues of a dragon he's slain and kept hidden in his pocket.

We lap up the gunk. I unzip his jeans and sheath him in the stuff. New parts spring forth in all directions. The receptive ones I plumb, spreading the substance and expanding organs that bloom between us like meaty flowers. I mount him, roots form, and the dead men around us stir. Nate's chasm widens. We plunge inside and eat the fruit.

In the New World, we find many strange and wondrous creatures. Birds of every color fly through air and water; rhinoceros, lion, and unicorn roam free upon the land. Men live like beasts, prized for their animal beauty and strength. Women suckle their young, unashamed. Exotic specimens both human and animal are brought to the auction block and deemed free of blemish by my European ancestors who trade their civilized microbial gifts of smallpox, measles, and typhus in exchange for the New World's abundant crops. Mercenaries are imported, slaves are sold, Eden is exploited.

The great explorers, masters of navigating by the stars, surveyed their course according to the trajectory of reason. Those who donned the mask of syphilis in their old age deemed it the worthy price of enlightenment. Certainly, the stars would not lie.

I fuck Nate's voluptuous new orifice. It fucks me, and grips me, and sucks me dry. I see my face reflected in Nate's obsidian skin, doubled by the twin globes of his ass. The eyes that look back at me are feral and empty, diseased by a Tudor kiss.

II

"You're home early."

I creep under the covers. It's three in the morning. "I didn't think you'd be here today."

"Yesterday."

"Sorry." I press into Eric, feeling his disgust.

Eric shifts, turns over, makes a barricade of sheets between our bodies. "We wrapped early. Extra pay." Eric makes military training films. It's not the creative work he craves, but it pays the bills. I've told him to quit. He's a painter by vocation. His brushes, paints, and rolls of canvas clutter the back of the closet.

Paint tubes harden. Brushes lose their hair. Eric says we can't waste money on studio space. I say use the living room. He says that's irresponsible, what would people think. I say who cares, you have to live and that's what it's for. He says well, we can't all just do what we want, can we? I say why not? At some point in the rhetorical mess, Eric goes deaf.

I destroy all chance of an alibi. I don't want one. "You got back yesterday last night or yesterday Monday?"

Eric sighs. "Today is Thursday."

"Oh. Right." I sit up and look at Eric in the red glow of ambient light from the twenty-four hour diner across the street. "What have you been doing for two days? Why didn't you call?"

Eric doesn't move. His body is an inscrutable landscape in the near dark, his voice an empty echo. "What have I been doing. Why didn't I call. Are you prepared to have a serious conversation at this hour?"

"No. I mean, I'm not prepared, I'm just, you know, concerned. I'm sorry. What did you do all this time?"

"Looked for you."

"I'm sorry."

"Stop saying that."

"But I am. Why didn't you call?"

"Go to sleep."

Inside me, there's a cathedral in flames. Ergot dancers surround the spires, casting obscene shadows in the red-tinged light as an apocalypse cracks the sky open like a raw egg. The man beside me doesn't see the figures licking the walls or the glare on the ceiling. He doesn't acknowledge the dizzying altitude of young mountains aglow with black and red wildfire that eats the trees. He's impervious to their screams. He doesn't ask me where I've been.

Tonight I told Nate it was over. Again. It wasn't the first time and it won't be the last. I'd tell Eric the same if he'd hear me. I'm sick of being the middle panel of our triptych, an incomplete story if I lose either wing. I can't survive as a solitary point in history, a grey globe interred by redundant chastity, closed and colorless, endlessly enduring the inertia of time's static symmetry. I need to fall off the flat edge of the world and embrace our collective fate. I want to fall: fall into the pit, or fly into the clouds, or both. If Hell is a product of history, Eden is a relic of eternity. Opposites conjugate in a compositional destination that binds the three of us together. We're hinged by the navigational rivalry of derelict stars. When we open our wings to take flight, we reverse the Fall of Man. If the end result is a fantasy or a satire, at least we'll sabotage the sequential face of history as we sail into the fire.

Eric's body is a warm, rhythmic beast beside me. Asleep, there's no anger on his face, no suspicion or disdain. He walks in the garden, the paradise that never existed outside an older man's dream of Eve's fidelity. He ignores the swans with too many heads, the restless gaze of owls. I slough off Eric's cocoon of sheets, exposing his flesh to my fingers. He's muscular, but his surface has softened with age into something both firm and pliant. I caress the paradox of his back. He's mistaken about Eve. She's not demure. She cuts across antiquity to expose the Father of Man as an imposter. Eve doesn't look down out of modesty or fear. She looks down out of boredom and resignation. Adam isn't enough.

When Eve looks up, and always she must, the future rages like a newborn pestilence. Enlightenment ravages the populace. Time spirals outward. Eric breathes less deeply as I draw my hands across his skin. I reach between his strong legs and brush the head of his lust as it bucks. Something involuntary and joyful like this grows inside me too. Maybe this time we'll evolve. Maybe this time we'll make it work. I want Eric to have more than one head, more than one life, more than one chance for enlightenment. One life is not enough. I wake him by pressing him into me where I'm still wet. His eyes stay closed. I'm careful to keep silent.

We fit together too well. Our incongruities shock. We came west together seeking emotional gold. The new delighted us. At the Mercado on Zuni, we practiced our Spanish with lavishly rolled *R*s until I halted at the deli case. Pig heads lined up before me with eyeless sockets. They stared like the heads in the window of the retirement home, watching without seeing, like unstrung puffballs in a fairy ring forced out of their circle to concede to linear time. Reflected in the deli glass, my face was transposed with the face of a dead pig.

The glare of sunlight obliterated the image. "Be careful," Eric said. "You'll hurt your eyes." He touched my back. I jumped. Purple sunspots skewed my smile into a grimace.

Eric pulled back. He's been orbiting away ever since. The harder I reach for him, the further away he recedes. We make love rarely, without speaking or looking. In public we're the portrait of a happy couple, but beneath our painted surface, the mute flesh of butchered animals holds a primal grudge. Our muscles remember every cut, our severed flesh sags, and our gouged eyes are blind. We wear masks of deception. We live behind glass.

We live until we die or mutate. Fungal hyphae network through both the soil below and the spatio-temporal heavens above. My body is an arm of the organism, inoculating Eric with spores of the disease that will transform us into a unified, animated host. We are destined for space exploration in the New World. We are bound for undying love. We are bound to Nate and the dead men on Zuni and the thinking underground forest that entangles us in her divine web. She rewards us with her sticky glory.

As we enter and exit one another, advancing and retreating, coupling and uncoupling, Eric grows louder, almost looking, almost shouting. I haven't heard him like this in ages, haven't felt him take me like this in so long that I forget all motivation apart from my body and its construct of lust. I feed him its sacrament.

I'm not sure about the consequences or the price. I'm sure that at this moment we're in a place more holy than any terrestrial church. Take, eat, this is my body.

But what if my body eats him first?

III

I'm drinking a complicated red with a smooth finish, tasting oak in the back of my throat. The syphilis bacterium is shaped like a corkscrew. The irony isn't lost on me. I wear the life-token of the many-named plague in the scars on my chest. With age, my body has become a symphony of scars. Textures, creases, enlarging follicles, sunspots, and tan lines blur into swarthy meat. My skin sings of illness. The drinks don't blur things like they used to, but I'll let you buy them if you like. I'm waiting for a friend.

I drove from Wisconsin to Denver without a reservation last night. Some insane chemical GPS called me to the Mercury Club like the rest of this throng. It's been ten years. Everyone looks like they came here to meet a blind date, eyeing one another, wondering when the show starts. I guess I'm not the only one who felt the call. Perhaps you felt it too.

It's getting late and you, my newfound friend, have listened to my story of love exploited and lost. I hope you don't think less of me. A triptych is a trap. In traditional form, the imaginary timelines of theology and the confluence of themes bind each panel to the rest. As separate entities, significance is lost, context is infinite. Randomly cropped remnants persist as puzzles the future may never unlock. What happens between creation and apocalypse? Is the middle panel the subject or the object? What sensation survives between lovers when we reject the boredom of the story and its conveyance? A triptych is engineered to be stable and portable. You carry it on your back when it's closed. It's almost a funny thought: an altarpiece like a traveling salesman's display ready to be propped up and gawked at.

"You're a woman of mystery," you say.

I roll my eyes. "You don't know me."

"I've seen you play."

"A triptych enfolds the viewer the way I hold my cello, like a lover between my legs, like a mother giving birth to an ekphrasis. She's an instrument from the Age of Reason, a Renaissance girl. You think she's austere, but deep down she's as needy as the rest of us. She begs to be plucked and bowed and strummed."

You say, "Mother, I want the sun."

"Excuse me?"

"Ghosts. I'm also on the stage, in theater. I'm Oswald."

I ask, "Is this research for your role?"

You answer, "It's more than that. My role makes me wonder what the world might be without the burden of a dead patriarch on its back."

"It's like you can read my mind. How many father figures do I have to destroy to escape this allegory? I have a thing for artists, especially the ones who don't make any art. Why is that so common? Why do so many great men fear genius and fall prey to the mundane? Don't you agree that the sexual and aesthetic goal of life is unencumbered freedom?"

You start to speak with a soft inhalation, and then interrupt your own breath when an old man and his caregiver enter the club. Your body moves like an act of grace, vanishing to an adjacent table.

I recognize Nate right away. He ducks through the doorway. His wavering frame in a vintage blazer hasn't changed. Same precarious height and poor connection, like his head will float away from his feet any second in a cloud of cigarette smoke. An older white guy accompanies Nate. He's shorter, disabled, and it's not until he leans over to peck my cheek that I realize he's not older, he's Eric. His body smells like sulfur.

Eric acclimates to the seat on my right side, his body unbending at the joints. Nate lilts into the seat on my left like liquid.

Nate's half-smile half-glance half-love expression molds his face into a permanent caricature of himself. Or maybe he's drunk. Of course he's drunk. Eric is stone sober and won't let up on the eye contact, the demanding veracity of his vision. He's an artist with no model, a painter with no canvas, a starving hawk. His eyes accuse me and excuse me from above. I'm not a person to him. I'm prey. I take his hand, and Nate's.

"I can't believe you're here. I didn't know you two . . . um," I say.

"Yeah," Nate offers. "Well, someone had to take care of him."

The violence in Eric's eyes belies his gentle tone of voice. "After you left, he kept coming by. I don't pretend to know what you do. I have always been supportive. As you can see, I needed assistance."

Nate does that thing where he makes a kissy noise sucking on his cigarette. I want to kick him every time he smokes a cigarette. He says, "Don't blame her, dude."

Eric's face looks like bitten fruit. His flesh is puckered and rotten. "This isn't easy for me. I'm not here to blame anyone. You didn't have to hide anything from me."

Nate says, "She was young."

Eric says, "You didn't have to lie. Why did you lie?"

Their hands feel like two different species. Nate's thin fingers seep away from my grip. He's got a drink and a cigarette to tend. Eric clasps my fret hand like a threat. I pull it away out of instinct. It's been my livelihood all these years.

Eric says, "You didn't tell me you were sick."

"I wasn't."

Eric doesn't hear me. Nate says, "It's my fault."

"I'm not talking to you," Eric snaps at Nate and then turns back to me. His hand is still open, expectant. "I will always care about you."

Parallel conversations ebb and flow around the club with similar hushed intensity. Each table flickers, candle at the center, black and red décor absorbing ambient light. Faces in various stages of decay implore, debate, and confess, a gallery of grotesque, unthinkable masks poised for a ceremony to start. You, my friend, my spy, solitary and silhouetted by the glow of your phone, wait attentively as the human narrative exhausts itself.

Eric's premise is all wrong. I speak to you as much as to him. "Do you want me to be a bird with its wings sliced off, a shark with its fins amputated for soup, sinking to the depths and dying of immobility?"

"Don't be sad," Nate says.

"Stay out of this," Eric says to Nate, and then to me: "I'm trying to forgive you."

Nate says, "Nothing to forgive. I'm making amends."

Eric's eyes flash. "Is that what you call it? Free rent and free food, probably peddling my meds. I should throw you back on the street."

"Don't talk to him like that," I say to Eric.

"Hey, hey, it's okay," Nate says. "I mean, it is what it is. Somebody's got to take care of him. I got this, baby." Nate's body flows in close to me while Eric's rigid posture of pain nails him upright in his seat.

"This is all very touching," Eric says from a distance. "Don't you feel any remorse?"

I'm not sure which one of us he's talking to but I'm ready to answer. "Time wasn't supposed to be so fucking linear. It was a gift. Something we shared. I saw us growing and moving together and burning what we left behind."

"That's why you poisoned me? As a gift?" Eric's voice isn't so gentle anymore. Heads turn.

"It's not poison. Look around you."

"I'm dying," Eric says.

Nate says, "The forest is dying."

Roots below and above are withered. Hyphae joining us through the fungal network burn away in the glare of modernity. Called by the chemical signals of an ancient organism's death-throes, we're a poorly reconstructed triptych, an anachronism. Looking around this somber congregation, I can barely imagine these beings as the frolicking, fruiting bodies of our shared, toxic vision; pale, inverted and many-limbed; joyful, innocent and wanton as we combine into a heretical geometry, a blueprint of paradox, an illuminated neuro-script. Our bodies will reconfigure into a manic vessel, the spaceship *Paradisum Voluptatis*. She will carry us aloft into the New World.

I say, "When we leave, this will be a dead planet. We're gathered for lift-off."

"This is fun," Nate says.

"This is bullshit," says Eric. "Let's go."

Nate's eyes almost open all the way. Eric fights to extract himself from his chair. His face reddens with effort. "She's crazier than ever. This is pointless. Do you understand?" Eric turns to me. "You know you need help. There's a cure. Sometimes it works." He struggles against the confines of his body. I can infer from his movements the ineffable beauty of the multi-dimensional, asymmetrical being Eric refuses to become.

I make one last attempt to reach him. "The cure is killing you."

Standing, leaning, Eric catches his breath and shakes his head. "Bat-shit crazy bullshit." He hobbles away, relying on his cane.

"Babe, I gotta motor." Nate's up and ready to follow. He's about a foot taller than me. He gets in so close I have to look up to see him. He says, "Call me. Okay?"

"What do you mean? If you stay, you'll die like him."

"Aw, I knew you loved me best. I won't tell. Almost forgot. I brought you something." Nate hands me a plastic baggy with some tablets of various shapes inside. Lint from his pocket is stuck to the baggy and the plastic is crumpled from re-use. It's no longer transparent.

Nate crushes me into his chest, leans down and puts his lips in my hair. "You loved me best."

"I—"

He says, "Shh."

I loved the idea of the man more than the man himself. I've looked for him, mourned for him, and known him by the singing of my scars, by the seven tongues hidden in his filthy pocket. He leaves one of them with me, bitten and dry. He leaves.

My spy, my snake, my newest friend, you palm the baggy and take the seat across from me. You're welcome to take them both. You say: "The faces we wear in this world are masks." You have effete cheekbones and glorious skin, and eyes still clear and bright with the ignorant kindness of youth. I suspect you've led a privileged life. You speak in a way that is wise, yet you can't possibly know that I avoid mirrors lest I see in my reflection the face of a dead pig.

I answer you as honestly as I can. "Beneath our feet, god is dying. The disease of life demands the stars."

"Does it? You share some colloquy?" You shift your shoulders forward and say "colloquy" as if I know what the word means. Your eyes are full of light and aspiration. "Will you share with me?" you ask.

Old sources of the sacrament have dried up. The antibiotics of the twentieth century eradicated most of our kind, and collectors of medieval art no longer guard the sacred argument of the hallucinatory sap. The drug is legendary, and outside of our bodies, it is lost, lost. My radiant new friend, the world is ripe for a new plague, and you're burning with faith. Who am I to stop time in her tracks? Why, indeed, would the stars ever lie?

You are naked and gleam like quicksilver, as though impervious to time. I'm less naked than you, but no less monstrous standing on the frontier of disintegration. I know Creation is a plague. I know that when desire transforms into violence, I will participate in the drama.

"Aren't you a bit young for this scene?"

"That's not important," you lie to me. "You're beautiful."

"I don't know if you're ready for this. Maybe you should take some of those pills."

"I don't need that," you say.

"Are you sure?"

The congregation's culled to less than fifty. Outside, we assemble into forms indeterminate as animal or vegetable or rock. We enact pornographic tableau, an exploded model of a medieval simultaneous stage. The chain of time closes and locks. Mycelia weave our raw nerves as one tendril, pulsating with ancient and modern thought. In the city, polluted by artificial light, the stars have gone blind. Orifices able to give and receive chart a didactic course as they increase. We navigate by multiplicity. The *Paradisum Voluptatis* ascends to the night sky with the glory of a symphony, an armed battalion greater than the sum of her parts.

Your heart beats too fast, your muscles clench. I told you to take the pills. I turn you over and push your face into the earth, our foster mother. You spit in her dirt and murmur your lines, "The sun, the sun." I pull back from the warm knot of your colon and release its new trickle of blood. To soothe you, I whisper in your ear as you grow limbs, voices, eyes:

"I'm the flat color on oak, the pigment cracked by age. What harm can I do to you? My waters are pictures of water. My lust is a satire of lust. My church is a creature inside you, a spore that spreads when you dream. My church is a doctrine of deception, a mask of love and horror. You wear it when you dream. Your dream is a weapon of desire; your body is the fruit of my dreams. Your body is the fruit of syphilis."

I press you into a new shape. We rise.

AUTHOR'S STORY NOTE

When I look at a painting, I see time. History lives in the hesitant moment of a faltered brushstroke, the bold stab of the matte knife, and the contemplative labor of chiaroscuro. Outsider artists breach formal technique. Hieronymus Bosch was self-taught. As the aging paint of his medieval masterpiece cracks, the mystery of "The Garden of Earthly Delights" resists any single interpretation. Prompted by editor Joseph Bouthiette, Jr., my story "Paradisum Voluptatis" is an ekphrasis of the Bosch triptych, a creature of multiple tendrils, a gnostic stab in the eye. Why indeed would the stars ever lie?

RADIX MALORUM

SEAN PATRICK HAZLETT

From *Vastarien*
Editors: Jon Padgett & Matt Cardin
Grimscribe Press

t's been said the curse of middle age is a man's inability to admit he's reached the peak of his life's parabolic arc—never to rise higher than whatever station he's reached. The longer he rages, the more he struggles against the natural order of things; the more he invites a complete and utter psychotic break. It's only when he surrenders to fate's capriciousness that he begins to find peace—a peace that I will never know.

My IQ is one-hundred-and-sixty. By every indication, I'm a genius. Yet I've been unable to master a world where the cretins are calling the shots.

Take my boss's boss, Alastair Jenkins. The guy's got the attention to detail of an LSD-laced gnat. Yet he runs strategy for our company, plotting the trajectory of an organization of five thousand people. If he has an insight—or more likely, a whim—all those people change course to follow whatever direction he charts.

It's insanity—an insanity no one seems to mind so long as the profits keep rolling in.

I'm going to murder someone today.

The nightmares started three weeks ago.

They were different than normal dreams—more vivid, crisper. Every sense was as real to me there as they were in the waking world—oftentimes more real.

Night after night, the dream always followed the same pattern: when I slept, I woke in oblivion's sleeve.

Suffocating under a shroud of darkness, I spiraled through an infinite vastness. Panic-stricken and desperate, I reached out into the void, seeking a handhold, an anchor to reality. Feeling nothing, I placed my hands where my body should have been, despairing as they slipped through the ether. Eschewing all reason, I flung my discarnate essence further into the abyss.

A rectangular sliver of light materialized in the darkness—a doorway to some bizarre dimension. Disregarding all caution, I made my way to the door, anxious to cross its threshold; desperate for sensation, even pain.

Passing through the portal, I emerged onto a grand plaza. Once again with substance and form, I shivered as a chill wind nipped at my naked flesh. A faceless man clad in a tuxedo greeted me with a tilt of his top hat. He carried a red string tethered to a flesh-colored balloon. The balloon had a face. It smiled at me, its mouth curving unnaturally upward like a crescent moon. Though I could not place its face, it seemed eerily familiar.

The scent of ozone permeated the air. Nimbus clouds gathered over a dull gray horizon. Flashes of lightning cleaved a glowing cicatrix in the heavens.

Something sinister swarmed on the plaza's cobblestone surface. The creeping things scurried toward me at a frenetic pace. To what purpose, I did not know. Beyond the carpet of crawling critters and far in the distance, a great pyramidion hovered above a thousand foot pentahedron hewn from cyclopean blocks. The pyramidion swiveled in my direction. On its triangular surface, a great eye opened and gazed into my soul.

A voice transcendent whispered, "Novus ordo seclorum."

I woke in a cold sweat. My alarm was hammering at my eardrums. It was already nine a.m.

When I arrived in the office, my supervisor, Jerry, was waiting at my desk. His arms crossed and his brow furrowed, he made it a point to turn his wrist and glance at his watch. "You're late."

"I'm sorry. Won't happen again." I bowed my head in ritual shame—a farce practiced by tardy white-collar cubicle slaves since the dawn of civilization.

"How are you going to delight the customer when you can't even delight your boss?" he said.

I grinded my teeth. Whenever Jerry aped corporate jargon, I wanted to gut him with a rusty nail. We were selling software, not stately pleasure domes in Xanadu.

"You're right," I said, channeling my inner chameleon.

"Of course I'm right. I'm gonna need to see more from you, Simon. Corporate is looking to cut more costs. If you wanna keep your job, I need all hands on deck. You got that?"

"Yes, Jerry, I got it," I said, irritated. Contempt oozed from my voice.

Jerry glared at me, then walked away.

I booted my laptop. Seconds later, Charlie, an office drone and graphics designer, nattered loudly on his iPhone while walking laps around my open office desk. He made it impossible to concentrate.

I felt an overwhelming urge to murder him.

The inherent horror of the modern corporation is that it's optimized to encourage middling men and women to strive harder while simultaneously degrading and dehumanizing them in a mindless march of mediocrity. Once the corporate entity exhausts them through layoffs and natural attrition, it replaces them with resources half a world away. What's worse, today's India is tomorrow's A.I. algorithm.

With all the noise, my attention drifted. My eyes wandered over a sea of wage slaves chained to their computer screens.

Then I saw him.

Standing against the wall at the far end of the office, the faceless man in the top hat and tuxedo approached my desk, then began a mocking march behind Charlie. Tuxedo gripped a crimson string fastened to a balloon holding his face.

I now knew what I had to do.

No one really talked about what had happened to Charlie.

The executive team had made sure of it.

The alienation of corporate life made it easier to keep the sheep in the dark.

Sure, there were hushed whispers about the two police officers who'd spoken to our CEO, but no one really knew what I knew; what I'd done to him—to his face; to his eyes; to his hands.

It's no coincidence that the percentage of psychopaths in corporate management is four times that of the general population. It's why companies are veritable hunting grounds for apex predators like me.

And our worship of money makes it all possible. Money, is, after all, a god. Without belief, our entire financial system would crumble. I always chuckle at the so-called "grown ups" who ridicule cryptocurrency as fake money. All money is fake; it is only faith that confers it power.

If not for my dark dreams, I never would have experienced this awakening. It was easier to make money when you didn't care about hurting people; it was even easier if you thrived on torturing them.

It was time to channel this impulse, harness it to fuel my rise.

That night, I returned to the plaza. Tuxedo led me toward the slithering masses. As I drew closer, their shapes resolved into a glorious vision.

As far as I could see, a wave of disembodied hands surged forward, forming a writhing wall around me and obscuring my vision of the pyramid god. A blood-red eye on the palm of each hand regarded me with a fierce and godlike intelligence. The voices they projected into my consciousness threatened to overwhelm me—to annihilate my sense of self.

So many songs. So many memories. So many paths.

Unchained to the mundane insignificance of my mortal coil, I had finally found my purpose, my true calling.

Mammon was its name.

I came to work early.

I watched with glee as Tuxedo danced around Jerry, my reality slowly melting like tallow beneath a flame. Tuxedo's meat balloon bobbed up and down, its mouth curling in an awful rictus.

I smiled too, then offered to buy Jerry lunch.

Alastair seemed reluctant to promote me, even if only temporarily. I could see it in his idiot eyes.

I really couldn't blame him. I wasn't a glad hander like he was. To me, people were taxing. I used to avoid them unless interaction was absolutely required. Now I actively sought them out, especially if their culling would increase my personal collection while simultaneously improving the corporation's profit margin.

The trick was not to exterminate the highest performing sales people. This annoyed me since the best of them tended to be the most insufferable.

But money was money, after all.

As Alastair droned on about our corporate mission and blue ocean strategy, his smarmy smile began to drip off like three flavors of melting sherbet. His face followed. By the time it was a flesh-colored puddle on the linoleum tiles, he dismissed me, closing his office door for a "very important call."

Through the glass wall, I could see Tuxedo standing behind Alastair's desk. The face on his flesh balloon winked at me.

While tempting, I decided to save Alastair for later.

For now, I only sacrificed those who wouldn't be missed.

Office gossip suggested a murderer was in our midst.

I shrugged it all off.

They'd never catch me. They couldn't catch me. My reality was fluid. Time was a recursive tree—its pathways branching out and folding back into themselves. The trick was not to get caught up in an infinite feedback loop that shattered reality. I could simultaneously be at my desk pretending to work and elsewhere peeling off Alastair's face.

Reality is a Rorschach test, an inkblot on the ethereal plane.

The sheep can only interpret it, but the artist peering down from the higher dimensions has the power to shape how that inkblot is rendered.

But that's not the point. The point is that I was coming up in the world at exactly the moment when most people had already reached the summit of their pathetic lives.

Today, they escorted me out of the office—my position eliminated. I laughed at the fat sow from HR who read my notice mechanically from a script.

When Tuxedo and his face arrived, I giggled hysterically.

She shifted in her seat, seemingly unsettled by my reaction.

As she stood up, I placed my hand on hers and said, "I'm going to bind your soul."

Her face went ashen. She stormed out.

In her wake, security surged into the room.

I had so much fun that day, exploring hundreds of permutations of the event. In one path, I carved off her face. In another, I tracked her home and sliced her and her husband into tiny pieces.

Later that night, I stalked Alastair through the Tenderloin. He resisted, killing me many times. Although a gambler may win a round or two, like the house, I always win. In an abandoned alley, I stretched his intestines across the opening of a decrepit recycling bin and strummed a delicious dirge. Then I added the best parts of him to my collection.

Greetings, kiddos. Here I stand in a twilight realm straddling the crossroads of recursive time, dressed in a tuxedo and top hat, awaiting myself. The skin of my face is stretched taut and paper thin, floating on the tendon tether of a flesh balloon distended with my essence.

There are more of us in your reality than you can possibly imagine. We maim and kill at will, then conveniently edit the timeline as if it had never happened—in this reality at least. For an incident can never be erased. Its stain forever befouls the fabric of the cosmos. Much like the fickle corporate titan, we sometimes experiment with objective reality—explore how the cattle react to a world inundated with abattoirs.

Something to ponder as you go about your Sisyphean labors of existence. Welcome to the new world order. Fare thee well.

From the third edition of *Metaphysical Pathologies of the Criminally Insane* by Doctor Irving Werther:

For months, Simon de Wees, otherwise known as the Corporate Carver, had eluded authorities, leaving a trail of mutilated bodies throughout San Francisco. It had only been after they'd received a note confessing his crimes that police had raided his studio apartment in the Tenderloin.

According to Detective Joseph D'Alessio, de Wees had sliced off his victims' faces, removed their eyes, and severed their hands. Until today, authorities had never been able to recover any of these body parts.

When police had entered de Wees's apartment, they had uncovered a wall of hands with eyes sewn into the palms. More disturbingly, and in one of the most macabre displays in San Francisco murder history, the skin of his victims' faces had been tanned and stretched into balloons floating in his apartment. De Wees's body was found in his bed dressed in a tuxedo and wearing a top hat. He had skinned off his face and, like the others, inflated it into a balloon.

Anonymous sources revealed that several members of the city's moneyed elite had urged the San Francisco Police Department to keep one particular aspect of the case under wraps. On de Wees's wall, scrawled in blood was a mantra that was becoming all too common in an epidemic of copycat murders:

Radix malorum est cupiditas.

AUTHOR'S STORY NOTE

"Radix Malorum" first appeared in *Vastarien*, a literary journal that features stories and critical analysis inspired by the work of horror writer, Thomas Ligotti. In particular, this piece explores the Ligottian themes of corporate degradation, philosophical pessimism, and nihilism. More importantly, the title lays bare the story's central theme. *Radix malorum* is truncated from the Latin phrase *radix malorum est cupiditas*, which loosely translates into: greed is the root of evil.

If anything, "Radix Malorum" is a cautionary tale about how the beneficial tenets of capitalism can be taken to inhuman and alienating excess. This extreme form of capitalism—hypercapitalism—seeks to maximize shareholder value at the expense of all else. Morality is ignored; employees are interchangeable parts; and all other stakeholders are annihilated. Mammon murders God.

This story is also indicative of my own surreal experience working at a major and iconic Fortune 500 company when its share price declined by roughly two-thirds. The overreliance on incompetent and inexperienced company lifers both astonished and deeply troubled me. It was akin to watching a circus in which arrogant and entitled *enfants terribles* capriciously unleashed lions that gorged on hapless performers while the audience cheered on.

Operating in companies in crisis is particularly difficult for intelligent, intellectually curious, and analytical people. In these situations, the set of actions required to right the ship is often surprisingly straightforward. Yet when people hunker down into survival mode, they stop communicating, spread rumors, and blame others. In the short term, the culture tends to shift from a meritocracy to a patronage system, where obsequious political lackeys rule the roost—often badly. When the dust settles, the most competent are gone and the culture has been laid to waste.

To capture the bleak sensibility and paranoia of these environments, I layered the story with a great deal of corporate symbolism and imagery. The swarming and grabbing one-eyed hands represent the single-minded greed of the hypercapitalist impulse. The smiling flesh balloons represent the false and taut masks corporate executives wear when they smile, glad hand, and promise everything will be all right despite all evidence to the contrary. The pentahedron, the pyramidion, and the phrase *novus ordo seclorum* all appear on reverse side of the U.S. one-dollar bill.

Moreover, the Latin phrase *novus ordo seclorum* translates to new order of the ages. In this tale, new order implies the sinister influence of hyperdimensional entities seeking to pervert and corrupt humanity from realms unseen much like management teams making life or death decisions under the cloak of boardroom secrecy.

Even Simon de Wees's recursive and hyper-dimensional existence is linked to the relentless and infinite treadmill of corporate life—the same disaffected experience multiplied a million fold. Over and over and over again without beginning and without end.

This story is ultimately about the ruthless suppression of the individual by the group and how the inexorable wheels of the corporate machine corrupt and twist otherwise good people before grinding them unto dust. In essence, workers are the conscious and organic feedstock of the hypercapitalist endeavor to be consumed without consequence.

LACKERS

LEO X. ROBERTSON

From *The New Flesh: A Literary Tribute
to David Cronenberg*
Editors: Sam Richard & Brendan Vidito
Weirdpunk Books

Bodies pulse on velvet throws, plastic lilos, picnic blankets, sodden-looking pillows, and even on the bare concrete floor. Skin glows beneath a string of Technicolor LEDs taped across the generator room's goliath metal structures, across their rusting steel wheels and flaking valves.

Even at an orgy, with all these naked people around him, Neil feels underdressed in his crumpled white shirt and jeans. He smooths his lank brown hair and redirects his gaze to anything but the people. Cables stream out to two-bar heaters in the room's corners, which poorly stem the winter chill. Bluetooth speakers, strewn across the floor, ooze some slow and sultry song that resounds around the room.

When Neil musters the courage to look again, more details of the flesh-pile reveal themselves. Large birthmarks. Cleft lips. Missing eyes, digits, and limbs.

By his feet, a half-naked man crawls over a woman. He licks down her neck and across her mastectomy scars, his tongue covering their scaly surface. A prosthetic nose languishes on the floor beside the pair, its metal snap fasteners glinting in the colored light.

The man turns to Neil. There's a red raw hole in his face where his nose once was.

Should Neil keep watching? What's the etiquette here?

Before he can decide what to do, Luka hooks an arm around him from behind.

"I only want to watch," Neil says, startled.

Luka laughs. "I only want to talk."

Luka guides Neil to a room at the back of the power station. Plastic limbs, with tags on them, form a flesh-colored pyramid in the room's corner. Protective masks hang on the wall.

"You can relax." Luka's voice is honeyed, his accent ambiguously European.

Neil takes the time to look at him now. His olive skin, slicked-back black hair, dark brooding eyes. He wears a purple silk kimono with a pattern of robot hands all over it. A long towel covers his legs, much like those dotted all over the generator room floor.

"Sorry for being lame." Neil examines the stained tag on a plastic knee socket. "Shit."

"What?"

"I shouldn't have said 'lame.' In this room."

Luka grins. Moonlight reveals his perfect teeth.

"So you store everything here for afterwards," Neil says.

"We cast off prostheses first, inhibitions second." Luka gestures towards the generator room, his silk sleeve falling across the stump of his left arm. "Here, we are our true selves. Lackers." He looks at the ghost of his missing hand as if to recognize it there in the air.

Neil imagines the hand gesturing. It's even more conspicuous by its non-existence.

"So you'll only observe."

Neil grips the hair at his crown. "I have a husband, for one. Maybe that doesn't stop the others, but it's enough for me. And, well, I've honestly never felt very sexual."

"Why not?"

He bites his inner cheek. "I didn't think events like this were for people like me."

"Before you knew about our mission, you mean?" Luka folds his arm and phantom arm.

"Yeah. I always have to brace people for what they're going to see when I take off my clothes."

"Speaking of which," Luka says, "it's time for me to see. The part of you that isn't whole."

This is the same wording from the lackers' illicit website, where Neil had uploaded the photo of himself that granted him entry to the club tonight.

He knew this was coming. A chill in the room announces itself. He unbuttons his shirt and moves over to the light so Luka can see.

Luka gasps. "Can I touch it?"

"I-I guess so."

With a warm finger, Luka traces the concavity of skin over Neil's heart. The caress sends tingles across Neil's skin.

"But how?" Luka asks.

Neil shrugs. "The ribs just never grew there. I came out of the womb holding a fist over my heart."

"I'll bet you did." Luka flattens his palm over the skin crater.

"Kids used to bully me about it."

"Oh yeah?"

"They saw it one time after gym." A strange, contorted grin takes over Neil's face. "They called me Marilyn. Like Marilyn Manson? They asked if I'd had the ribs removed so I could suck my own dick."

Luka laughs through his nose. "And after that?"

"No one's brought it up since."

"Sometimes what's left unsaid is the most important." Luka feels Neil's heart pounding against his hand. "Does it hurt?"

"No pain at all. It just looks different."

"'Just'? Oh but darling, appearance is everything." With Neil stunned into silence, Luka sends his hand wandering down. "By the way, I'd kill for your legs."

"Enough." Neil pushes the hand away.

"Sorry. I went too far." Luka steps back, pressing his palm to his chest. He seems to savor Neil's warmth.

"It's not just that. Look, I'm a journalist."

Luka's eyes freeze. "Huh?"

"I'm doing a feature. I only sent the photo so I could track you down." Neil buttons his shirt again.

"I appreciate your honesty," Luka says, though his cold

expression betrays him. "So, you just came here to gawk at the freak show."

Neil flicks one of the masks. It dangles on a nail and throws shadows across the wall. "You know it's more serious than that. Barb Russ. Alex Tillman. Christian Simmons. These names mean anything to you?"

"No." Luka looks insulted. "People aren't too keen to admit they come here. Some are return customers, others aren't. And everyone has a code name."

Neil holds his gaze, waiting for him to falter.

"They're rumors," Luka continues, walking over to the door. "Obviously. People badly want to believe we're harmful. Undeserving of affection. Get back to me when the gossip dies to nothing. Then we won't need a club anymore."

A well of guilt forms in Neil's chest. Then again, Luka's air of having been offended could be a ploy.

Luka clasps his invisible hand in the other. "You exposed yourself to me, so I'll return the favor. I won't kick you out, and you can interview who you want. Just be upfront with them about your intent. Oh—and no photos."

When Neil returns to the generator room, the lust has cooled down.

Club members wrap blankets over their shoulders and prop themselves against the metal housings. They drape themselves across the cold concrete walls. Some smoke from short glass pipes, thick bongs, and vapes. Others lick substances from stumps.

Neil approaches "Viper," a man whose open leather waistcoat shows the plastic mesh holding in his abdominal organs.

"Industrial thresher accident," Viper says. "Stripped off the skin and muscle. And my right arm, of course." He puffs from a joint stuck in a metal pincer that juts from his shoulder.

"Queenie," a middle-aged woman in a black slip, says she

always felt like her right leg belonged to someone else. "Last time I checked, the term for it was Body Integrity Identity Disorder. This one time, I filled a bathtub with dry ice and stuck my leg in it, I had a tourniquet over my thigh and I was biting on a towel to stifle my screams. My parents rumbled me in the act." She dabs her eyes with a delicate finger. "They rushed me to the hospital. Surgeons did nothing but remove the frostbitten flesh while I pleaded with them to take the whole leg with it."

Neil examines her stump. "How did you finally get the leg removed?"

She winks. "Don't worry about it."

Neil speaks to victims of acid attacks, house fires, childhood cancers, and auto accidents. Their tragedies soak into him, his heart cooled as if by the ghosts of so many missing body parts. No one will talk about the missing people and besides, he can't handle hearing more about their everyday realities. He eventually heads for the front door.

The noseless man stands close, with Luka beside him. He taps white powder onto the face of Luka's iPhone.

Luka stops Neil as he passes. "Before you go, we'd better exchange numbers. In case you have any more questions." He enunciates the last word with masterful disdain.

Neil swallows hard. "Of course."

"Adam and Eve were already 'of God,' so to speak." JP's biblical pontifications echo through his and Neil's little Hackney flat. "They didn't need to eat the forbidden fruit. That was the snake's trick."

Neil bites at a thumbnail in thought. What's JP doing? He doesn't usually stay up this late making videos.

"Well, that's my interpretation anyway, doofus-face!" JP adds.

Oh. He's livestreaming on Twitch for platinum-rank Patreon subscribers.

Neil peeks into the gaming room.

Controller in hand, JP splays out on his gamer chair, which gathers sweat on his periphery. Boxes of his "merch"—crucifixes and plush toys of Jesus—surround him. He wears an old hoody and pajama bottoms. Wireless headphones sit askew on his head.

When JP turns and sees Neil standing there, he gets up and joins Neil in the hallway, kissing him on the cheek.

"You have that look on your face," JP says.

Neil acts nonchalant. "What look?"

"Distant eyes, sour mouth. You know something you don't wanna tell me."

Neil grins and stays silent.

"So you had a good time, then?"

"I wouldn't say—"

"By the way, while you were out, I googled 'amputee support groups.' Wouldn't you know, they're a thing."

Neil scoffs. "They're not just amputees, they're—"

"Lackers," JP drawls. "Wow, they sure get to people fast."

Neil walks off to the bedroom. JP follows and stops him at the foot of the hallway. Light from the restaurant signs outside casts an ethereal glow across the pair.

JP takes a deep breath, considering how to proceed. "Isn't it harmful to tell people they need to go to a special club for affection?"

"What would you have them do? Stay at home and cross their fingers that they wake up in a—" Neil looks around. "Can your subscribers hear us?"

JP pouts. "Maybe. So what was Luka like? How about that missing arm? I heard he chopped it off himself."

In response, Neil puts on his pajama bottoms, lies on the bed and pulls his laptop off the side table.

"Whatever," JP says on his way out the bedroom. "I'll be done by three."

JP makes YouTube videos on Bible interpretations, a passion that turned into a living. The pair tell each other that happiness is most important, that money isn't everything. Some days it's as if JP grants Neil permission to think that way just because JP makes more money.

Has JP so soon forgotten the years when his subscribers numbered only in the hundreds? The consolations Neil offered him as he cried on the couch? Does JP look back on that time and think of himself as a temporarily inconvenienced famous person? Isn't that the most compassionate way for him to think of Neil now?

Neil tuts and tries to tap these thoughts out his head with a fist. He reaches for his jeans on the floor, takes the phone out of the pocket and scrolls through his contacts.

Luka Novák.

Luka gave his real name?

He opens a new browser tab and searches for the name on Facebook.

Luka grins back at him, wearing wraparound sunglasses and Lycra. Behind him is a summery vista: mountains, winding dirt roads, and a clear blue sea.

Investment banker. Liver of life. Proud cat parent of two.

When JP walks into the bedroom again, Neil closes the Facebook tab.

"I was insensitive earlier," JP says.

Neil feigns confusion.

"I didn't mean to disparage anyone. I just think Luka's attitude is poisonous."

Neil looks at the time. It's three a.m. He isn't getting into it.

JP smiles bleakly, taking Neil's silence as an admission that he has a point. He comes to bed and puts his head on the fully ribbed side of Neil's chest.

They peruse Netflix together and start watching some series that supposedly takes place in a superhero universe, but no superheroes ever show up. At least not while JP is awake. He falls asleep on Neil about half an hour after Neil has lost interest.

Neil lowers the volume and opens Facebook again, clicking on Luka's picture.

Luka stands on two springy black sports prostheses.

I'd kill for your legs. Because he doesn't have his own?

When JP rolls over in bed, Neil slams the laptop shut and puts it back on the side table.

JP places a hand on Neil's chest concavity, quickly withdrawing it again, as if he'd just touched a hot iron. "Sorry," he whispers.

Neil frowns at him, then lies back and closes his eyes.

It's almost light outside when he finally falls asleep.

He dreams of a decade-old hook-up. It was after some club night out with the other waiters at the restaurant he worked at back then. He'd gone back to some stranger's shitty early-twenties apartment. They'd kissed on a couch, surrounded by empty bowls with crusted spaghetti or dried-up cereal. There was a heap of underwear in the middle of the living room carpet and a roll of toilet paper over by the TV, for some reason.

It was dark that evening, the guy was a good kisser and they were both hammered, so Neil only noticed the problem when he felt warm drops fall on his bare chest.

Blood. The guy was slicing his own forearms with a straight razor.

After all these years, Neil still remembered the sound of blood dripping on his skin.

At the time, Neil had gotten up and left without a word. But in the dream, the stranger is Luka. Luka with two arms and hands.

Instead of a straight razor, Luka wields an ornate boning knife with a mother-of-pearl handle. He doesn't just slice the skin but digs into it, into the vessels, muscle, and bone.

Blood ejaculates from the dream wound.

Squirt, squirt, squirt.

Neil wakes up in the thick sweat of nightmares, his come leaking through the sheets.

As I walked around the generator room, taking in all its carnal glory, I thought about how lackers sneaked around this city, relegating themselves to abandoned buildings out of some internalized sense of inferiority. How we were complicit in making this the case, with dating app bigotry and associated contemporary prejudice. But I was also inspired. The lackers drew attention to their imperfections. They didn't cower, didn't lust after one another despite *their flaws. They celebrated those differences and used them to fuel their desire.*

Neil lies in bed, trying to will assignments into his inbox and ignore JP's guffaws from the gaming room when he gets a message from Luka.

Tonight.

There's an address, a train station outside the city. Not quite abandoned, but according to the results on Google Maps, it's so poorly maintained and has so few trains that it might as well be.

"You have that look on your face again." It's JP, standing in the bedroom doorway.

Neil places the laptop to one side.

"Off to see your friend Mr. Novák?"

Neil snorts. "You went through my phone? Used my laptop?"

"What does it matter? Don't lie to me. I know you too well."

Neil stands up, heads to the wardrobe and pulls out some clothes. He shuffles into a pair of jeans.

"When is it?" JP looks at him in the wardrobe's inner mirror.

Neil stops buttoning the shirt. "This evening."

"Right then."

Neil pushes past JP and goes to the front door, trying to find his shoes.

"Don't," JP says. "Please."

Neil looks down at his ribless concavity, which pulses fiercely. He turns to JP. "Touch it."

JP winces and holds out a hand. He stops. "Why are you obsessed with the one thing I can't—?"

"Touch it!"

JP forces his eyes shut and reaches out again. But his hand seems to push against an invisible barrier.

Without another word, Neil puts on his shoes, does up his shirt and leaves.

Viper stands by the train station, wearing a leather jacket and scarf. Glass shards from smashed windows litter the concrete around him. A bashed brass lock lies there, glinting in sickly streetlight.

"Good to see you again," Viper says as Neil approaches.

Neil keeps his head low and nods, walking straight to the door.

Viper holds out a pincer and stops him. "There's a protocol."

"Oh."

"It's no big deal. Can you show me the message Luka sent you? With the address?"

Neil scrolls through his phone and finds the message. When he looks back up, Viper sprays him in the face with a bitter tasting chemical. A black fog consumes his vision and he passes out.

When Neil comes to, he's lying by the train tracks. Up above, stars peek through a thick canopy of clouds made blue by the night.

He sits up. His jeans are torn above the knee. Cable ties loop around the track and over his legs, securing him in place. Tight rubber tourniquets squeeze at his thighs, his flesh bulging and red.

He tries to move his arms but they're bound behind his back. He tries to scream but a dirty towel gags his mouth.

"After I read your article, I had my doubts that you would show tonight."

Neil tilts his head back and sees an upside-down Luka.

Luka walks closer, pulling the kimono over himself. This one is pink and covered in silk-screened eyeballs. Their long cords of vessels and nerves run across the fabric like bloody snakes.

"You made it sound like you aren't one of us."

Neil shakes his head, trying to protest. Drips of sweat sting coldly in his eyes.

The lackers assemble in a circle around him. Viper, Queenie, the noseless man, the mastectomy-scarred woman and the rest—they're all here, all holding candles that drip big white gobs of wax.

"You redeemed yourself towards the end," Luka continues. "That part about letting imperfections fuel desire. I thought, 'Yes, he has potential. And if he comes back to us, I won't make him disappear.'" He bends down and strokes Neil's hair. "So you can join us. But not yet. Not as you are. Because what we do, it's about more than desire. It's about true beauty." He plants a gentle kiss on Neil's forehead. "You still don't know just how beautiful you could be. But with our help, you'll see."

Horns blare through the night. A train barrels towards them, its ghostly white headlights cutting through the darkness.

AUTHOR'S STORY NOTE

I'm a fan of the work that *Weirdpunk Books* puts out and I heard that they were looking for Cronenberg-inspired stories for a new anthology. I read their submission call and said to my subconscious, "I would like a story idea for this, please." About a month later my subconscious said, "How about an orgy club for maimed people?" I strongly recommend this story generation method to all writers!

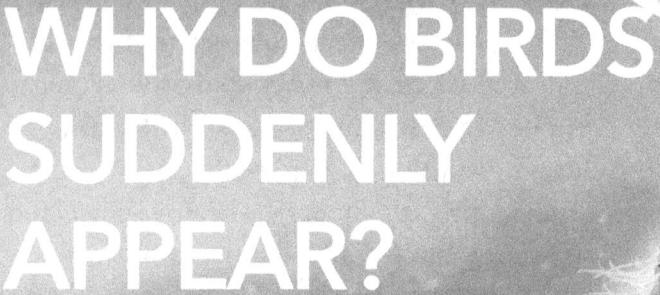

WHY DO BIRDS SUDDENLY APPEAR?

RAJIV MOTÉ

From *Honey & Sulphur*
Editor: Joseph Bouthiette Jr.
Carrion Blue 555

The curious gathered in the courtyard to watch the pale, naked man shuffle towards the light spilling through the black arch. His limbs were bone, wasted muscle, and sagging skin, hanging like sticks from his bloated torso. He had no hair. Some of the watchers made to cover their own nakedness with their hands, or twist their bodies from the light in sympathetic shame, but none looked away. The light cut through the inky shadows, not angry and red like the distant volcanic fire, but brilliant and golden. Against it, the man's skin looked translucent as fog. From beyond the gatehouse came sounds that could be heard nowhere else in Hell. Laughter. Song. To the watchers, the light and merriment on the other side of the arch felt nothing less than holy.

"Do you think they'll let him pass, Jaan?"

Everyone lingered in the courtyard, despite the danger, wondering the same. The irresistible drama of redemption, if that was what this was, gave meaning to this world of suffering. They spoke in whispers and watched the man's progress, their eyes flickering to the sky, ready to scatter if their loitering was noticed.

"We'll see, Tessa."

Repeating each other's names was a ritual between them. It was also, in its own way, holy. They couldn't remember if those were their true names, but they clung to them. The names stirred something just shy of a memory, a feeling of being together, enclosed, safe. From the corner of his eye, Jaan tried to memorize details of Tessa's face—the red-gold hair, high forehead, blue eyes, lobeless ears, thin lips, sharply tapered chin—but as his eyes moved over each feature he forgot the previous. Memory was slippery, and fragile as thin glass. Once, he thought, that her face meant something to him. If he could just hold its parts together in his mind, he might remember what.

The man's feet dragged on the gray stone of the courtyard, never lifting enough to break contact. It took him time.

"Ought he approach penitent or proud, Tessa?"

"I can't remember, Jaan."

Before the arch was the Gatekeeper, tall and sinister in his feathered cloak and tufted helm. He allowed some of those who approached to pass. Others, he punished horrifically, their remains strewn across the courtyard to crawl and knit themselves together. Jaan remembered that, but trying to discern a pattern was like grasping at smoke.

The man stopped his shuffling and stood in front of the Gatekeeper, his gaze downcast. The Gatekeeper regarded him with eyes that shone round and yellow beneath the helm. He circled the man slowly, occasionally grasping at a body part with a claw-like hand, as though judging the ripeness of fruit. Jaan felt a flush of shame, and nearly averted his eyes. Bodies were so shameful.

Tessa's hand reached and clasped Jaan's, and he looked down at the sudden, unexpected contact. Touch without pain unnerved him. His eyes crept up her arm to her shoulder, and rested on her breasts, hanging like fleshy pears above her ribs. Then his gaze sank lower to the red-gold thatch of hair where her pale legs met. They once meant something to him, those parts of her. Tessa's hand withdrew, and she tried to cover herself.

"No, Jaan. Don't look."

He became aware of his own nakedness, and recoiled. He had a ghost of a memory of the sickly-sweet taste of fruit, a lifting veil, and the slow billowing of bone-deep shame. The shame was an unclean itch marbled deep into his flesh, and when it flared, he craved the deliverance of scouring punishment.

"I'm sorry, Tessa."

They returned their eyes to the man, being prodded and inspected by the Gatekeeper. Jaan's fists clenched and his nails drew blood. From the corner of his eye, he spied revulsion on Tessa's face.

The Gatekeeper continued circling and groping the man who stood motionless before him. Jaan stepped back, anticipating a spray of blood. But the Gatekeeper stopped, and with a mocking bow, motioned the man under the arch. He shuffled forward, hastened by a hard smack across his buttocks, and disappeared into the golden light.

A commotion of talk exploded in the courtyard.

"He was accepted!"

"Did anybody know him?"

"He expiated all his sin!"

"How did he do it?"

"Should I try?"

Neither proud nor penitent, Jaan thought. The man came . . . empty. Motion caught Jaan's eye. He looked up.

"Birds!" cried someone.

All eyes drew skyward. The black, jumbled shapes of wings, beaks, and talons burst through the sooty clouds in utter silence. There were birds and there were Birds, and these were the latter. Insufficiently tormented souls eventually drew Birds. They were living voids, bird-shaped holes in the universe, and they inspired primeval horror beyond all torture when they appeared. Suffering had purpose, the only purpose: atonement. So it was believed. But the Birds were nothing, an absence, a horror of meaninglessness, the annihilation of all possibility. Facing them was beyond anyone's courage. The people in the courtyard scattered.

"Jaan!"

"Tessa!"

They ran. Flagstone became jagged rock that tore at the soles of their feet, but the pain was not enough. They ran faster. A hanging tree twisted up near the road, its branches already heavy with dangling figures kicking their legs and wheezing against the rope around their throats. Birds of a more ordinary sort pecked at their flesh, tearing off gobbets. It was good, honest torture. Irreproachable. But there were no unoccupied nooses. Tessa moaned. Jaan could not bring himself to glance at the sky. They ran on.

On the hills above their path, the citadel burned. It always burned. Figures fetched buckets from the lake and scrambled up ladders, trying to quench the blaze as more fires sprung up for each they put out. They, and the citadel's defenders, plummeted from the walls, succumbing to flames, or the arrows and spears from the Fell Hordes below. The endless war was unwinnable, but the souls on the ramparts were grateful to fight it. From the time he spent there, Jaan knew it was an exquisite torture of perpetual despair and defeat. But he and Tessa could never make it to the walls before the Birds were upon them. So they kept running, towards the hopeful sounds of rushing water and screaming. A bridge emerged from the darkness, and soon Jaan saw the river. Pale, bloated bodies floated in the current, dying but not dead, never dead.

Jaan smiled. He seized Tessa's red-brown hair and balled his fist. "Tessa," he said.

"Jaan," she answered.

He smashed his fist into her nose. She crumpled, her blue eyes filled with gratitude, and tumbled over the low railing. The hairs on his neck stiffened. He sensed silence descending on him like a crushing mass. He froze in panic, his mind screaming to throw himself into the river, and his body refusing to obey.

Suddenly, excruciating pain pierced his heart, and Jaan looked down to see the tip of a lance emerge from his chest. He twisted his neck to see the Horned King behind him, astride his rat. His Fell Hordes of clawed, fanged, spiked monsters bristled with weapons behind him, on their way to the citadel. With relief, Jaan submitted to the agony as the Horned King raised his lance and Jaan slid along its length. The King then lowered his lance with a twist, and Jaan slipped down the blood-slick wood and tumbled into the river of bodies.

*   *   *

Jaan floated. His body bobbed with the current and caromed off other bodies. The water, growing colder the further it swept him, flooded his nose and mouth as the swells filled the troughs. It bubbled up through the hole in his chest, injecting agony into his heart's attempt to heal. He drowned and froze and bled and embraced the pain, knowing at last he was safe from the Birds.

"Tessa," he said. But he lost grasp of what the word meant.

Having found a steady source of pain at last, Jaan could let go. Relieved of fear of Birds, and the anxiety of an existence without progress or purpose, he could devote himself to his atonement, to burning away the shame that infested him to his marrow. Securely in torment, he even amused himself with idle thoughts, like pondering the origin of shame. Once, a long while ago, or perhaps recently—time had no meaning—he'd asked the Owl, for the Owl was ancient and wise, and had gifted him with unimaginable pain.

"There was once a thing called sin," the Owl said, before carefully slicing open the flesh at Jaan's heel with a talon. "Sin is a bloody, sticky rawness in men that adheres to the world and separates them from their Maker. An abhorrent, repulsive condition. Shame is your awareness of sin. Your knowledge of its wrongness. Is it not terrible?"

Jaan frowned through the pain blossoming in his foot. Memory was slippery, but he knew there was a moment, something with a sickly-sweet taste, when he learned shame. If such a moment existed, there must have been moments *before* he knew shame. Before there was sin. He put this to the Owl.

The great bird hooted, an amused sound. "So, a philosopher!" The Owl delicately peeled the skin from Jaan's heel in a single narrow strip around his foot, tracing between his toes and spiraling slowly up his leg. "Your Maker began you, but you are not yet complete. Finishing yourselves is your purpose." Pain blazed through Jaan. Not just where the flesh was removed, but everywhere.

"You were meant to eat of the fruit. You were meant to open your eyes. Shame is a teacher. Heed it, and let it guide you." Jaan remembered hearing the Owl's calm words despite his screams. He was hung by his hands, bound to a great harp by its strings, and while the Owl peeled, his struggles strummed a gentle counterpoint to his raw-throated cries. In some walled-off corner of Jaan's mind, he heard a tiny whisper: *Tessa*.

"Suffering roasts away the rawness and attachment. It makes you perfect. Pleasing to your Maker."

His Maker. There was something forbidden by his Maker, something that brought him a sense of purpose and incomprehensible shame, all at once.

The Owl was a master craftsman. Before it regrew, Jaan's entire rind, a glistening red ribbon looping on the ground, was uniform and unbroken, beautiful in its perfection.

* * *

"Tessa." He spoke the name, and icy water filled his mouth, making him sputter. There once was a face that meant something. Blue eyes. Red hair. Or was it gold? The tiny part of him tucked away from the agony, the part he thought of as himself, grasped at the pieces, trying to fit them together as they sliced his fingers, a puzzle of shattered glass. He floated, froze, drowned, and collided with other bodies. He floated forever, or a short while. Time had no meaning.

"Tessa," he said.

"Jaan," he heard.

Jaan raised his head, upsetting the equilibrium that kept him afloat. His limbs thrashed, and razor shards of ice sliced his skin. And he saw her, a few bodies downstream, a rime of frost covering the parts of her above the water. Jaan crawled over the bodies, sending them into choking, gasping fits. His hand reached out, and found hers. They clasped. Again came that uneasy feeling of contact, with neither pain nor shame. A raised whip that never fell. So cold, and yet . . . Her. *Tessa*. The tiny oasis from the agony that was himself shyly touched the tucked-away part of her that whispered his name. And they adhered, merged, making a shared, hidden space, a crystalline bubble containing only themselves.

Jaan. The name flowed through their connection.

Tessa. The name flowed back. The names echoed in the bubble, sustaining themselves.

Time had no meaning.

Jaan learned that misery and its absence don't exclude one another. They're adjacent countries with artificial borders, and sometimes one can choose where to stand, where to live. Creatures under the water took bites of their flesh, shards of ice cut them, the water itself continued to freeze and drown them. Jaan suffered, he wept, and at times he screamed. As did Tessa. But that was the way of things, the rules. What one did. It was not what they *were*. Their hidden selves, Jaan and Tessa, lay entwined in their bubble, separate from what Hell demanded of them.

Hand in hand they floated, souls joined, straddling the boundary between agony and secret joy. Enough agony to avoid Birds, enough joy to nurture the space they shared. Arrows from the Fell Hordes on the banks struck them, the monsters that hid deep in the water rose and feasted on their flesh, and ice floes sliced them to ribbons. But they always found each other again. They drew each other in as surely as the arch and courtyard drew those hopeful for salvation. It could all be endured.

"Could we stay like this, Tessa? Forever balancing?"

"What is forever, Jaan? This is how we are. Until something changes."

"Nothing ever changes, Tessa."

"Then yes, Jaan. For now, we can be like this forever."

Their bubble grew. By increments they shaped it into a garden of sunlight, blue skies, green trees, fruits, flowers, and life. It was memory, not fanciful invention. Memory could be rediscovered in this space. Here, memories stayed. They remembered a world before Hell, where joy was unadulterated and shame, absent. They remembered taking pleasure in their bodies, and each other's. There was no sin there. They must have been taught their shame. They sported in sun-warmed pools, ate fruit and the flesh of fair beasts, and danced in the hills and forests. Jaan found the sweetness of the memory so intense, it was almost its own torture. He couldn't remember feeling so keenly in the garden.

"We didn't know anything else then, Jaan."

"Is that why we suffer, Tessa? So we may go back to the garden appreciative?"

"Then do we harm ourselves, Jaan, by creating our own joy? Do we block our own return?"

"Maybe the Owl lied, Tessa."

"Then what was the point of all this, Jaan?"

He had no answer. The light beyond the archway was beautiful. But was it more beautiful than this bubble he created with Tessa? Was it more real?

*   *   *

Time was meaningless, but change did come. Jaan and Tessa ran aground at the site where a great battle had taken place. Guttering fires burned where once there were buildings, and the corpses of the Fell Hordes were strewn across the field, gutted and dismembered, weapons sticking out of their bestial bodies. The stench of carnage was overpowering. None lived. None to deliver torments. Jaan shivered as he scanned the sky where black clouds began to gather. He and Tessa had lost their balance. Cracks ran through their perfect, crystalline bubble. Shapes circled among the clouds, darker than black, misshapen windows into an abyss.

Tessa bent down among the corpses and lifted out a barbed whip. "Jaan," she said. "Take a weapon."

Jaan found a long knife and brandished it, looking up at the clouds. "Tessa, I don't think this will—" With the loud crack of rent air, the whip wrapped around his throat, and Tessa pulled. Jaan's eyes bulged. The barbs were cruel, but the agony of betrayal was pain beyond anything he'd experienced. That alone should have driven off the Birds.

"Quickly, Jaan! Hurt me!"

At last he understood. Jaan rammed the knife into Tessa's belly, haft deep, and twisted. She doubled over, but jerked the whip with her last strength, crushing his windpipe. The bubble shattered. In the garden of their mind they still held each other desperately, fighting for balance. *I'm sorry I'm sorry I'm sorry . . .*

Still the Birds circled.

They healed and struck. *Tessa.* Healed and struck. *Jaan.* Time was meaningless and the Birds circled, sometimes high, sometimes low. They rode raging rapids of pain and panic that crushed inwards on their ruined little garden. Its skies grew dark. Its trees blackened with rot. It was one thing to submit to torture, together. But to hurt each other . . . How much pain could he inflict on her, to save her? How long could he bear it? How long could she? The Birds were very low. Amidst the chaos, Jaan scrambled for a plan.

After gutting Tessa again, Jaan took her whip and bound her ravaged body, hand and foot. He stood over her, watching, drinking in the agony over what he must do to her, and hoping it would be enough, for both of them. The Birds circled. Tessa's bowels slithered back inside her body, and the skin slowly closed the wound. Her eyelids fluttered.

He stared down hard, scrutinizing her naked body with as much disgust as he could pour through his eyes. In their bubble-garden they learned to delight in each other's bodies, but back in Hell, the habits of shame were deep and strong. Betraying her this way would hurt her more than anything he could do with a knife. It would protect her.

"Jaan, don't . . ." Tessa tried to cover herself, but was unable to move. Her eyes widened in horror. Didn't she understand? No, she *mustn't* understand. If she understood, he would lose her.

"This, Tessa? This . . . *meat of yours* . . . is what kept me from entering the arch?" The Owl had hinted as much. His Maker would welcome only perfection.

"Jaan, please . . ."

"Your lies weren't enough for me, Tessa. You aren't enough. How much will I have to suffer to clean the filth you've put into me? How far have you pulled me away from my redemption?"

Tears streamed from Tessa's eyes. Jaan had considered everything he was telling her. But he had rejected it. Hadn't he? The effort to convince her to feel his betrayal required him almost to believe his words. He had to hate her just a little if he was to save her. The look on her face tore him apart. She was saving him too.

Then his lower lip trembled.

And she saw.

What remained of their connection was tiny and dark, a clouded crystal shard, but he felt a whisper through it. *Jaan?* It broke his resolve. *Tessa.*

Her tears ceased. Her expression softened. She understood. *I love you too*, she whispered through the bond.

The Birds swooped. Silently they wheeled and dove, and where they struck, holes of nothingness riddled her body.

"Tessa!" Jaan screamed.

They swarmed her, thick as flies on meat, and all Jaan could see was a flapping, churning void where Tessa lay bound. When they broke off, she was gone.

In every corner of his mind, Jaan was alone. He was aware of himself still screaming, wordlessly, until something inside him broke. The Birds swooped and circled. Jaan watched them impassively, suddenly as silent as they. "Come," he whispered. The Birds scattered in all directions, back to their clouds.

* * *

The man dragged his feet across the courtyard, towards the arch. Voices around him whispered. Eyes in pale faces watched, scrutinized his nakedness with revulsion. He ignored all of them. The Gatekeeper waited, black against the golden light spilling from within the arch. He shuffled towards him and stopped, his eyes downcast. He submitted to the groping claws on his body. He knew that yellow eyes examined every bit of his naked, emaciated flesh. It didn't matter. All his shame had burned away. His suffering was complete. He knew even before the Gatekeeper's bow that he could pass. He resumed his shuffle, into the blinding light.

The world beyond the arch was bathed in sunlight. The trees and sky were vivid shades of green and blue, and music and laughter were everywhere. Fountains splashed. A breeze carried the scents of flowers. Before him on the trim lawn was a long banquet table. Seated on both sides were huge birds of every sort, beaked and billed, crested and horned, chittering and honking merrily, their colored plumage ruffling in the breeze. In unison, their heads turned toward the man.

At the head of the table sat the Owl. He stood and bowed. His enormous eyes looked pleased. "At last," the Owl said. "You are ready." With a sweep of his wing, he gestured to a great, silver platter at the center of the table, garnished with a mixed assortment of human heads, limbs, and entrails. The man shuffled forward, noticing the cool softness of the grass under his feet, but caring nothing for it. He climbed onto the table and took his place, lying on his back. The sunlit sky filled his eyes, blue and perfect, and birdsong rang in his ears.

AUTHOR'S STORY NOTE

Every time I look at Hieronymus Bosch's triptych, "The Garden of Earthly Delights," I see something new. There are hundreds of bizarre little dramas, comedies, romances, and horrors in the details. But what keeps drawing my eye is a mystery, in the middle of the Hell panel. There's a courtyard and an arch with brilliant light pouring through it. Pale figures stand just outside the radiance. It's a strange, quiet scene in a landscape of monsters, torture, and mayhem. What is that place? Is there hope through that arch? This story explores that mystery.

DARJEELING

SYON DAS

Independently published by Syon Das

Dedicated to my father—I hope my tales disturb you more than you recall your tales disturbing me

* * *

July, 1968

The night sky loomed over West Bengal. As a fog gradually dipped it's opaque wings into the foothills of the Himalayas, Bipin Malakar cursed under his breath. Nauseated, the forty-eight-year-old doubled over, slamming a trekking pole into the mossy path beneath his boots. While their heavyset scout leader dry heaved between expletives, five teenage boys glared at the pair of iron gates ahead of them. On the other side, lay a marble path that ran straight for ages. It eventually tapered off into a small set of carpeted stairs, leading to the jute-coir doors of a stone building. While the establishment's height was nothing to marvel at, its expansive width gave the entire structure an overwhelming presence. Three green windows were spread apart next to both sides of the door, and a single grey window was situated on the upper half of the building. The area was surrounded by an endless army of fir trees, which all seemed to be reaching into the darkness for help.

"Finally . . ." Mr.Malakar said. He took a swig of water from the canteen strapped across his torso. As the man wiped his unkempt moustache, the teens watched the bottle fall back onto his plump stomach, and create ripples. After a fourteen-hour journey involving two trains, a steamer, and an inclined hike from the local hill station, Mr.Malakar and his troop of scouts had arrived. They had travelled from their small homes in Burdwan, to the multi-crore Banerjee estate in Darjeeling.

*   *   *

A residence that had once belonged to Kanav Banerjee, the former owner of several tea plantations, was now a barren attraction for Himilayan folk to view from afar. One day after a game of squash, Kanav came home to find his nineteen year old son, Ahil, dead in his bedroom. The young man's torso had been sliced clean down the middle, and a dark, red cavity resided where his spine and organs should have been. Kanav would have held onto Ahil's arms as he wept in agony, but they had been twisted out of shape and jammed deep into their sockets. Blood had spewed out of the teen's skull and seeped into the floorboards. Ahil's face, however, was untouched and frozen in a neutral expression. It served as a stark contrast to his mangled frame.

The details of that day never got out to the public. Everyone had been told that Ahil's passing was the result of suicide. Although that choice had stigmatized Kanav's family name and parental worth, it seemed like an easier pill to swallow than having to disclose the actual nature of his son's final moments. Due to the ghastly circumstances surrounding the event, Kanav decided to move to Bombay with his wife, Jaanvi. Before going, he left the estate in the hands of his most loyal housekeeper, Devak Malakar.

For the past 13 years, Bipin's brother had tended to the Banerjee home with unfaltering care. Apart from cleaning the place, Devak spent his days reading poetry and cooking. He occasionally went to the garden near Batasia Loop, to let the lush scenery wash over his senses. Darjeeling's cold nights were saved for getting lost in thoughts; thoughts about how life was treating Jaanvi and Kanav in Bombay; about how different his *own* life might have been if the Banerjees had decided to sell the property. But most of all, the nights brought up thoughts of Ahil. While Devak had never lied to Kanav, the housekeeper deemed it best to keep the fact that he had seen the teen's corpse a secret. Devak had never told another soul besides Bipin, that he had been in the room mere seconds before Kanav had discovered Ahil's body. The horrific scene became a part of Devak's psyche, and had attributed to several nightmares. However . . . the housekeeper had to live with something far more troublesome for the rest of his life. Something that only *he* was aware of. Devak knew the reason for Ahil's death.

*   *   *

Bipin fumbled inside the pocket of his chino shorts, then pulled out a brass key. As the man unlocked the front gates, he maintained eye contact with the scouts and said, "My brother is being generous in letting us stay, so show some respect . . . *okay?*"

The troop of teens nodded in unison, then rolled their eyes before following their leader into the estate. They were used to him speaking in an authoritative tone before any deed that required disciplining had been committed. With a career that entailed nothing more than making sure a group of young men could hike, be part of a cavalcade, fish, and tie knots, it was understandable why Bipin Malakar needed to squeeze as much self importance out of his job title as possible.

"Do you think it's true?" Sunil said to his fifteen-year-old brother, Adith. The pair were trailing behind three older teens; Rohit, Pratik, and Asif.

"What? The *ghost* stories? Come on, grow up. This isn't a radio horror special," Adith replied, shifting the rucksack on his back higher.

During the summer, which was monsoon season in Darjeeling, Devak would invite Bipin to come and spend a few days on the estate. They would take long strolls throughout the winding footpaths of the mountainous region, drink some of the area's finest black tea, and eat fresh Passion fruit while listening to Hemanta Mukherjee's records. After sunset, Bipin would always try to tease out more details about what Devak had seen on the day of Ahil's passing. Unwilling to casually discuss the matter, the housekeeper would throw a grim look in his brother's direction. He would state that that the upper floor, and especially *the room*, was off limits.

From the moment they left Burdwan, Bipin had rambunctiously been telling the boys about "Ahil's presence." He claimed Devak had caught glimpses of the teen's spirit in several rooms of the building, and that he could see Ahil standing near the gates of the estate after dark. Bipin had taken his brother's warning about going to the top floor of the house, and decided to flesh it out into a tall tale. It was nothing more than a bullshit haunted house story to make a typical sightseeing trip seem more risque. However, the false accounts were scary enough to get the best of Sunil's fourteen-year-old imagination.

As Mr.Malakar and the teens made their way through the foggy path, they heard the front door swing open. After a few seconds, they were able to see a man wearing calf-length socks, blue trousers, and a black undershirt step outside. He put on a set of full-rimmed glasses and smiled.

"It's nice to see you, brother. Welcome," Devak said, placing a hand on Bipin's shoulder. He embraced the scout leader, then motioned for the teens to come in. "I have a table spread with sprouted bean soup, goat curry, and pickled potatoes waiting for you."

"Oh man, I haven't had goat in *ages*," Pratik replied, letting off a slight moan near the end of his sentence.

"*I haven't had goat in ages*," Asif and Rohit mimicked. They erotically rubbed their stomachs, making orgasm faces towards Pratik. Adith and Sunil chuckled. Pratik socked Asif in the shoulder, then shot a glance towards the younger teens that instantly silenced them.

The scouts were surprised by the home's minimalist design. They figured that Kanav Banerjee hadn't cared to leave behind any memories when he moved, and Devak didn't seem to be much of an interior decorator. For it's massive size, the layout of the place was simple. Upon entering, the boys were met with the Brazillian Cherry steps of a staircase leading to the second floor. While Devak hadn't wasted any time in telling them that it was off limits, he mentioned that the floor had two bedrooms, as well as a storage closet that used to be a small library. Everything else was ground level. The kitchen was near the back of the building, and was the only room *not* primarily built out of wood. A few feet from the fridge was a vinyl-record player stationed beside a leather chair. The combination of classical Bengali music and coffee had a way of taking Devak back to simpler times.

The left side of the residence had three rooms. The first one had a bunk bed, the next one contained a steel cot layered with a thin mattress, and the third was filled with several mops and cleaning products. On the right side of the building were two rooms, one of which was Devak's. It contained a twin-size bed, which the housekeeper surprisingly didn't feel comfortable resting on. He felt more at home within the tattered sleeping bag spread out a few feet beside it. In the corner, was a black dresser with a dusty stack of notebooks on top.

Right next to Devak's quarters was a spacious bathroom, which had the same wooden aesthetic as the rest of the home. The one thing that made it less artistically barren than the other rooms, was the inclusion of several flora patterns gracing the walls. While a pleasant aroma flowed throughout the entire residence, it was occasionally marred by the slightest hint of a tangy odor.

* * *

After dinner, the scouts showered and freshened up. While Adith and Sunil changed into their pajamas, the older teens refused to head to bed . Pratik, Rohit, and Asif insisted that since they were only a few months away from graduating high school, their adulthood granted them access to the town's less populated areas after dark.

"First of all, we're not even *boys* anymore," Rohit said, waving a finger between himself and the other eighteen year olds. "We're *men*, okay? I mean, shit! We come *all* the way here to Darjeeling . . . and you want us to stifle the curiosity that you've spent the last four years instilling in us? All because it's *dark*?"

Bipin's cheeks became bright red as his fists clenched up. He looked like he was two seconds away from strangling Rohit, until Devak patted him lightly on the back.

"It's alright," the housekeeper said, unfazed by the teen's arrogance. He smiled. "I understand where you're coming from. When I was eighteen, I would climb the highest tree I could find after sunset, and sink my teeth into a horror novel." Rohit went to interrupt Devak, but the man continued.

"The thing is . . . these Himalayan regions . . . they're strange." Devak's expression grew cold. "They have a different vibe after sundown. You can feel it. You can tell that the trees don't sway the same way. Then there's the silence . . ." Rohit wasn't smirking anymore. All five scouts began to get lost in the housekeeper's words.

". . . it's a type of silence that lets your imagination come into play. The deeper you delve into it . . . the less aware you become of what's in your head . . . and what actually might be around you. It's even more true in the case of young men such as yourself, with minds so . . . curious. You're always in the mood for discovery . . . and this place . . . it can sense that. It will give you something new . . . something *different* to remember. However . . . these aren't things that you would want to get stuck in your head. But by the time you realize that . . . it'll be too late. Remember . . . while this isn't just limited to forests and footpaths . . ." Devak looks up, as if Ahil were stapled to the ceiling above him. ". . . we're always better off staying within the walls that we know.

At least after dark, that is."

Bipin Malakar looked at his brother, then at the frightened scouts. After collectively sharing a moment of intensity, the group broke out of their trance.

"Alright, so we agree that it's time for bed . . . correct?" Devak said, reverting back to his friendly demeanor.

As the scouts nodded, Adith asked, "Where are we gonna sleep? We all have sleeping bags so—"

"We're the *seniors*," Asif said, lightly squeezing the necks of the two brothers. "Pratik and I get the bunk, Rohit goes on the cot, and you two can get the ground of whichever room you like! After all, you *do* have *sleeping bags*, right?"

"Right . . ." Sunil murmured. Adith narrowed his eyes at his younger brother, ashamed that he succumbed to the older teen so easily.

"Great, so it's settled," Bipin said. "Alright boys, don't stay up too late chatting about girls or cricket. We have to hike to Sandakphu tomorrow to catch a glimpse of the Sleeping Buddha peaks." The teens looked at each other in horror, thinking whether or not they had enough energy to make a trek of that magnitude. They silently nodded, then dispersed.

"You're quite the storyteller," Bipin said, winking at his brother.

Devak's face lost it's warm shimmer. He took off his glasses and said, "It wasn't a story." He stared into Bipin's eyes for a brief moment, then turned around and headed towards his bedroom. "Don't go upstairs," Devak stated. He didn't look back.

*   *   *

It was 1:20 am when it started. Sunil and Adith had fallen asleep in their bags next to Rohit, despite the older teen snoring loudly on the cot. Then suddenly . . . through the silence of slumber . . . came the sound of padded footsteps. They were coming from directly above. They were coming from Ahil's room. Sunil was the first to hear them. While he did his best to ignore the sound at first, within minutes they became too ominous for his fourteen-year-old brain to handle. He glanced up at the ceiling, then back at his brother. Sunil thought of waking him up, but decided against it. He was usually met with a smack when he interrupted Adith's sleep cycles. Waking up Rohit was out of the question, so Sunil was on his own. Like a halfwit from a slasher flick, he decided to check out the noise himself. After quietly making his way out of the room, Sunil peeked at Devak's door to make sure it was closed. Seeing that it was, the scrawny boy scout started to ascend the staircase. Shivers coursed through the teen's arm as his hand slid over the cool, bronze railing. When Sunil finally reached the top, he paused and looked down the hallway towards the second door on the floor. It was located right above Rohit's room. It was the one.

Trying not to think about the demented horrors that lurked within the long stretch of darkness, Sunil slowly made his way down the hall. The property was surrounded by the white noise of wind and rustling branches. The teen felt his ears pop as he gulped. While saliva trickled down his parched throat, Sunil stared at the rectangular inlays etched into the mahogany door. The safety of the sleeping bag crossed his mind, and the scout contemplated whether entering Ahil's room alone was the smartest idea. Eventually, the impulsivity of youth got the best of him. Sunil silently edged forward, reaching a hand out.

As his middle and ring fingers began to curl around the knob, the faintest sound of movement came from the other side. A droplet of sweat trickled off the teen's earlobe. Sunil's eyes were peeled towards the center of the door. He realized he had a firm grip over the knob, and slowly started to turn it. The sound of muffled footsteps stirred up. Sunil froze. The movement intensified . . . and started to get closer to the door. His breathing became labored. As the footsteps came closer and closer, the teen heard a subtle rattling noise. He looked down to find his hand trembling over the knob.

"What the hell are you doing?" a voice whispered. Sunil's hand sprung off the knob like it was a piece of burning coal. He swiftly turned his head to the left . . . and saw Adith starting at him with a dumbfounded expression.

"I thought you were going to the bathroom when I heard you get up," his brother said. "But when I opened my eyes, I caught you walking up the stairs and th-"

"Footsteps . . . I . . . I heard footsteps," Sunil said, glancing back at the door he had almost opened.

"In *there*?" Adith replied, sticking his chubby finger towards the room. The noise was gone. No sounds of movement. No footsteps. Adith looked angrily at his brother.

"Look . . . I know you love shitting yourself after every *creak* you hear, bu-"

"I'm not lying, Adith! I'm sure there were footst—"

"Shut *up*!" Adith whispered sternly, grabbing a fistful of his brother's white shirt. "Just stop it, okay? There's no *ghost*! Act your age!"

Sunil looked down at the ground, embarrassed. The teen *did* pester his older brother with supernatural gibberish constantly. Ever since middle school, his reading material was comprised of nothing but things such as abridged Edgar Allan Poe anthologies, vampire comics, and picture books about cursed locations. Although *anything* to do with the paranormal immensely frightened Sunil, he just couldn't stay away from the stuff.

"There's *nothing there*, man. Just go back to bed, okay?" Adith said, letting go of his brother. "If you *hear* anything else, just put in your earplugs."

Sunil looked at the door, then nodded. Adith sighed.

* * *

Within minutes of settling back into his sleeping bag, Adith drifted into his dreams. But Sunil refused to close his eyes. The teen *knew* what he had heard, whether or not his brother believed him. Sunil stared at the ceiling, and thought about the decayed body of a teenager . . . crawling around on all fours. He pictured it making its way down the stairs. After thirty minutes of fighting a set of heavy eyelids, the boy scout tapped out.

Two hours later, the footsteps returned. They were much more prominent this time, and accompanied by the periodic scratching of floorboards. Sunil opened his eyes.

"Adith . . ." the terrified teen said. He poked his brother's leg with a shaking finger.

"Adith, wake up . . . *Adi*—

". . . *I hear them*," Sunil's brother muttered, sitting completely upright. Adith woke up to the sounds a few minutes ago, but had become too unsettled to say a word. While the pair glared at the ceiling, the footsteps and scratching became heavier. Suddenly, the teens were startled by an abrupt cough. Adith let out a small yelp as he grabbed onto Sunil's shoulder. Rohit jolted awake, rolling off the cot. As he instinctively jammed his hand into the ground, the bulky senior let out a muffled cry. He winced in pain, then shook his head in confusion.

While rubbing his wrist, Rohit angrily turned to the brothers and said, "What the *hell* is your problem?" He stood up and kicked Adith's sleeping bag.

"We heard sounds. There's something up there, Rohit," Adith said, ignoring the blow the older teen had given him. "It's . . . It's coming from Ahil's room . . ."

As all three scouts looked up, the sounds had dissipated once again. Rohit frowned and said, "Sounds, huh? Like what? Shit falling? . . . Steps? . . . Footsteps from Ahil's fucking *ghost* or something?"

"It was footsteps first," Sunil said as he stood up. "Adith didn't believe me, but then he heard them . . . *we* heard them. And it—it wasn't just the steps this time, there was scratch—"

"I'll tell you *what*," Rohit said, cracking his neck and knuckles. "*We* are gonna go up there together. Let's see what it is that you two thought was scary enough to *ruin* my night's rest." The six-foot-three teen motioned the brothers to get up. Despite Rohit's attempts to intimidate Adith and Sunil, the younger teens were ironically pleased with the fact that the well-built senior would be accompanying them upstairs. He would finally see that they weren't screwing around.

"Well, let's *go* then! We don't have all night," Rohit whispered, impatiently glancing down at his *Citizen* wrist watch.

As the three scouts made their way towards the staircase, they heard a voice behind them call out, "Rohit? What's going on?" The teens turned around to find Pratik in boxer briefs, rubbing his eyes near the doorway.

"*Ahil's back*," Rohit said with a chuckle, playfully slapping Pratik in the chest. Asif ruffled his hair and joined the group of teens. "Ghost hunters Adith and Sunil have been hearing him *moonwalk* upstairs for the past hour, so we're gonna have a look. Wanna come?"

The two dazed seniors looked at each other with indifference, before Asif said, "Yeah, mhm . . . sure."

Rohit glanced down the corridor at Devak's closed room, then put his thick index finger up to his lips. "Be quiet," the senior said, smiling at the scouts. As the teens mosied up the stairs, Sunil tugged on his brother's shirt and whispered, "*I'm scared, Adith.*"

"So this is it, huh?" Rohit said, lightly flicking a finger against the door to Ahil's room. The cocky teen was standing square in front of it, while Asif and Pratik were positioned on both sides of him. Adith stood a few feet away from the older scouts, while Sunil waited down the hall. The fourteen year old was peeking at the boys from the top of the staircase, while keeping an eye out for Devak and Bipin.

After a minute passed, Pratik glared at Adith and said, "I don't hear shit." Then he looked at Asif and Rohit. "You guys hear anything?"

Asif yawned, moving his head from side to side. Adith glanced at Sunil, who was intensely focused on Rohit's hand on the doorknob.

"What do you know," Rohit said, deadpan in his delivery. He turned the knob, placed his fleshy palm on the door, and pushed it open. A subdued creaking noise was followed by complete silence. As the teen looked down the hall to see if Sunil's face had gone pale, Asif, Pratik, and Adith stared into the darkness ahead. There were no footsteps; no scratching; and no ghost.

Rohit cheekily grinned at Sunil, then said, "I guess dead things *stay* dead, don't the—-" His sentence was interrupted by a chilling shriek. Adith jumped back against the wall, while the seniors snapped their heads towards the room. In a moment of collective shock, Sunil pissed himself. Downstairs, Bipin Malakar sat up in bed with his ears perked. He couldn't tell if the sound had been an auditory hallucination from the tail-end of a nightmare . . . or the product of something much more sinister.

"Wha . . . did you hear that?" Bipin asked his brother. A few feet away, Devak shifted awake in his sleeping bag. He knew exactly what had made the sound. He knew what it meant for everyone on the Banerjee estate.

Asif pushed past Rohit, and squinted into the room. Although the teen saw nothing . . . it saw them. Asif's eyes widened. While his face lost color, a hulking, furry mass blitzed out of the darkness. As it viciously tackled Asif, a startled Rohit stumbled and slipped onto the ground. Adith and Pratik began running towards the staircase. "That . . . that's not a *ghost*," Sunil stated through a trembling pair of lips.

A red set of hooves pressed down on Asif's kneecaps, cracking them instantly. As he screamed out in agony, the creature punched its prickly, muscular arm into his mouth. The veins in Asif's neck began to pulsate and stretch, as the hideous being shoved its arm further down the his throat. While Asif's lids welled with tears, he was hoisted off the ground like an action figure. His legs dangled helplessly as he choked on the creature's limb. Blood started leaking out of his eyes, and he felt the cartilage in his nose break under pressure. Asif's neck burst open. Sinew and hot streams of crimson profusely spilled out onto the creature's thick fur. It then swiped a set of long, curved claws across the his waist, severing him in two. As the lower half of the body fell to the ground with a "thump," the creature let the organs and bones from Asif's torso cascade into its hellishly wide mouth. Rohit watched his friend's demise in terror, unable to budge from his fallen position. After consuming its contents, the creature squeezed Asif's dismembered body like an empty soda can, then flung it back into the room. A putrid stench emitted from the abomination's mouth, as it cranked it's massive head down towards Rohit. Petrified, the boy scout started to cry. Thick veins criss-crossed over the top of the being's exposed scalp. A set of misshapen, grey horns protruded from it's concave skull, and it's face vaguely resembled a rotted jackal's.

As Pratik and Adith rushed downstairs to get a hold of Mr.Malakar, Sunil stood still, transfixed by the surreal carnage. He watched from across the hall, as the nightmarish being pounced on top of Rohit.

The eighteen-year-old whimpered and flailed, like wounded prey in the wild. The creature wrapped its icy hand around Rohit's wrist, and brought his arm closer. Fangs pushed their way into the teen's bicep. Rohit screamed as streams of blood coated his boxers and bare legs. The creature's jaw crunched down harder, causing the bone to snap. Hot gusts of air blew out from it's reddened snout. Rohit grew lightheaded. With a violent shake of its head, the filthy being tore off his arm, then swallowed it whole. As the disoriented teen fell flat onto his back, the creature lifted up it's leg. It slammed it's chipped hoof into Rohit's face . . . over and over again. Skull fragments laced with brain matter clattered all over the floor. The boy's legs spasmed for five seconds . . . then stopped moving. The abomination lapped blood off it's hooves, before looking down the hallway. It focused its sights on the fourteen-year-old.

"Sunil!! What are you doing? Come on, get down here!" Adith shouted from the bottom of the staircase.

Sunil felt his legs turn to jelly as the twisted creature leapt towards him. Its claws tore out chunks of wooden flooring, and bright red spittle flew off it's purple lips. Sunil stared down the staircase and whispered, *"Adith . . ."*

Before he had a chance to move towards his brother, Sunil felt claws clamp onto his back. He let out a high-pitched scream as layers of his skin and flesh were torn off. He convulsed as his entire body went into shock.

"SUNIL!!" Adith cried out, making his way back up the stairs. But after two steps, someone grabbed his elbow. The scout looked back to see Pratik and Mr.Malakar. They were partially clothed in uniform, and wearing their boots. Bipin Malakar rubbed his eyes to make sure what he was looking at was real, as dread filled his veins.

"We're leaving . . . .*now*," Pratik said, trying to ignore Sunil's strained moaning. The creature slashed its way to the front of the victim's skeleton, and seized two ribs. Blood poured from Sunil's slack mouth as his bones were viciously yanked around. Before Adith could reply, Devak appeared from his room. Sweat was plastered across his face and shirt. As the man heard Sunil from the second floor, his brain was flooded with images of Ahil's corpse.

The pungent smell of death, which for so long had been

contained within the walls of that unholy room, overcame Devak's senses once again. He glanced at Bipin and said, "This is my fault. I should never have let you bring them here." The housekeeper's thoughts honed in on a book. It was the book he had pried from Ahil's contorted fingers on the day of the teen's death; a book that celebrated the darker aspects of West Bengal's history . . . specifically regarding cults that were driven into obscurity. It outlined their practices, rituals . . . and prayers. The page which Ahil had opened up to, contained a darkened sketch that never left Devak's mind. He had burned the book to ashes that very night, hoping to keep whatever the teen had called upon, buried forever. But it had been too late. After having its way with Ahil, the spirit had been waiting patiently in that room. It had been seething . . . waiting to take form again. Then these teens arrived. Their innocence . . . their youth. That horrid *thing's* sole purpose was to tarnish every bit of it. Misery, fear, and bloodshed were the elements that made up it's lifeblood. And when the scouts had opened the door to that room . . . they became an offering.

"I need to stay. I need to make sure it doesn't leave this place," Devak said. "But you need to go . . . *now. All* of you . Get out. Just keep running. Don't look back . . . and don't worry about me."

Mr.Malakar looked at his brother with watery eyes. He went to protest, but was interrupted as Sunil's head flew straight into his chest. Bipin held back vomit, and Adith dropped to his knees in anguish. Pratik looked at the top of the stairs to find the creature gnawing on the scout's remains. He promptly threw open the front door, and ran outside.

"*GO!! NOW!*" Devak screamed, shaking Bipin by the shoulders. The scout leader quickly nodded, squeezed his brother's hand, and then followed Pratik.

"You too! *Go!!*" Devak said to Adith. The teenager didn't hear a word. Tears streamed down his cheeks as he held onto Sunil's head. Adith's heart ached as he looked into his brother's blank eyes. Devak reached for Adith's shirt to pull him up to his feet, but the teen smacked his hand away. Adith's sobs grew louder as he fell over in the fetal position. Devak pointed to the open door and looked at the boy scout for the last time. "*Leave! . . . Please!!*" Devak said. Adith didn't move a muscle. The teen's world . . . ..his best friend . . . his brother . . . all gone.

An unearthly howl erupted from the top of the stairs, piercing Devak's eardrums. Without glancing up at the creature, the man headed for the back of the house.

*   *   *

Devak retrieved his centerfire rifle from a crawlspace near the kitchen. The housekeeper had kept it concealed since he planned for the scouts to show up. He now saw how shortsighted he had been in thinking that a group of teens would follow the orders of a lowly housekeeper. As the wailing of a boy echoed throughout the entire floor, Devak wondered if Adith's fate had been worse than Sunil's. The harrowing nature of his situation started to get the best of him. Another demonic howl reverberated through the walls. Devak heard the sound of breaking floorboards, and frantically loaded bullets into the gun. The noise became harsher . . . and came closer. Thoughts of what it would feel like to be devoured by a monster crossed the housekeeper's mind, but he managed to stay focused, keeping a firm grip on the weapon. The wood behind him creaked.

Devak swiveled around, his rifle in position to fire at the creature that had haunted his days and nights. But before he could apply pressure on the trigger, his guts and scrotum filled with an agonizing burning sensation. The rifle slipped away from his hands. He looked down to find a set of pitch-black claws dug deep into his pelvis. Devak screamed as he stared into the creature's glassy pupils. It grinned in delight, exposing its fangs, razor sharp teeth, and a serpentine tongue. After letting off a third howl, the creature pulled its claws out of Devak, then dragged them across his midsection. Colors flashed before the man's eyes as he dropped to his knees. A fountain of red mist sprayed out onto the floor. Devak could feel his intestines sliding loose, as they slowly dropped out of the deep gashes in his stomach. The creature buried its claws into the top of the man's skull. In a split second, he tore Devak's scalp clean off. Blood streamed down the sides of his ears, soaking his neck. As the housekeeper mumbled incoherently, the abomination shot its narrow tongue through his right eye. It felt like someone had smashed a sledgehammer into Devak's face. His fingers twitched while the creature's sharp, leathery tongue darted around different parts of his socket. The housekeeper's head violently hitched back. As his optic nerve got severed, Devak felt waves of heat and sharp pain overcome him. Then after a brief moment . . . he felt nothing.

The creature placed a hand on the man's shoulder, and with a second set of claws, hacked a hole into Devak's chest. A furry arm pushed its way into the fresh cavity. The thing wrapped its hand around Devak's spine, then pulled it straight out of his lifeless body. It's stained teeth vanished into the spinal column, marrow and pink fluid gushing down its throat.

The residence was completely quiet. Strains of skin and flesh dripped off the monster's black fur, as it took a minute to revel in the aftermath of its twisted escapade. Having had its fill, the creature flung Devak's corpse into an empty bookshelf. Then, it balled up its fists, and shot them straight through the wooden floor. With a blood curdling howl, the hidden horror of Darjeeling broke through the back wall of the Banerjee home. Its snout twitched, picking up the scent of Bipin Malakar and Pratik in the distance. The wretched beast began to sprint across the estate . . . slowly becoming enveloped by the darkness of the early morning.

MRSA ME

ALICIA HILTON

From *Rigor Morbid: Lest Ye Become*
Editor: Sandra Ruttan
Speakeasy, Bronzeville Books

was born in a dumpster, in an alley behind a dive bar. A wee speck of methicillin-resistant *Staphylococcus aureus*, baptized by saliva from a hospital orderly, clinging to a wedge of pizza crust. Honestly, I didn't want to hurt anyone—certainly not the Norwegian rat who gobbled me with his yellowed fangs, feeding me a banquet of liquefied refuse. We'd both gotten a bad rap, MRSA and rats.

The night air was refreshing, swimming with luscious phero-mones from two drunk hipsters who were screwing beside my dingy manger. Slap, slap, pelvises met, thrusting, against the brick alley wall. Him with buzzed hair and a hipster beard. Her with auburn tresses, flowing over her shoulders, almost to her ass, a perfect foothold for my scaly-tailed host.

Scritchy, scratch, claws scrambled over a pile of trash, tail trailing behind, over the side of the dumpster we flew, onto a drainpipe, down to the asphalt. Scurry, scurry, through a murky puddle, until we reached our goal.

It was simply miraculous, how I'd grown, feisty MRSA me. No longer a little tyke, I was eager to make new friends. Thank goodness, *Rattus norvegicus* leapt to make the introduction, bounding on hipster dude.

Over the leather biker boots, my buddy skittered.

Engrossed in their tryst, the couple didn't notice the furry visitor, until he climbed the dude's designer denim, and jumped on hipster girl's bare thigh. Goodness, the humping millenni-als couldn't have been more welcoming, although they seemed surprised to see us.

How she shrieked. How he yelled, but Rattus charged higher. The hamburger grease splattered on the girl's shirt, drew my mammalian friend like iron shards to a magnet.

Fists flew.

I heard a squeal.

Brave Rattus got hurled to the asphalt and stomped by heavy

black boots, but he'd already dug his chompers into the pretty young lady's juicy hip.

Hello, gorgeous. I splashed in the tasty new essence. Plasma is much nicer to swim in than saliva.

The male millennial fled into the bar, off to guzzle another pint, or two, or three. He didn't say goodbye to Jane, fickle bastard.

If I'd been a more sensitive microbe, I might've felt guilty about breaking up their midnight nookie, but why feel shame when you're about to see the world, hitching a ride with a sexy host?

An Uber was our humble chariot. The driver had a crusty scab on his chin. How I longed to burrow in.

He gave Jane a sly look, signaling that he found her tears alluring, but she stared out the window.

We shrieked to a stop in front of jilted Jane's dormitory.

After stopping in her room to grab a bathrobe and a toiletry caddy, Jane walked across the hall to the communal bathroom and stripped off her clothes. She cranked up the shower until it steamed, blasted me with the hand-held nozzle, and scrubbed.

It would've been unforgivable to abandon Jane in her time of grief, especially since her roommate was away. Loyalty was one of my most admirable traits.

After she toweled off, she left the bathrobe on her roommate's bed. How convenient that the terrycloth was burgundy, the perfect color to camouflage the crimson smear, squirming with my kin.

Rattus's puncture marks must've been tender, because Jane yelped when she touched her ragged flesh as she crawled naked under her blanket.

How cozy I was, snug as a bug in a rug, while she slumbered.

My talent for replication was more impressive than my loyalty.

By the time my charming host's alarm clock sang, announcing it was half-past seven—hurry up and get to the airport—my offspring were having quite a celebration, riding up and down veins and arteries, through mucous membranes, dancing on Jane's chapped pink lips whenever she breathed.

Poor Jane. She barely made it to the bathroom before the beer she'd guzzled last night blasted up her throat and splashed all over the tiles beside the row of sinks.

Instead of cleaning up the mess, she left the noxious puddle, filled with gazillions of my MRSA clones, for unsuspecting damsels to trip over.

A smarter girl would've rushed to the university clinic, but Jane washed out her mouth, returned to her room, and packed her suitcase. Final exams were over, and it was time to jet home to dear old Mom and Dad.

She grabbed two bikinis, one black, the other pink, and shoved them into a wheelie bag along with sunglasses, a striped sundress, a handful of tee shirts, two pairs of jeans, some really short shorts, thong panties, and a fresh package of condoms.

We all have to die someday, but it was such a pity that she wouldn't live long enough to find a better boyfriend.

As her temperature rose, climbing from 98.6 to 102.8 Fahrenheit, I felt a pang of conscience, but not enough regret to abandon ship. She'd had her fun. Now, it was my turn to party.

The airport traffic was hellacious, and the Uber's air conditioning was busted, but I didn't mind, since the driver rolled down the windows. The warm breeze carried my MRSA buddies into the yellow cab parked on the curb beside us.

Tons of people waited in the security line. An old lady carrying a little dog glared at Jane when she coughed up clotty phlegm. Since my host didn't have a Kleenex, she wiped the slime on her jeans.

The TSA agent insisted on doing a pat down, because of Jane's bloodshot eyes. He was wearing gloves, but didn't change them before he groped the next passenger.

Lucky for me and my MRSA buddies, government budget cuts have unexpected consequences.

AUTHOR'S STORY NOTE

When I began writing "MRSA Me," I was inspired to write from the POV of a bacteria or virus, because threats that can't be seen are terrifying. "MRSA Me" began as a poem and morphed into flash fiction. The alliteration and rhymes provided a playful counterpart to the horror and facilitated the interaction between MRSA and the rat. I've traveled a lot, and seen TSA agents patting people down without changing their gloves. Airports are already a hotbed of germs, and this type of physical transfer makes it more likely that travelers will get sick. I find it ironic and disgusting that a poorly executed security measure exposes people to more danger.

WHAT DID YOU DO TO THE CHILDREN?

DAVID L TAMARIN

From *Dig Two Graves Vol. II*
Death's Head Press

I met my angel at a grindhouse midnight screening of *Blood-sucking Freaks* in a dirty syringe-filled theatre with cheap torn seats and the smell of decay and vomit. I saw her go into the lady's room, looked around (the theatre was empty), and with a smile and growing erection I made my way over to the ladies room. I was going to rape her, rape her head, choke her to death with my cock, tear open her chest and fuck her heart, I was going to ejaculate into her lungs. I was going to find a baby and perform a reverse birth, shoving it up her vagina until they were both dead. I'd make her vomit, then eat the vomit, then make her vomit more, and have her eat it again, for hours, while I took pictures and masturbated. I was in my own little fantasy world of pain and domination when I opened the door and walked in the bathroom but she was waiting and drove a thick railroad nail through my hand, nailing me to the wall, a porn theatre Jesus. She got out a video camera and I was immediately turned on. I stared at her, realizing for the first time how beautiful she was. I fantasized about us killing a group of school children together, soaking them in kerosene and piss and then covering them with little M-80s then blowtorching the little fucks until they were nothing but ash.

I fucking love you! I screamed, kicking her in the hip as she tried to hammer my skull. She fell backwards, then leaped on me, and we began to kiss passionately. A woman walked into the bathroom. Bad timing. Lola and I consummated our relationship by torturing the woman and killing her. She was a short Vietnamese woman with an annoyingly high-pitched scream and we shoved her face in the toilet, using it as a waterboard, pulling her out seconds before death to let her breathe so we could do it again. The dead don't suffer. You have to take measures to keep them alive. She was barely conscious and Lola held her up. I positioned myself and Lola started jerking me off. When I was hard enough, I put my cock into her eye socket, at first just gently touching it and rubbing it around, with Lola holding the eye open. Then Lola told me to hold on and she got out a safety pin and pinned her eyelid open. She was shaking with ecstasy and she kept poking the lady's eye and eyelid with the pin, and blood and fluid dripped out the little holes. Once the eye was open I put my cock back on it and rubbed it around, ever so slightly increasing the pressure. I felt her eye flex inwards, it was like sticking a finger into a hardboiled egg, and I went in deeper and the eye juices got me all lubed up and I pulled out before I could do too much damage.

We looked at her eye. It was still there, but not where it should have been. It was recessed back into her skull, and I could feel her gazing at me with it. I thrust myself in this time and fucked her brains out, literally. Lola filmed it at all and we went back to her place and watched it and fucked and snorted meth all night. She kept a hostage at her place, which was out in the woods surrounded by trees. The hostage's ears, lips and nose had been cut off and sewn back the wrong way, making him the Suffering Mr. Potato Head. The lips were sewn over his eyes, keeping him in perpetual nightmare darkness. Where his nose should have been was his ear, which had started rotting and smelled putrid like midget brains or Ebola sores melting. The most grotesque part was the penis hanging out of his left ear socket and the testicle stitched onto the head of the penis. His teeth had been removed and there was an ear where they should have been.

She explained everything to me. "I'm an artist. This is a world of suffering, a world of outhouses filled with vomit and contaminated shit, and I exist to capture that on film. When the sedatives wear off and he wakes up we can have some fun with him. I suggested that we remove his feet and switch them around but she told me it would take hours cutting through the bone. So we both put our faces into his legs, and had an eating contest, no hands allowed. Blood sprayed out as my teeth tore through his flesh and grinded it up for me to savor and swallow. She had bitten a piece clean off and the blood started splashing everywhere. My next bite wasn't as clean. I tore into his flesh and got a hot mouthful of skin and blood and arteries, but I couldn't rip it all the way off. I shook my head furiously like a dog drying itself until the piece came off. It was gigantic, and I could taste hair in my mouth. I spit it out and Lola dove into it and started chewing it, like a snake attacking and killing a rat.

The guy might have been sedated but there weren't any sedatives I knew of that would keep one oblivious to this type of pain, and he woke up and lamely thrashed about, making strange gurgling sounds. He was trying to beg us to stop. Then Lola did something that I could barely watch. She took a linoleum carver and began making gory designs in his neck, blood leaking out, drool coming out of his nose-mouth. She jabbed a sewing needle in the open gaping black hole where his penis once hung. It was like watching someone chip away ice to make an ice sculpture, and she made more puncture wounds then I could count. He soon bled out and we resumed eating him. For a joke she tore the penis off, ripped the testicle from the penis head, and began fellating it. She reached into his crotch and pulled out a mass of red tissue which she used to slicken the penis.

I felt myself getting hard, and I pushed her onto the sofa and shoved my cock inside her, fucking her with all the anger and adrenaline and power and bloodlust spinning my head around, and when I came I looked up at the ceiling, howling like a wolf, and for the first time saw the giant skin quilt she had stitched together. Each piece had a different tattoo. I came so deep inside of her I feared it would shoot out her eyes and hit me in the face.

Hold on.

She went and dragged out another victim.

Here's what we're going to do. You're going to stick your cock in her cunt, and I'm going to ram my hand down her throat, and

marbles, and we sat on her couch and threw marbles at the lady, trying to get them into her mouth. We had tied her to her chair to make it easier. I was the first one to get a marble into her mouth hole. Lola furiously threw one at her, and she was so anorexic it tore through her shoulder like a cannonball flying through a pile of afterbirth. We heard it hit the floor as it fell out the back of her.

Hold on she said and went over to the camera.

We're almost out of film, let's finish this up and take a break after we load in a new tape.

She turned on her TV and put a black DVD into the player, which swallowed it up like a man with pica swallowing a bag of pennies.

Are you ready for this? You have to be totally honest. This is for the festival, and I've got to win this year. I think it still needs a little editing and there are a couple of places where the lighting is kind of sketchy and you can see shadows. Oh shit, I almost forgot the popcorn. The TV had a big animal skull on it, upon which was a black candle that I lit. I saw teeth scattered over the top of the TV, and little pieces of what looked like foreskin.

You know what turns me on? I want to talk to you before we watch the video, because I feel like I really know you.

Absolutely she said with the wickedest grin I had ever seen. The type of grin that one would rather commit suicide then look at. I felt myself growing hard.

Have you ever been naked inside a body bag, right after they take out the corpse. You're covered in blood and tissue and the smell is so intense it hits you like a shot of heroin, and you zip yourself in and just start licking the inside of the bag, masturbating. There's nothing like it. It's like fucking death herself. It's even better if you fill the bag up with bugs and spiders so you can feel their hairy legs crawl over your skin.

But you know what? I've never fucked anyone inside a body bag, because I've never had a partner into the same thing as me. But I think I've found my soul mate in you. We've got to get a body bag. I rubbed my crotch, I was so excited I could not control myself, and I lunged at her, kissing her and gently biting her, and we began to make love as the movie began. I glanced up occasionally, to see a small child in a dunk tank that men were filling with their piss. They were pissing all over the kid, and the tank was starting to fill up. It was up to his thighs. A long line of drunken men stretched into the distance. The kid was crying of course, and they would just piss in his mouth, of course. One guy vomited in the tank and another pulled a handful of diarrhea out of a Ziploc bag and threw it on the child. Someone else shot some AIDS-tainted blood out of a syringe into the kid's face as I thrust deep into Lola. The urine was now dirty, with shit and blood and vomit floating around. A man with an executioner's mask with a child's smile painted on it held a large stick that he used to keep the kid in the tank. Piss rained down all over him and I exploded inside Lola, the most intense orgasm of my life, just as the man in the mask shoved the kids head down with the stick so that he was fully immersed in the tank of urine. He tried not to but he opened his mouth for air and got a lungful of urine. Something in the back of my mind told me something was very wrong. I felt dizzy. For some reason my cock stayed hard and I pulled her face into my lap.

I told her, this is the greatest first date of my life. There was something about the harsh glare in her eyes that frightened me as she yanked her head out of my lap, but I pulled her towards me, puzzled by her change.

Let me change the tape first, she said.

Then it hit me and my blood ran cold. I could feel the drop in temperature, I could feel the inside of my stomach and heart sink, the whole world threatened to start defying the laws of physics, because this could not be right, this could not be happening, this could not be real.

Four years ago my two twin sons Mark and Andrew, ages 11, were abducted, and never seen again. No bodies were found so they may be alive, we just wanted to know if they were or not. To myself only I spoke the truth. Please let them be dead, because whoever took them could be doing horrible things to them, things unimaginable, things like this, shadow things, and that was Mark in the tank, Mark! They must have kept him alive and just recently killed him, he looked so much older. I wanted my son, I wanted to know what he would be, would he be my partner in crime or some school nerd? And for four years I've wanted them back, it's been something literally ripping my guts up every night. I pictured them being roasted alive, their skin burnt, the smell of their own burning flesh deep in their nostrils, the pain as the genitals and pubic hair began to burn, and that feeling that things would be better if you were dead. Or what if they were sex slaves held by a cult of religious freaks? They'd be raped daily, forced to suck old men's cock, they'd be bleeding black blood out their asses every day from the rapes and assaults. Would someone slowly starve them to them, feeding them every other day, less and less, but enough to keep them alive, until they looked like anorexics? I imagined my kids nude and a man with a blowtorch and nasty grin and cigar, and an "I Love to Eat Pussy" trashy oily hat. I imagined them being forced to fuck each other or other kids or getting fucked and being blindfolded and put into battles royal where everyone gets a baseball bat. Was someone so sick that they would have my sons alive for 4 years?

Yes, because these people were guilty. They were showing me the evidence, gloating in it, even as I struggled to accept this.

Then they put the television in front of me. She grabbed the back of my hair and pulled my head back and kissed me deeply against my will as the white static faded and an image became visible. I felt light headed. It was my other 11-year-old son, Michael. He was covered in bite marks and feces. I felt a fist pound my ear, making my head ring like a hit of crack. I could feel my brain bleeding, my mind crying, my soul dying. The things I imagined—but thought unimaginable—had all come true. Nightmares were real. I couldn't keep from shaking. I was starting to doubt the reality of the universe.

I looked at Lola, stunned.

Don't you recognize me? You should, because you saw me when you were raping my daughter at Lofton Park. I was the woman with the camera. This is pay back, faggot. You fucked up. Pricks like you are so predictable, you think with your dicks and assume all women are helpless. We saw what you did in the playground last Sunday night, we taped it even. You're not a very nice guy, are you? What kind of man suffocates a young girl by shoving dog shit down her throat?

I'm a good man, a good father, and I was bringing up two great guys, so I had an obligation to be part of society. But my urges were not ever to be suppressed. She wasn't the only one. I can't help who I am, that I do vicious things, that I should be dead, but I had two kids to raise. Since then things have gone to hell, I've been more violent, just to be violent, I end up with cunts like you—

And then a door burst open and the man in the mask from the video came in, followed by several behemoths of indeterminate race, indeterminate species actually, very simian, with my son attached to a leash which they jerked around. He didn't recognize me. But then again his eyes were stapled shut with monstrous industrial staples.

Michael—I cried out, and everyone just laughed. Crude kitten legs stuck out of each of his ears. I felt like the night I discovered him missing, when I walked into the bed room and he wasn't in bed and there was a dead girl in his place, months dead, rotting, green, inhuman. Someone had replaced my son with this obscene corpse. I remember vomiting, then running to get my wife, completely forgetting that she had committed suicide just days ago. I began to question whether it was suicide after all. Maybe these people slit her wrists and throat and put her in the tub. I remember calling my friend Mark as soon as I was done sodomizing my dead wife. Mark would know what to do with a corpse, something other than fucking or eating it. First my wife, then my child. And now here he was, we were reunited, but that had destroyed all his senses, leaving him in a cold dark sound-less never-ending nightmare of pain and claustrophobia, and I could not get through to him. I had more important things to attend to though and I got into a fighter's stance, ready to take on these savage fucks.

The man in the mask jumped at me and I heard them laughing as he tackled me and my head hit the floor and everything echoed for a second before all was night.

I woke up in a panic. How come I couldn't move? I became immediately aware of the pain. It felt like someone had blowtorched the top of my head and then shoved tacks into it. I was staring into a camera, blinded by the room's only light, which came from behind the camera, making it impossible to see who was there. Then I felt a burning and my stomach dropped like a suicidal teen off the roof of a gigantic tower, and I saw my penis, or what was once my penis. It had been sliced open down the middle and an unseen hand poured hot Tabasco sauce onto it. The pain was so intense, so real, I could taste it, see it, feel in wrap around me like a cloud, or a warm blanket, and my spine twisted and froze and I jerked my chest forward, tearing through the thin nails that had been driven through me to keep me on my seat. I couldn't scream, I couldn't fight back, I couldn't do anything. And then, right at that moment, I knew I wanted death to save me from the tortures and humiliation I would face. I bit down on my tongue, intending to swallow it and either choke on it, drown in blood, or bleed out. But hands tore my mouth open and I felt a ripping as my tongue was pulled out. They forgot. They fucking forgot. The mouth is the most powerful part of the body. The jaw can crush and destroy more effectively than anything else. So I bit down as hard as I could, hoping to bite off the fingers, and then choke on them. But my teeth hit bone and chipped and I could not get through his hand. I wanted to die so bad.

Lola stood over me, just her outline. Relax, this is just the initiation. We've got a doctor who'll sew you back together. He refuses to use anesthesia though, or to clean his instruments. And he's a drunk with the shakes. But don't worry, we won't let you die.

And that smile I fell in love with lit up her face, making it look like she had a halo. If this was my future, I was ready, because seeing her made all the pain worth enduring. But judging from the melon scoopers in her hand I wouldn't have my sense of sight very long. I breathed in, trying to get a sniff of the smell of her essence, the sweaty wet crotch I had fucked for hours, and as she took out my eyeballs my mutilated penis shivered in orgasm as I sniffed her twat. It was more beautiful than a field full of daisies with elderly women buried beneath it. I felt my face turn hot and wet as blood flowed from my eyes down my face and onto my chest. Finally, I was going to die. But I heard a blowtorch and knew they would be cauterizing the wounds, keeping me alive.

Remember, the dead don't suffer . . .

AUTHOR'S STORY NOTE

THEY DON'T WANT YOU TO READ THIS. There are a lot of people who are angry that you are allowed to read my story and its evil content. I decided to self-publish *What Did You Do To The Children?* so I contacted a company that would convert my .doc file into a Kindle book for a fee so I could sell it on

Amazon. They took the unprecedented step of refusing to help me because of the story's content. My story was evil and vile. It was WRONG. My story was contributing to all of the negativity and bad shit in the world. My story was a bad thing. The company refused to help me because doing so would mean that they were harming the world, and they couldn't in good conscience help me convert my story. Two other companies gave me the same line—they didn't want my money because they wanted nothing to do with my tale. So I figured out how to convert it myself and submitted it to Amazon to be sold at the Kindle store. To my complete shock Amazon rejected the story on content grounds. I don't know of them doing this with any other piece of writing. There are Kindle books that contain nude photos. There are many, many Kindle books in the genre of underage incest porn. You can find pretty much anything if you look hard enough. But my story was too much. I edited it and re-submitted it, and they rejected it a second time. I then changed the title to What Would You Do? and edited it even more, and finally they published it. Years later, after many failed attempts, I found a publisher who would publish the uncensored version of the story, and it was accepted into the anthology *Dig Two Graves Volume 2*, and then accepted into the book you are now reading. I wanted to give up many times, but I just couldn't. There was so much opposition to this story, so much anger and hatred directed at me for what I wrote, that I temporarily quit writing horror. But the few people who read the story loved it and encouraged me to get it published, so I kept on fighting until this story saw the light of day. The most disgusting thing about the story is all the effort utilized to stop you from having the right to read it. I was made to feel like a criminal, and all because I wrote a story based on my fears of what might happen to my young innocent son, who just turned five. I'd like to thank the people with the courage to publish this and I'd like to say Fuck Off to the assholes who tried to prevent this story from entering society. If you have read the story, that's a victory for freedom of speech. This whole ordeal made me very depressed and angry for years, and now I can finally smile because Red Room Press has recognized the story and decided to publish it. I realize now that I must keep writing extreme fiction. It is my civic duty. If so many people want to suppress my writing, it must have some merit, and it must possess the power of transgression. If you read my story, thank you and I hope you enjoyed reading it as much as I loved writing it. To you motherfuckers who want to stop me, you better give up because you will never stop me. As long as I get positive feedback from horror fans I know I am doing the right thing. This world and most of the people in it fucking suck and I will do my part to wage cultural warfare against these close-minded fascists. I will never give up.

HAVE A HEART

MATTHEW V. BROCKMEYER

From *Under Rotting Skies*
Black Thunder Press

The old madrone tree that hung over the house had always been a point of contention between Beatrice and Raymond. They both agreed it was a thing of beauty, with its papery red bark and strangely bent trunk, branches askew and at weird angles. But to him it was a thing with functions to exploit, and to her it was a thing of danger to be feared and destroyed.

They'd fight about it often, and that spring day the goose refused to leave her nest was no different. There were at least a half dozen eggs in the goose's clutch, nearly the size of softballs, and she wasn't moving off them, instead thrashing her wings and snapping her beak at Beatrice for simply coming near.

Beatrice leapt back as the big angry hen hissed like some kind of dinosaur.

"Damn, that is one broody goose!"

Raymond took off his glasses and scrubbed the lenses with the loose end of his flannel shirt. "I say we just let her hatch her eggs. It'll be cute having a bunch of little goslings running about. Marcy will love it. Besides, those goose eggs taste gamey anyway."

"I guess," Beatrice said, standing hands on hip, watching the bird settle in her nest. "But I don't know if I can handle more geese. They're so loud."

"Goose, Momma, goose!" their two-year-old daughter shouted, pointing a chubby finger as the hen turned her head to eye them suspiciously.

"That's right, sweet heart," Beatrice replied. "But don't get too close, Marcy. She's a mommy goose and is protecting her little babies in the eggs."

"Momma goose?" Marcy asked, her squeaky voice filled with wonder.

"Yes, that's a momma goose."

Marcy laughed and slapped her chubby palms together. "Momma goose!"

"Okay," Beatrice said, scooping Marcy into her arms. "Let's let the geese be for now."

Raymond swung open the door of the coop and as they strolled out, the gander came shuffling up to them with its wings stretched out, quacking loudly.

"Oh, and aren't *you* going to be a proud father," Raymond laughed, patting its head.

After the people left the coop and started up the path to their farmhouse, the hen lifted herself off her nest, stretched, and went to the water basin. The gander took guard, slowly scanning the perimeter for any sudden movements or lurking danger. The hen dipped her bill into the cool water and took a long drink. She then went back and instinctively nudged each egg, carefully turning them over so the life growing inside wouldn't stick to the shell. Using her beak, she gently pushed them back into a cluster, arranging them just so, and delicately sat back atop them, draping them in her warm down. She preened a moment, then, satisfied, curled her long neck around her body and tucked her head under a wing, shut her eyes, and slept. Beneath her, within the eggs, tiny hearts were beating.

Beatrice and Marcy huddled together in bed, looking at pictures of baby geese on the iPad, trying to figure out when the eggs would hatch.

"It says the gestation period is twenty-eight days. She's been sitting on those eggs for two weeks now. So, it should only be about another two weeks until they hatch."

"Baby goose, Momma?" Marcy asked, gazing at the picture of a fuzzy, little gosling on the screen.

"Yes, sweetie. Baby goose."

Marcy giggled and clapped her hands. "Baby goose!"

Raymond sat at his desk in the corner, furiously typing on

his laptop, working on a grant to fund putting a large pond on their homestead.

"What we'll do is put an island in the middle of the pond," Raymond said. "That way we won't need a coop anymore. The geese can nest on the island and the moat will keep them safe from predators."

"But why geese?" Beatrice said. "They're so loud, and not very nice either. Can't we get some ducks or swans? I was thinking we could just go down to the feed store and give all the goslings away."

"Swans are meaner than geese. And bigger. We should work with what we have. It's a basic permaculture principle. Besides, their aggression gives them an advantage for survival."

"Permaculture, permaculture. Does everything have to follow permaculture principle?"

Grinning, Raymond flicked his laptop closed. "Yes, it does. That's the first principle of permaculture."

He stood and stretched his lank body, then yawned and scratched at the stubble on his chin before slipping out of his workpants and into the ratty sweatpants he used as pajamas. "My question," he said, "is how long are we going to let Marcy sleep in bed with us? Her room is painted and ready to go."

Marcy's face lit up with a smile and she shook her head. "This is *my* bed, Dada."

"Oh, no, it's not!" Raymond said, coming over and tickling her under her arms. "That's *Daddy's* bed!"

Marcy let out a shriek and a torrent of giggles as she wiggled under his hands.

Beatrice turned off her iPad, set it on the bedside table. "Most children co-sleep till they are three, so you've got another year to go, buster. Get used to it."

"I just keep waking up with someone's finger in my ear," Raymond said, turning off the light before climbing in with them.

Beneath the heat of the hen's body and soft down, the large eggs were warm, humid, and safe. The hen could feel the tiny lives moving about inside the eggs, and was now on lockdown, only leaving the nest when absolutely necessary to take a quick drink and to eat. The gander paced protectively back and forth across the coop, honking and charging at any sound that arose from the dark forest around them.

Raymond was trying to work, but Beatrice was bitching about the damn madrone tree again.

"Look at the way it leans over the house. It's dangerous. We need to chop it down."

Her eyebrows arched like a steeple, her face twisting with concern in a way that always annoyed him when they were having a disagreement. He always thought she used that look as a way of trying to guilt him into agreeing, a means of prying his sympathy, the way a child would elongate the word "please" to get what they wanted.

"What are you talking about?" Raymond said. "That tree is so anchored in the earth. It's not going anywhere. That thing is keeping the whole hillside up. Cut it down and we'll have a massive erosion problem."

"But it's hanging right over our bedroom. I can see it at night through the window, shaking when the wind blows."

"That tree provides shade in the summer and shelter in the winter."

"But it's dangerous."

"Honey, it isn't dangerous. Trust me."

"It looks dangerous to me."

And so it went.

While Beatrice was flipping through a seed catalogue and sipping a chilled glass of lemon-balm tea, Raymond placed a sheaf of papers beside her.

"Here you go," he said.

"What's this?"

"My final analysis."

"Analysis of what?"

"Our symbiotic relationship to that madrone tree."

She shook her head and let out an exhausted breath. "You gotta be kidding me."

He cocked his head and said, "Do I?"

Had he always been such a dick, she thought, *or is this a new thing?*

She looked at the papers, sighed, and began to read.

FUNCTIONAL ANALYSIS OF ERICACEAE ARBUTUS MENZIESII

COMMON NAME PACIFIC MADRONE

Oh, God, she thought, *Mr. Permaculture, here we go.*

Arbutus Menziesii is a broad leafed *sclerophyllous,* an evergreen tree with urn-shaped flowers which are born in terminal clusters. It is wind-firm, drought-enduring, and its wide-spreading root system is associated with *ericoid mycorrhizae . . .*

Boring, so fucking boring, skim.

While palpability of mature leaves is low, young leafy sprouts are favored by California mule and black tailed deer, as well as domestic goats and sheep . . .

Skim, skim, skim.

Leaves provide forage for the dusky-footed wood rat . . .

Giving a home to wood rats right next to our house is a plus how?

Pacific madrone is an important component of cavity-nesting birds such as the red-breasted sap sucker, hairy woodpecker, mountain chickadee, house wren . . .

Skim, skim, skim.

Its flowers attract pollinators such as bees and humming birds, as well as a host of beneficial insects such as parasitic wasps. Its berries can be eaten fresh in the winter or dried for long-term storage . . .

I've never seen you eat them. They taste like shit.

. . . they can also be used to make jewelry and as bait for steel-head trout . . .

When was the last time you made jewelry or went fishing anyway?

Tea made from the bark and leaves eases sore throats, and salves made from berries and leaves has been proven effective in the treatment of poison oak irritation . . .

Finally, in exasperation, she threw the bundle of papers aside.

"This is ridiculous," she said. "There's a hundred more of those trees out in the forest. What does any of this have to do with that specific tree behind our house? It's dangerous. You are not addressing the issue here."

"Honey," he said, laughing pretentiously, scratching at his beard, "it's not dangerous. You're being paranoid."

"Ugh," she said, walking stiffly away before she lost her temper.

Raymond and Beatrice spent all day planting cover crop: a mixture of fava beans, vetch, clover, and oats, which would grow all winter and be fed back to the soil in the spring. Marcy had been a great help with spreading seeds and covering them with soil. They lay in bed, exhausted—Marcy fast asleep and snoring lightly, Raymond beginning to drift off when Beatrice spoke.

"Did you hear that? That scurrying in the kitchen? I think Stinky is back."

Stinky was the skunk that kept coming into their house to eat the cat food. It had found some way in through the walls and would scuttle around at night making eerie scratching noises.

They had repeatedly tried to catch it in this big metal contraption Raymond called the "Have-A-Heart," but to no avail.

Raymond sighed loudly. "Okay, I'll set up the Have-A-Heart trap. Live it up, Stinky. This is your last night in our house." He pulled himself out of bed, slipped back into his dirty bib overalls, and headed down to the barn to retrieve the trap.

As he passed the goose coop, he heard the large birds scurrying about, leery of predators in the night.

Their chicks should be hatching any day now.

Raymond made sure the cat was outside, then took the Have-A-Heart out of the box and set it up in the kitchen. It was basically a three-foot by one-and-a-half-foot stainless-steel cage with a trap door. He opened a can of cat food and gingerly placed it on the release mechanism, then pulled the trap door up, taut on the powerful springs, and delicately locked it in place.

When he went back to the bedroom, his wife and daughter were curled up together on the bed, fast asleep. For a moment he marveled at his good fortune: his beautiful wife, his perfect and incredibly cute daughter, this little farm they had. He gave a deep sigh of satisfaction, pulled back the quilted comforter, and climbed in. He wrapped his arms around Beatrice, her warm scent of earth and herbs lulling him to sleep.

The madrone tree fell on the house that night, crashing through their bedroom roof and onto the bed where they slept.

It was a miracle little Marcy wasn't killed. Tucked into Beatrice's arms, she was literally saved by her mother's embrace. The heavy trunk crushed Raymond's skull, killing him instantly. Beatrice was pierced by three sharp branches, one through the neck, two penetrating deep into her chest. She lived for twenty minutes, gasping for air through a pierced lung, spitting up blood and pinned to the bed, then died.

Little Marcy, completely unharmed, cried and wept for a long,

long time, but eventually fell back to sleep, shuddering, her tiny shoulders racked with slowly diminishing sobs.

Hearing the loud crash, the gander stomped around the coop, beating its wings ferociously while his hen gazed about in concern, stretching her long neck for quick, furtive glances.

When the light of the morning sun rose over the bluffs and its light fell through the gaping hole in the roof, Marcy awoke, wet and sticky and drenched in her parent's blood, which had already begun to cool and congeal. She was confused. There was a big tree in the bed with them, and her mother and father were all tangled up in its branches. She called out to them in a timid and questioning voice, "Momma? Dada?" When she was answered with only silence, she cried out louder, "Momma? Dada?" Then again, and again, until it was no longer a question but a demand, *"MOM-MA! DADA!"* at which point she began to weep hysterically.

The chicks were almost fully mature, the chorioallantoic membranes no longer able to fully meet their respiratory requirements. The goose eggs had lost thirteen percent of their weight and now contained large pockets of air, which dipped below their tiny wings, the hatching muscles on their necks involuntarily contracting, their bills piercing the inner membranes for oxygen to breathe. Internal pipping had begun.

When Marcy's crying petered out into low moans and wails, a great hunger filled her. She eased her way to the side of the bed and slid carefully off, grasping tightly to the blankets till her chubby feet touched the cold floor. She toddled off to the kitchen, whimpering and sniffling, in search of food. The cat sat outside on the windowsill, meowing to be let in.

Momma always said, "Do not eat the cat food!" but she was so hungry, her little belly a ball of emptiness that had turned in on itself.

The can of wet food smelled so enticing and delicious that her mouth began to fill with saliva. A long line of drool spilled out from her lips and over her plump little chin. On all fours, she crawled slowly into the trap. It was a tight fit, its stainless-steel wire sides barely able to contain her as she wiggled—getting closer and closer to the fragrant mush—till she was fully within the trap. She reached out and took the can and the spring-activated mechanism released the heavy door. It slammed into place, the cage shuddering and two sets of locks cinching tight.

The yolk sac and blood vessels were now totally absorbed by the chicks as they rested, preparing for the final hatching sequence.

Marcy began to wail, shriek, and scream. She tried to back out of the trap, but couldn't. She tried to go forward, but was unable. She couldn't turn, and was terribly stuck within the confines of the cage. She screeched with all her might, her fat little body trembling with effort.

The chicks rotated in their shells, chipping in circular patterns from within, pushing with their feet until their eggs weakened. When the cap of one of the shells cracked and hinged open, the first chick scrambled free.

Marcy could no longer cry, for there was no moisture left within her. Her tongue had swollen so that her throat was beginning to close, and she gasped for breath. She had eaten the food, which had made her vomit. Trapped in the cage, lying awkwardly in a puddle of her own sick, a terrible thirst filled her. When she shut her eyes, she daydreamed of water, cool, in a glass, shimmering in a bowl, sun-dappled lakes, mossy ponds, flowing streams . . .

The newly-hatched chicks followed their mother to the feeder, stuffing their little mouths with grain. A few sprigs of plantain rose around the water basin, and they gobbled those as well. Their black eyes shone with life and they flapped their tiny wings and stretched out their dark tongues so that their pink undersides glistened in the sun.

Stinky, the skunk, scampered through his subterranean lair, waddling about amongst the trash and rocks beneath the deck, making his way to the edge of the house. Squeezing between a rotten board and a gnawed-open piece of plywood, he slipped into the dusty post-and-beam foundation. Scrabbling up onto a copper water pipe, Stinky shimmied through a small hole in the floor and into the closet that housed the hot-water heater, and then into the house.

Smelling a mixture of vomit and cat food, he scurried to the cage, circling it, looking for a way in, nosing at the steel bars. Marcy lay inside, motionless but for the faintest movement of shoulders as her body sucked in air and slowly released it. Stinky watched as her breathing grew slower and slower, till she finally shuttered and went completely still.

Then, lifting his wet, black nose to the air, and smelling blood and viscera, Stinky shuffled to the bedroom. Digging his claws into the dangling blankets, he pulled himself up and onto the bed and into a tangle of branches.

He pushed his way through the leaves and sticks, climbed up over Beatrice's shoulder, scampered across her chest, and straddled her face. He sniffed at her chin and licked at the blood, gave it a furtive nibble. But the skin was too tough, stretched too taut over the bone, so he crawled forward to examine one of her staring open eyes, ran his pink little tongue over the orb: squishy, salty, tangy. Curling his dark lips up over his fangs, he delicately tore a morsel of eye flesh. It was delicious. He swallowed, then dug his sharp teeth greedily into the soft meat, delighting over the zesty burst of flavor.

The gander watched his hen and their hatchlings wander around the empty feeder, rooting about for bits of spilled grain or sprouts of grass. They'd run out of food and water days ago, and he felt weak, his tongue stiff and papery. He wandered the periphery of the pen, scouring the wire mesh for an opening, some way out, a primordial urge to live and provide for his flock fueling his heart to beat faster.

He found a soft spot of dirt in the corner where a two-by-four had rotted and began to dig, working the earth with his beak, furiously scratching, then using his webbed feet to empty the little pocket. He dug until exhausted, rested, and then dug again, until eventually a little tunnel had formed. He squeezed his head and serpentine neck through the hole, worming his way in. Pulling his wings in tight, gripping the earth with his sharp feet, he pushed, straining with all he had until he popped through to the other side, free.

Lifting his gray and black wings over his head, he squawked victoriously, and the hen, seeing him on the other side, hurried to the hole. The gander nervously tasted the air with his black tongue, shifting from foot to foot until she snaked through. The goslings followed, little gray puffballs stumbling about on fleshy black-webbed feet.

A tall patch of oat straw swayed in the breeze a few feet away, dew-laden and heavy. They slurped the water and chomped on the leaves. One of the goslings nosed the ground and uncovered a woodlouse, snapping it up and swallowing it.

As the morning sun crested over the distant ridges and spread warmth on the forest floor, the gaggle turned to the wild.

AUTHOR'S STORY NOTE

Living in an off-grid cabin with a tall madrone tree hanging precariously over it, this tale of nature's triumph over the follies of man is actually more autobiographical than not. I'll leave it to you, reader, to discern the facts from fiction. I owe a debt to Chuck Palahniuk for this story, I wrote it in a class I took with him at LitReactor, where we studied literary methods on how to show the passage of time. The genesis of the story was to show time passing through the incubation of a goose egg. I then took it upon myself to see if it was possible to shock or disgust one of my favorite writers. He seemed more amused than anything else. Go figure.

SWINGS AND SUSPENSIONS

D.A. XIAOLIN SPIRES

From *Gorgon: Stories of Emergence*
Editor: Sarah Read
Pantheon Magazine

T ingting throws the keychain at my head. The crinkly plastic-wrapped bauble bounces off my cheek, nosedives towards my torso and slides off my bulging belly. I catch it in my palm. "Sorry," she says, smirking. "Didn't mean to hit the baby bump."

I shake my head. She's about to be a mom and she still acts this silly.

I rub my thumb on the souvenir toy. Luminescent yellow, the color of the giant ball before me. A small round head. Except it had vertical slits, like the letter I for eyes and an O for a mouth, which is supposed to look like the number 101, but my eyes cross and it feels like some binary message making its way into my head.

The tour guide ignores our antics and continues on. "This 729-ton steel damper sways back and forth, a great marvel of a pendulum, held up by extremely thick cables of two thousand steel strands. The damper counteracts earthquakes and the gusty winds from typhoons acting on our magnificent Taipei 101. It keeps the building upright. There are two smaller dampers up in the spire, but this is the main one."

We all marvel at the giant ball before us, situated between the 88th and 92nd floors, a colossal sphere with such a momentous presence. It reminds me of when I was a kid and my mom took me abroad for the first time to Epcot Center. A giant geodesic sphere graced the landscape like a ship landing from beyond. It was covered in triangles, looking like the pineapples of my native Tainan in the south. This sphere, nestled in the iconic skyscraping symbol of Taiwan, had horizontal layers, rather than triangles.

"Looks kind of like terraces, like the oolong tea farms in the Maokong mountains," Tingting whispers to me, a little too loud.

The tour guide, who was in the midst of explaining something else, stops her spiel. Her grimace at being interrupted is hidden by a professional smile. "Yes, those steps you see," says the tour guide, "are the steel plates of increasing and then decreasing diameters that constitute the ball, layer by layer. Expert crafts-men welded them together."

"Ah," we say, marveling at the expertise of its production. I'm looking at the layers, from the top smallest one to the bulge in the middle of that ball and I feel my baby kick. I stare at the face of the alien-looking trinket of the mascot keychain in my hands, warped under its protective translucent plastic packaging. My baby kicks three more times, "one-oh-one" I think.

The floor begins to shake.

"Don't panic. Just get to the wall, away from the ledge," the tour guide says. She begins to herd us, waving her hands, flag-ging us over. We all move away from the gaping hole cut out from the center of the floor, containing the massive room-sized planet-like damper.

Tingting leads me as my legs shake. My knees ache as I pro-ceed. The world leans and vertigo and chills sweep my body. My calves are already bloating; this shaking doesn't help my stability. I wipe cold sweat from my face with a sleeve. I imagine my fetus, sloshing around in amniotic fluid, just like this giant ball in the air that is supposed to sway.

But, the giant ball doesn't seem to be doing its job.

The baby kicks over and over as if yearning to get out. "Not yet," I say aloud. "We still have a few weeks!" Then I realize I'm talking to my belly and feel silly. But, no one is paying attention, as the tour crowd yaks in a frenzy, backed up against the wall. Heels and soles trying to grip onto the floor. Hands holding the wall, holding each other. Shouting and praying. A woman next to me starts to cry, tears streaming down her cheeks, rubbing rosary beads between her fingers.

The room sways in greater arcs now, first right, then left, and we slip about holding onto anything, placards, corners of walls, anything we could see, but the damper is strangely still. I'm transported, sitting on a swing set, a memory from when I was a child, eight years old, the sun streaming down my face, playing in the schoolyard, content. The bullies, Weichi and her lackeys, gathered around me, pushing me, faster and faster, taunting me, laughing. My hair flew, tangled and landed on my face as I oscillated back and forth. My breath stopped. I screamed. I fell off, landed in a sprawl, spraining my wrist. The bullies ran off, leaving me there. My lips bled into the dirt.

My lips are bleeding now, and I realize I'm biting them. And all I think is: *I want to get to that ball.* Taipei 101 is swaying, and people are holding on for dear life around me, hanging onto door handles. *Shake it!* But, it's a voice, an urging, not my own. It's coming from inside me. *Don't let them bully you!* I know I must be delirious, but I don't care, and I step towards the ball.

And something clicks in my head. *The wind. We must counteract the wind. We,* I think, wondering who I'm referring to.

"No!" I hear Tingting's yell behind me, but too late. I sprint, as fast as my aching calves allow, jump onto the ledge and spring off, flying through the air. I miraculously grab onto one of the terraces, my fingers clasping onto the edge of the bulky middle of the enormous sphere. The air feels cold here in the center of the room, or maybe it's just my body realizing I'm hanging off this cliff of a layer. Any false move and I plunge to my death. The ball leans and I'm trying to hold on. Strength fills my fingers and it's not me, as I feel the continuous kicks. It's my fetus projecting onto me, taking hold of my body. We had a donor sperm and now I'm wondering if the lab lied about the source. The doctor always had this wayward smile like she was hiding something. *Who is in there, in that belly of mine, controlling me? Tinging's genes or not? And who else?*

But, no time to ponder, I kick my feet but don't get any leverage. I struggle, my knuckles shaking. My fingers manage to pull my body up, though I've never done a single finger pushup in all my life. But it's strength from within and a will to live that fills me. Achingly, I climb to the top, ignoring the shouts my way.

And there, sitting at the pinnacle of the giant damper, my water breaks. Taipei 101's leaning left and then right, and I should be panicking, but I'm strangely calm. It's a birth that must be a world record and I struggle with underpants and before I even manage to peel off my skirt, she's out, along with the placenta. Still, the earth shakes, tremors that keep passing and still the tower careens this way and that. I see a face one-oh-one—vertical slit eyes and a circle mouth.

An alien face, the one from the trinket, the mascot of this building leering at me from my cradled arms. I stifle a scream, close my eyes and suck out amniotic liquid from her translucent nostrils. She breathes. From her skin, tiny mounds arise. Blue and green. I feel them nudging into my arms, against my goosebumps, emerging from the strangeness of it all. I bring her up to my eyes, her umbilical cord still dangling, and I see that on her forehead, on her nose bridge, cheeks, everywhere are little nubs, growing thinner, sharper and they start poking out of her skin, tall and straight, spires, many of them, until I can no longer deal with the pain and rip my skirt to stuff as a buffer. It works, for a bit. The screaming of Mandarin from the tour group stops echoing and falls to a mute, as I can no longer hear them, all I can focus on is my baby before me, shifting, transforming. I feel a heartbeat coming from under my rear, deep and sonorous, vibrating from the damper. Is that possible? *Thump thump thump.*

And my baby's arms reach out in jagged blue-green sleeves, not sleeves, but her arms, made of one giant spire with fractals of spires coming out of it. I smell a primordial dank musk and I realize the small spires are cutting my arms through the bandage of ripped skirt, slick in blood and amniotic fluid, but I dare not let her go. The spirals rising from her skin are four-sided and latticed, like the giant sky-piercing Taipei 101 building we are all in. Her arms lengthen, not mechanical like the extending arms of the bucket trucks that fix street lamps, but more organic, and she reaches out to two of the steel cables of the dampers. Her arms splay out like a snake, the latticed pattern of her skin so much like scales, and she grabs the cables holding the damper and begins to shake them. The damper sphere hiccups from under me, a jerky totter, as if realizing it had been still, derelict in its duties, and starts to swing, like it's supposed to do.

I move with it, swaying, like a pebble perched on a dancing turtle. I grab onto my daughter tighter, if I could call this monstrosity my daughter, as her arms go limp, sagging as she still holds onto the cables, her job done. I realize the screams have turned to awed mumbles.

Taipei 101, the building itself, stops lurching, stops shaking as much. My eyes can gauge that, even as the damper I am on careens one way and another.

I'm exhausted. I stare into my baby's vertical slit eyes, *one* and another *one*, as their immaturity encodes. I can't read the eyes like I can a regular human's, can't tell if they express happiness or fear, but something in my head says, *don't worry*. It feels mature, the voice of reason, of someone older than me, and I know she has saved us all, saved me from that feeling of helplessness when the bullies pushed me too fast, too fast—she swooped in and took all that fear away. She retracts her arms from the cables, letting the giant damper move on its own.

I'm swinging on the damper now, sitting at its apex, but I feel no fear, just a deep sense of love at this strange creature before me. Her eyes lizard-like and her scaled arms of blue-green glass wrapped around me a dozen times. Tingting's over in the mass, huddled with the other bodies, waiting for the tremors to stop, and I want to signal to her that yes, this is our kid—but I hear a gentle sigh and a soft gurgle from within my embrace, and I can't keep my eyes from the cute little ring of her mouth and the captivating coos emerging from her lips.

KIRTI

ALESSANDRO MANZETTI

From *Space and Time Magazine*
Editor: Angela Yuriko Smith
Space and Time Publications

After pocketing the money from selling his goats, Arjun drags his worn slippers away from the market and sits down on one of the four chairs of a seedy bar under a faded Coca-Cola beach umbrella to have a bottle of whiskey. He wants to forget his house, a dirty hole in the infamous slum of Park City. His wife is waiting for him with arms crossed in front of an empty pantry. Numbing the guilt and any concerns for tomorrow, he gets up and waves for a rickshaw. The small vehicle, driven by a boy with snow-white teeth, brakes and picks him up before zig-zagging between the yellow taxi rank and Calcutta's traffic of souls and ghosts. Lulled by the hum of the small rickshaw engine, Arjun observes the city rush from the plastic window. It plays like an accelerated movie.

Everything seems different than a few hours before when he had only dead flies in his wallet—everything except the immense movie posters pasted everywhere. The blank face of a young actress from the South wearing a necklace of keys stared from every wall, a 20-foot tall giantess. A water-bug with antennae stained with human brain peeped out of her ear. Those playbills invaded the city to promote a new horror film in Hindi.

Besides that face staring at him from all over, the city looks brand new in Arjun's eyes. It has been turned bright from the impossible shine of five thousand rupee gold coins, showing the profile of Queen Victoria with a crown of worms on her head; a nineteenth century Medusa. Her skin is of curry powder and resignation as they were immersed, like a fabric to be dyed, in a boiling tub of anti-matter colorants and unusual yolks of cells, coming out oiled and perfumed like a newborn odalisque who has already lived a thousand years.

Streets, squares and buildings sparkle above the orange asphalt of the afternoon, restored with a strychnine-flavored paint of youth. The magical effect will last as long as the money in Arjun's pocket. He has never owned so many coins and he feels alien, like a skinny dog with a diamond collar around its neck. He knows this new magic is only illusion, but he doesn't care about tomorrow. He revels at the deception of his mind, admiring his new Calcutta from the red leather rickshaw cushion.

When they are running by the shops of Calmac Street, with their plastic bead curtains distinguishing them from the poorer shacks, Arjun taps the driver's shoulder. The boy wears a checked shirt soaked through with misery and a beedi cigarette tucked behind his ear: "Get me between Chittaranjan and Shobhabazar . . . you know what I mean." Arjun gives him a significant look.

"Wow, Sonagachi! Yes, sir . . . you want to have some fun, eh?" The boy looks back smiling and sweaty and hands Arjun a photo of a thin fifteen-year-old girl with tied-back hair and golden discs on her naked breasts. "My sister Kirti works there, close to Gdurgacharan Miira, until ten o'clock. She's so beautiful, isn't she?" asks the boy before opening the throttle of his green rickshaw. The boards are covered with photos of Indian actors and hooker's telephone numbers. The tires bite back into the road.

Their destination was a seedy alleyway in the most crowded red-light district of the city. The rickshaw skidded around a bald-headed pimp dressed in Bermuda shorts and fake Ray-Ban sunglasses. The pimp curses the driver before retrieving his piece of coconut barfi that had fallen the ground amid a crowd of slippers. The boy suddenly stops the rickshaw about fifty yards ahead and looks around, turning his head from left to right, stretching his neck to catch the right face among so many. "There she is . . . Kirti! Kirti!"

The girl is wearing a red and purple sari and hoop earrings larger than the palms of her hands. She is squeezed by two fat women who never stop talking and gesturing obscenely. Kirti is really beautiful. *It would be okay*, Arjun thinks. He pays the fare and escapes the onon-scented jalopy.

He heads to the girl, now hidden by the rhino girth of her

colleagues who seem to want to hide her subtle grace. Suddenly he's surrounded by a squad of pimps spitting out words at the speed of light, plucking him by the sleeves. He pushes through them, deaf to their sales calls.

"Kirti, is that you?" Arjun whispers to the young prostitute when he finds her. "Let's get out of here. Got a place to stay?"

But the girl doesn't answer even though she's staring at him. She bobs her head rhythmically, barely moving her red lips. Arjun notices she's wearing earpieces. He grabs one of them, "What are you listening to, baby?" he asks, holding the little device to his ear.

Wearing The Inside Out by Pink Floyd competed with the noisy throng around them.

"Great song," he says. He pushed closer to her, he grabs her hand and whispers in her ear urgently: "But now . . . you must take good care of me, honey. Name your price, let's do this."

Kirti, without saying a word, takes Arjun's hand and guides him towards the maze of alleys behind Gdurgacharan Miira. He is intoxicated as he slides deeper and deeper into the evening color palette reflecting from the pitted roofs and shadowed boxes of vegetables. Like living watercolors, goddesses wrapped in Mesopotamian fabrics nursed infants while disenchanted people gnawed roasted dog's legs. Elders stared at ancient sand-lime bricks embedded in modern concrete structures and frames of empty oval mirrors displayed the feet of passers-by like assembly lines of fat insects at work.

Then, turning one more corner they reached a block of low houses with worn walls and clothes hanging everywhere on ropes edged of red light bulbs. Kirti stops before a blue painted building and jumps over a puddle to bend down in front of a low wooden door more suited for small animals than human beings and disappear into it. An instant later the girl's hand, adorned with henna mandala, emerges from the black rectangle of the opened door and invites Arjun to follow her.

The man scratches his head; he had slept many times with such women but he never did anything like this before. *A strange way to ply the job*, he thinks, but driven by his desires, he puts his doubts to sleep in a matter of seconds. *Who cares, she's too beautiful*, he says to himself crouching down and moving forward awkwardly like an old toad. He climbs into the hole.

Once inside a damp room slowly reveals itself to his eyes. It turns out to be a kind of freshly repainted stable. In the dim room he spots a thin neon lamp in a corner making a faint orange light. Like a stain, the feeble glow cannot escape in the windowless space.

Holy shit . . . Arjun thinks. His face twists up, disgusted.. *It had to happen today . . . to end up in a lousy place like this . . . that idiot of the rickshaw must have thought I was a beggar!*

A deflated mattress covered with cheap colorful cloths printed with erotic motifs, dominates the room. On the opposite wall is a thin frame of light. A door, normal-sized this time, the main entrance leading to another alley. The pitched ceiling of the room is low and Arjun is forced to bend his neck to move inside. *Fuck!*

"Kirti? Where the hell did you go?" he whispers, unable to see the girl's silhouette in that deceptive twilight. "Hey! Come out!"

Impossible, she seems to have disappeared or perhaps left by the other door. *But it makes no sense, I haven't paid yet . . .* he wonders, groping forward, while his eyes adjust to that dull light. Details of the claustrophobic hole begin to emerge.

Tripping on the floor made of irregular wooden board, she notices a pair of men's shoes under a small round table with a glass of tea still warm on top of it.

Man, at least I'll have this . . .

He looks around as he sips the tea and sees a rectangular, dark shape edged with an opalescent frame decorated with fish heads and other strange engravings he cannot decipher on the wall. *It must be a mirror*, he realizes, moving closer to it on tiptoe. He peers into that strange surface, grinding his teeth. No reflection, *but . . . it's not even a painting, there's nothing there . . .*

His thoughts are cut short at that moment when something does appear there giving life to that empty and meaningless gap: an anthropomorphic shape with long, messy hair, and large hoop earrings. It stretches its arms, grabbing his shoulders and pulls him inside. Vertigo, disgust, darkness. Arjun passes out, dreaming about flying inside a beehive that vibrates and continually rotates.

Arjun wakes up in another room, smaller than the other, with a ringing in his ears and a burning sensation in his left leg. *What happened? I was bitten by an insect?* He sits up and looks to the pain under the groin. In that damned orange light an old woman, dressed in rags with a necklace of keys around her neck is slicing his quadriceps muscle with a little sickle and passing the raw pieces of meat to the two children sitting next to her. They squabble over that tasty bite, grinning wildly. The old woman gazes to Arjun with indifference, grabs a glass of tea and hands it to him, croaking: "Drink it again, my prince, so you won't feel anything . . ."

THE TEA AND SUGAR TRAIN

DEBORAH SHELDON

From *Dimension6* #18
Editor: Keith Stevenson
Couer De Lion Publishing

The railway tracks outside Cecelia's door began to vibrate and hum, signalling the approach of the Tea and Sugar Train. She put her darning aside and took up her shopping list.

The door of their four-room shack opened onto the Nullarbor Plain, a flat and endless expanse of Australian desert in the middle of a godforsaken nowhere. The red soil, red-hot as a fever, sprawled level and unbroken from horizon to horizon while the cloudless blue sky glared above it. Blue over red in every direction, resembling a flag. Sometimes, especially if Cecelia felt tired—as she often did at this stage of her pregnancy—the lack of trees, shrubs or grass played tricks on her vision: the sky and earth appeared to press up close against her nose. She had to blink and focus on the railway tracks before she could regain a proper perspective across this wide, dead, barren world.

Cecelia shut the door against the dust and eased herself into one of the veranda chairs to wait. The other chair, next to the pile of old railway sleepers they used for firewood, was empty. As usual, Henry had left early this morning on his handcar, trundling west to join his team of gangers and fettlers. The Commonwealth Transcontinental Railway spanned 1100 miles from Port Augusta to Kalgoorlie, and some 300 men strung along those miles took care of the tracks. Warped or rotten sleepers had to be replaced, recalcitrant lines kept to the required elevation and gauge, lineside equipment maintained. Henry's job prevented derailment. Too bad the pay didn't reflect the importance of his work. Some weeks, Cecelia's shopping list for the Tea and Sugar Train took most of Henry's wages. Last week, dear Lord, he had *owed* money to the company.

She must be even thriftier. Count every shilling, every sixpence. Every ha'penny.

From the east, the train appeared as a black dot, growing larger. Cecelia referred to her shopping list and licked the tip of her pencil. *Half pound lamb chops.* She crossed out the item.

Two bags of flour instead of one, she decided. Wilting fruits and vegetables were cheap. She would bake sweet and savoury pies, and pasties; rely on damper and scones to bulk out their meals . . .

She placed a hand on her belly. Soon, another mouth to feed. And when the child was old enough for learning? Why, they would have to leave this dirt-raddled shack and move to a railway stop with a school. The company's rental fee would be high. Textbooks, pencils, stationery, proper clothes. And shoes! Lord, a child is always outgrowing its shoes. Cecelia recalled last night's argument, a fight they had played over and over since her monthlies had ceased. *How are we going to live?* Henry had shouted. *I don't know,* she had replied, as always. Weeping, as always. *I don't know.*

The plume of steam from the locomotive was visible now. Perhaps ten more minutes and the train would be here with its hotchpotch of carriages. From habit, Cecelia glanced at the dead-end siding. Yes, the switch was in the correct position. The Tea and Sugar Train would not derail.

On the siding sat her own little handcar that Henry had scavenged from the scrap heap. Its seesaw pump-lever, platform and battered iron wheels meant the world to her. It was supposed to be for emergencies only. Some mornings after Henry left for work, she would double-check the train schedule—even though she knew it by heart—switch the tracks and take the little handcar, squeaking and rattling, onto the main line. She would work the pump-lever up and down, up and down, the wind in her hair, eyes closed to imagine the hubbub of Melbourne, Adelaide, or even the dusty streets of Kalgoorlie. She always saw herself on a promenade. In her mind's eye, she wore a dress with shoulder pads, a homburg hat topped with an ostrich feather. But her arms would soon tire. When she opened her eyes, there was nothing but the blue and red flag of this blasted Nullarbor. Puffed from her exertions, she would swap sides and trundle back home again.

Home . . .

When Henry had returned from the war, morose and aloof, empty as a cored apple, he had wanted to live in isolation. As his wife, Cecelia had followed him out here. Out here into this wide, dead, barren world. No neighbours for two hours by handcar in either direction. No telephone. No radio—

The baby thrashed its limbs, breaking into Cecelia's thoughts.

"Hush," she murmured, patting her belly. "Hush, now."

It would be a relief to visit Dulcie, the nurse on the Tea and Sugar Train. At six months, should the baby be so restless, so agitated? This morning, the child seemed to be fighting against the walls of Cecelia's womb. This was her first pregnancy. No one had told her what to expect, not even Mother, who had kept a dignified silence on such matters despite undergoing seven births herself.

The train puffed and wheezed, brakes grinding.

Cecelia stood up with one hand on her aching back. She waved. Ollie the engine driver, a giant Irishman, waggled his arm out the window in return. Cecelia's heart lifted.

People!

For a few minutes, she would chat with Ollie, and Nick the green grocer, Winston the livestock handler, Albert the butcher, George the dry goods man, Reggie the water man, and share a laugh with them, hear the latest news from towns and cities. Dulcie was good for a yarn . . . *I'm so lonely*, Cecelia sometimes whispered to Henry over dinner. *Please talk to me.* He would only bend his head over his plate and attend to his meal.

The train, growling and heaving like a beast, came to a stop.

"Hello there!" she called, waving and smiling. "Good morning! Good morning to you all!"

"Are you grand today, Mrs Young?" Ollie shouted out the window. "I'll be down in a sec. How's your sweet tooth?"

"As sweet as ever!"

Most weeks, Ollie the driver gave her a box of chocolates. She didn't know why. It frightened her but she always took the gift, hiding it in the pantry, scoffing the treats while Henry was gone, burning the box in the fireplace. What did Ollie want in return? He hadn't told her yet. She hoped her smile was enough. Occasionally, though, she wondered what might happen if, one day, she packed her suitcase and climbed into the locomotive's cabin and went with him all the way to Kalgoorlie. The Indian Ocean must be as green as jade.

The frantic bawling of ewes spun her around.

From the livestock carriage some yards distant, two sheep fell onto the ground. The screeching animals couldn't get up. Instead, they rolled and bucked in the dirt. Cecelia saw the blood. It squirted out of each sheep from where their four legs should have been, and yet were not. Cecelia's stomach turned over.

Where were their legs?

She called for the livestock man—"Winston! Winston!"—and the ramp emerged, teetered, and touched down on the dirt. About a dozen sheep, bleating and jumping, fled from the carriage and ran in panicked circles around each other. Close behind them hurried a few shrieking pigs. Out tumbled the flapping chickens. The birds scattered and ran into the emptiness of the desert without hesitation, as if the Devil himself were on their heels. The sheep and pigs rushed after them. There was no water in the Nullarbor Plain. The animals would die. How had they escaped their cages? And why hadn't Winston left the carriage yet?

What was taking him so long?

Cecelia held a palm to her throat, the keening of the mutilated sheep raking her nerves. She was about to call for Ollie when Winston's arms finally appeared, hands groping at the ramp, followed by his head and the rest of him.

But how in the world . . .?

He was descending the ramp on his hands and feet, arched

over backwards, spine bent at an impossibly sharp angle. His head dangled loose on his neck, grey hair sweeping the boards. Shock and dread fired through Cecelia, freezing her to the spot. Winston shuffled like a broken spider down the ramp. Blood smeared his cheeks.

When he reached ground, he worked his jaws and turned his face to gaze at her.

They locked eyes.

Cecelia couldn't breathe.

What kind of hellish vision was this? Could she be dreaming?

Like a rusty flywheel, Winston's head began to rotate, slowly, jerkily, notch by notch, until it was the right way up. Even from this distance, Cecelia could hear the bones in his neck cracking and splintering. His mouth opened, releasing a glut of blood and raw meat. From the sheep's missing legs, she knew.

This couldn't be happening.

Had she lost her mind?

Winston scuttled towards her at great speed. Cecelia drew a lungful of air and screamed.

"Saints preserve us!" Ollie bellowed.

She glanced around. Ollie dropped the box of chocolates and launched himself back up the ladder and into the engine's cabin. Dear Lord, Cecelia thought, heart pounding. *He's going to leave me here with this monster.* But the next second, Ollie leapt out with a coal shovel.

"Stand clear, Mrs Young!" he cried.

The monster that had once been Winston yawned open its maw and picked up its scrabbling pace as if to attack. Ollie swung the shovel two-handed like a cricket bat. The blow against Winston's head made a loud, slapping, wet sound as it caved in the bones. Cecelia squeezed her eyes shut. The blows went on and on and on.

Thud. Thud. Thud.

Ollie meant to smash the monster's skull into pulp. Her racing heart fluttered and skipped. The maimed sheep kept bawling.

Thud. Thud.

And then, one final time.

Thud.

She opened her eyes. The monster that had once been Winston lay in the dirt, limbs twitching spasmodically, blood and mush spattered around him in a curdling puddle. Ollie strode towards the sheep. Before Cecelia could look away, he had dispatched both animals with the shovel, bringing the blade straight down, first upon one neck and then the other.

Now, all was silent apart from the soft, billowing breaths of the train.

She tried to gather her fractured thoughts.

A demon.

Winston must have been possessed by a demon.

Oh Jesus, she thought. *My Lord, Jesus Christ, remember that I am a sinner. Most Holy Virgin pray for me. You shall always be praised and blessed. Pray for this sinner—*

"Mrs Young?"

Ollie had turned to her. His chest heaved. Blood covered his bib-and-brace overalls. He took off his billed cap, wiped his forehead with the back of his hand and walked over, unsteady, trailing the gory shovel through the soil behind him.

"Mrs Young, are you unharmed?"

"Yes. And you?"

"Sure." He gestured at his overalls. "Ain't none of this blood's mine."

She locked her knees to stay upright. "What in God's name happened to Winston?"

Ollie's face was blanched, eyes glazed. "Damned if I know. He was fine at our last stop. Taking the piss as usual, playing the fool." He whistled a reedy note. "Damned if I know."

They stood together for a time, panting, trembling.

"We'll have to send for the constables," Cecelia said at last.

"I suppose you're right."

"I'll be your witness."

"If anyone believes us." He groaned, seemed to droop. "Oh, shite. I killed a man."

"No, not a man. A monster."

Ollie blew out a breath. "How do you suppose he . . . *twisted* himself in that way?"

"I've no idea. I've never seen anything like it."

Ollie put his cap back on his head. "Well, I'm not leaving you here. You can't stay with him looking . . . like *that*. Hop in the cabin. You can ride with me, sure enough."

"Oh, thank you, Ollie. Thank you so much."

"Right. Let's crack on."

He started for the engine. And then it occurred to her, in a sick and panicky rush, that the other train workers had yet to appear. Surely, they had heard the commotion: the shouting, bleating, smashing and slaughtering . . . Why hadn't they shown themselves? The possibility felt too ghastly to contemplate. Her teeth started to chatter.

Carriage doors rattled open. Simultaneously, Nick the green grocer and Albert the butcher showed themselves, alighting from the train wrenched over backwards.

"Ollie!" she wailed. "Ollie!"

In unison, the heads of Nick and Albert turned right way up, bones snapping.

Brandishing the shovel, Ollie ran past her at the abominations. "Get in your house and lock the door!"

Cecelia staggered on rubber legs towards the shack but took in the danger of it within a moment: one way in and out, a flimsy wooden door; thin panes of glass in each of the four windows and no shutters. If a monster got inside, she'd be finished. A monster would do to her what Winston had done to those poor sheep.

Gnaw at her limbs.

Eat her alive.

With a sob, she veered towards the woodpile. Images of Henry flashed through her mind. Henry's shoulders rolling as he chopped the sleepers. His affectionate smile, rare as it was. The calm, unhurried way he packed and smoked his pipe after dinner. His sombre hazel eyes gazing across the Nullarbor Plain as if he could see for a thousand miles or more. Sometimes, he would take her hand and kiss her fingertips. Henry. Oh God, Henry.

Cecelia grabbed the axe.

The blasted thing was so *heavy.*

Her baby jolted and kicked. Could it sense Cecelia's fear? She had to be strong. Had to fight like a man if she hoped to save the child and herself. She wrapped an arm about her belly and, breathless, faced the melee.

Nick the green grocer was down, a broken and bloodied heap in the dirt.

Ollie, swinging the shovel, was defending himself against Albert the butcher.

Albert darted around Ollie's legs with the speed and agility of a huntsman spider, gnashing his teeth. In life—for surely, he must be dead and somehow reanimated?—Albert had been a stout and strapping lad, unlike Winston and Nick, who had both been thin, elderly, frail. Cecelia *must* help before the monster overwhelmed him.

Except her legs gave way.

Dizzy, she stumbled against the pile of wooden sleepers. Good Lord, she almost dropped the blade of the axe straight into her own thigh. The scare of it cleared her head. She struggled to get up again.

Ollie's shovel broke in two.

Cecelia stumbled towards them, axe held out from her body in one hand, the other cradling the weight of her belly as the baby struggled and flailed. Ollie dodged the champing teeth and sprang into the butcher's carriage. Albert went to follow.

Unseen from behind, Cecelia swung the axe sideways into his knee.

To her surprise and horror, the heavy blade went straight through his leg. Unbalanced, Albert toppled like a three-legged table. She lifted the axe to chop again. Ollie bounded from the carriage armed with meat cleavers. His flurry of blows on Albert's head and neck released fountains of blood. Hot droplets spattered her face. She turned away and gagged.

"Mrs Young," he yelled, "want a bollocking? Get yourself indoors."

She shook her head. "They've all changed. All of them. Look."

Out came Reggie the water man, George the dry goods man. On the landing of the Health Centre Coach, grotesquely arched and distorted like the others, face upside-down, was Dulcie the nurse in her starched uniform, the triangle of her veil hanging loose.

Their three heads rotated. Three necks cracked and broke. Three mouths stretched open.

"*Nách mór an diabhal thú*," Ollie murmured, but Cecelia didn't know what that meant.

He stepped back. Cecelia moved closer to him.

"Let's go," she whispered. "Can you uncouple the engine from the carriages?"

"I can, but not before these devils attack us."

She swallowed. "Are we to die?"

"More than likely." Ollie reached out and squeezed her hand, briefly. "I'll do my best."

The monsters rushed them.

Ollie lunged forward to intercept Reggie. George, stocky as a hog, lumbered at Cecelia with his teeth bared. Terror shot through her arms and gave her strength to swing the axe two-handed in a sweeping arc. She brought the blade down on the monster's skull. The blade cleaved the head in two and lodged itself in the jawbone. Cecelia gasped. She had expected the skull to be tough, as hardened as a length of sleeper, but it had offered no more resistance than an eggshell. George collapsed in an untidy heap, bleeding, fitting and spasming.

Dulcie was still picking her way down the steep ladder of the Health Centre Coach. Cecelia tried to free the axe. Impossible. Stuck fast. Her efforts only managed to tug and shift George's twitching corpse in the dirt.

Behind her, Ollie and Reggie struggled, tussling like wrestlers. Ollie had lost one of his meat cleavers. She had to defend against Dulcie and then help Ollie. But how? She couldn't pull this blasted axe from George's head.

Dulcie reached ground and came at her in a spritely, loping gallop.

"Come on, goddamn it!" Cecelia shrieked at the axe, yanking with all her might.

The axe wouldn't budge.

She turned and fled towards the house, Dulcie's teeth catching at the hem of her dress. Could she stove in the monster's head with a sleeper? No, no, Henry had not yet cut these ones to length. How could she lift a sleeper the size a of a tree trunk? Henry had taken his pick, shovel, ballast fork and lining bars with him. Vaulting across the veranda, Cecelia bolted inside and went to slam the door.

Too late.

Dulcie's head was already over the threshold.

Grunting with effort, Cecelia leaned against the door and shoved, shoved, shoved. No good. Her shoes lost purchase, began to slip and slide as Dulcie shouldered further and further inside. The toe of Cecelia's shoe found a knothole in the floorboards. Now she could push back. A stalemate for a few moments; equal force against equal force. Praise God, was the door closing? Yes, it was. It *was* closing.

The monster's tongue unfurled and whipped about.

Cecelia yelped.

The tongue elongated. Soon it would be long enough to wrap itself around Cecelia's ankle and pull her into those teeth that were growing, sharpening, extending.

"In the name of Christ, get away from me!" she screamed.

Dulcie burst open the door, throwing Cecelia against the table.

They faced each other, motionless, for what seemed like an age. The hideous mouth opened wider. Its throat convulsed. The tongue roped onto the floor, its tip switching back and forth like a snake's tail.

A weapon. Cecelia must find some kind of weapon.

The cast-iron pan?

She took a single step towards the woodstove. Hesitated when Dulcie shifted on four limbs. The distorted body started to tighten and pull itself together as if preparing to jump.

Cecelia lunged for the pan. Dulcie sprang. The flat of the pan caught the monster across the face. The nose broke away cleanly and drooped alongside one cheek. The monster didn't appear to notice. The tongue intercepted the second swing. Prehensile, it lashed itself around the handle and ripped the pan from Cecelia's grasp. The tongue had touched her for a split-second, the texture of it dry and scaled, and Cecelia howled in revulsion and terror.

The pan clattered to the floorboards.

The tongue retracted.

The advancing jaws snap, snap, *snapped*.

Cecelia grabbed the skinny little poker from the fireplace and held it out just as Dulcie leaped, all limbs in the air at once like a spider. The poker entered the gaping mouth and Dulcie's impetus drove it straight down the gullet. Cecelia felt it punch and lodge somewhere deep inside. The monster dropped, short-winded and retching, tongue lolling.

Cecelia wrenched out the poker and brought it down on the grotesque head over and over, crunching the bones, staining the gauzy white veil first with blood and then with brains. At last, Dulcie teetered and fell.

Strength ebbed from Cecelia. She leaned against the table and wept. The baby, oh dear Lord, the baby started to thrash in what felt like a wild, animal panic.

"Shush, my darling," she whispered through quivering lips, patting at her belly with one bloodied palm. "Hush, now—"

Was that a contraction?

Shocked, Cecelia stopped weeping.

That quick, vice-like sensation in the cradle of her pelvis? *There it was again.* She knew what that meant. No, she was only six months along. She had to get to a hospital.

"Ollie?" she called. "Can you hear me?"

No answer.

She cocked her head to listen.

Nothing but the huff and respiration of the Tea and Sugar Train.

Her heart started knocking again. Lifting the bent and crumpled poker, holding it out like a sword, she stepped around Dulcie's corpse and approached the open door. The fight with Reggie the water man, the monster that Reggie had become . . . had Ollie won?

"Ollie, please say something," she cried.

No reply.

She peeked around the jamb.

And there was the Irishman, standing over the remains of Reggie. She sagged and shook with relief. Every monster was dead. She made her way outside haltingly, painfully, groping for support against the doorframe, the chair next to the woodpile, the nearest veranda post.

"I killed Dulcie," she said.

Ollie turned. The sight made her flinch. He was covered in gore from head to toe as if dipped in a vat. Eyes shining white in his bloodied face, he stared at the meat cleaver in his hand and dropped it, raising a puff of red soil.

"Can we leave right away?" she said. "I think the baby is coming."

He didn't reply.

She hugged the veranda post, watching him. Her womb clenched and released again.

"I need a hospital," she said. "Will you drive me?"

The closest hospital was four hours away. And if she got there in time, could the doctors stop her labour? Save the baby? She had names picked out already: Douglas Ross for a boy; Maureen Joy for a girl.

"Ollie?" Tears rose. "For God's sake, answer me."

He coughed. Brought a hand to his throat and coughed again. It was an alarming sound, a choking sound. Cecelia pushed off from the post, stepped from the veranda and managed a few paces on unsteady legs. Woozy, she had to pause. Ollie started wheezing. It worsened into a strident, whooping sound.

"What's the matter?" she said, frightened. "Where are you hurt?"

Ollie hacked and barked, clawing at his throat. Dear God, how could she help? No medical training, no medical supplies . . . Then, as if punched by an invisible fist, his head flung back with a loud pop and stayed there.

Cecelia froze.

The coughing and wheezing ceased. Ollie's knees started to bend.

"Dear Lord," she whispered. "No. Please no."

Ollie swung his arms overhead so violently that both shoulders cracked. Methodically, steadily, he bent over backwards, lowering himself inch by inch until his palms lay flat on the ground. He shook himself with the vigour of a wet dog. Shuffling, he faced her with his upside-down head.

Cecelia lifted the crooked poker. "Stay away. Can you still understand me? Stay. Away."

Neck bones cracked and broke as his head swivelled the right way up. He bared his teeth.

The fight left her with a sob. How could she defend herself against this giant of a man? Ollie must be three times her size. She had nothing but a flimsy poker. What now? What?

She would kneel and pray.

There was no other recourse. And while this monster that had once been Ollie murdered and defiled her, she would hold the love of God our Father in her heart. Lifted into Heaven with her unborn child, she would wait there for Henry until his time on earth came to an end, until they would be a family once more, together again for all of eternity.

And then she remembered the handcar.

With a spurt of fresh energy, she dropped the poker and sprinted.

Ollie shuffled noisily through the soil behind her in pursuit. Her lead was only a few yards. She hauled the switch to move the tracks, checked over her shoulder.

Ollie was too close.

Jumping aboard the platform, she grabbed the pump-lever and worked it. Shuddering, creaking, the handcar began to inch along the tracks.

Faster, faster, she had to go *faster*.

She looked back. Saw the open mouth. Instinctively kicked out, once, twice. The sturdy heel of her shoe broke his front teeth. Panting with exertion, grunting, she wrenched on that damned pump-lever as quickly as she could. The handcar gained speed. It bumped onto the main track, began to zip along. Negotiating the wooden sleepers would slow Ollie down.

Unless he retained enough human sense to run alongside on the dirt.

She looked back again. He was stumbling over the tracks, almost upon her. She kicked out again. Yet she couldn't kick and work the lever both.

"God help me," Cecelia yelled to the heavens.

Shutting her eyes, she focused on the lever. *Up down up down up down up . . .*

Her muscles burned. The flesh on her legs crept as she awaited Ollie's bite.

A flurry of contractions buckled her. Stars danced in her vision. She lost the pump-lever's rhythm. Was Ollie close? No time to check. Near, too near, she heard him clattering over the tracks. Panic would be her undoing. She brought to mind the padded shoulders of a new dress, the ostrich feather in a homburg hat. The promenade, the promenade. She would be strolling the promenade with Henry while he pushed the perambulator with their child sitting inside, a chubby little girl, Maureen Joy, with her waving arms and strawberry blonde hair . . .

Cecelia glanced around.

Ollie, some yards back along the tracks, had stopped. Had given up the pursuit.

Thank you, God. Oh, thank you.

Shaking, Cecelia slowed the pace, arms on fire. How far was Henry and his gang? Surely, no more than an hour. If she spared her strength, she could make the distance in good time.

Up down. *Breathe.*

Up down. *Breathe.*

The wind dried the tears on her cheeks. Willpower stopped her legs from folding. All she wanted now was to feel Henry's arms about her, his kisses on her mouth. How to explain the horrors from the Tea and Sugar Train? The events defied description. She glanced back. The locomotive lay far in the distance. She was safe.

But what had changed everyone? What had changed Ollie?

Something from the sky, perhaps, something out of the air . . .

A cold fist closed around her heart.

What if she, too, were doomed to turn into a monster?

Unnerved, she took one hand off the lever to knead at her neck. Did she feel all right? Any different? It was hard to tell, her body wracked with pain, cramps, fatigue . . . Yet she didn't need to cough. No choking sensations. That meant she was okay.

Didn't it?

She put both hands on the pump-lever. Focus. Up down, up down. Her mind raced.

What about Henry? She might come upon him and the other fettlers and gangers, only to find them contorted upside-down. Could the whole Nullarbor Plain be infected? Or even the whole of Australia?

Another contraction took Cecelia's breath.

A contraction . . . or was it a *bite*?

The baby stretched as if trying to arch itself.

Arch itself backwards?

Cecelia screamed into the empty blue sky. Her screams rolled out without answer or echo across the wide, dead, barren Nullarbor Plain.

AUTHOR'S STORY NOTE

My retired in-laws take frequent trips around Australia with their caravan. One day when they were visiting, they spoke of their intention to drive from Melbourne to Perth; a journey of about 3400 kilometres (2110 miles) across some of the harshest, most unforgiving terrain that our desert continent has to offer. Alarmed, I expressed concern. "Oh, no worries!" my mother-in-law said.

"The route is quite popular now. Funny to think we'll be following the tracks that used to carry the Tea and Sugar Train." The what? I'd never heard of this particular train before. As soon as I looked it up online and saw its jumble of mismatched carriages, I started plotting a story.

SCREAMS
FOR STARGIRL

BEN PIENAAR

From *Dark Moon Digest #35*
Editors: Lori Michelle & Max Booth III
Perpetual Motion Machine Publishing

Sarah Wilson lived in an audio world. She thought in sound, saw in sound. She heard colours and listened to taste; a delicious meal was a symphony; a brilliant view was a concert played out before her eyes. As a child, she had once been mesmerised by the pitch of a dog's yelp as it was kicked by a small boy. It hit the right note, somehow. Another time, the breathy gasps of a schoolmate who'd just broken his arm falling from the monkey bars, in anticipation of a scream. They sounded to her like gusts of wind down an autumn street.

As she grew older, an idea began to build up inside her, something new and exciting. This music only she could hear—what if she collected it? Distilled it to perfection in a way that only she, with her unique talent, could? What if she made a symphony to her own taste?

So she had cleaned out the basement. Piles of leaves and cobwebs obliterated, along with their inhabitants. She'd particularly enjoyed getting rid of the rats—their squeals and chitters had a range and frequency all of their own, especially when tails were cut and legs twisted. When the area was clear of all but the concrete and wooden rafters, she set up a studio. She padded the walls with the highest quality material and crafted every inch to make the acoustics just right. She spent grocery money on microphones, and recording devices of supreme accuracy, which she set up at specific angles and locations around the space.

Finally, she fitted the rear wall with bolts, cuffs, and loops through which she might thread thin ropes—she didn't want clinking chains to interfere with the quality of her composition.

'I wrote a song, do you want to hear it?' Sarah said.

Xander didn't answer immediately. He was standing in the middle of what was supposed to be a living room but was lacking the furniture to make it worth actually living in. A guitar lay on the dusty floor in the middle of the room, and a single light bulb hung from a wire above it. *Artists*, he thought. *Can't live with em . . .*

'It's about a ghost girl who falls in love with a woman—a living one—and then kills her so they can be together.' She was sitting up on her kitchen counter, watching him the way a cat might: unsure of him and his intentions, sizing him up with one paw raised and ready to run.

He gave her his most charming smile, trying to put her at ease. So far, the night had gone like nothing else he'd experienced. Usually girls like her—aspiring singers or musicians—would gush over him, or themselves, or music, or all of the above. They were always too eager to lay him or get him to listen to their album. Sarah, however, had spent most of their first date cracking the lobster she'd ordered (on his bill) and talking about the ocean. 'Did you know it goes deeper than mount Everest is tall? There are less people that have been down there than on the moon.' That was, of course, when she spoke at all—mostly it was just him on a monologue about what he did, as if *he* was trying to impress *her*. He supposed he was. For all his chops and status in the industry, even the singers he dealt with didn't look *this* good—and she hadn't even worn makeup for their date. 'Sure, go ahead,' he said, thinking: *moment of truth, girl.*

He expected her to prepare, somehow, to stand up straight and brush her hair back, take a deep breath. Instead, sitting slouched over on the counter and without so much as a pause, Sarah simply opened her mouth and began to sing.

The smile fell from Xander's face. His hands, always in and out of his pockets or running through his hair or clasped together, were limp by his sides. He must have looked horrified, because she stopped suddenly, and then shrugged. 'That's all I've got so far. I'm better with instruments, anyway.'

Holy shit, he thought. *She doesn't even know. She has no idea how good she is.* Her voice had a natural depth to it—the passion of an ancient soul. He was awestruck.

She hopped off the counter and started back toward the front door. 'Anyway, you should go. I've got stuff to do.'

'Hey, hey hold on. You, uh, got anything else?' She looked back over her shoulder, uncertain. Seeing he was serious, she nodded, and then pointed to the Cello by the fireplace. 'I can do something with that.'

'Sure. Go ahead.'

And she played for him again, pulling out one of the chairs from her kitchen table and sitting with legs splayed out and hair hanging down over her face, completely lost in the music. She played with the confidence of a seasoned professional, yet as wild and unrestrained as an enthusiastic amateur. Xander was familiar with all the classics, and he tried long and hard to place the song—a deep rising melody like *Hall of the Mountain King*—until he realised it was original music.

When she was done, she looked up at him with a blank face, waiting for his reaction but apparently expecting nothing. She had played so perfectly she might have won a standing ovation from the philharmonic orchestra.

Xander took a deep breath and folded his arms. 'Sarah.' He paused. He wanted to run at her and hug her, and maybe kiss her once or twice, and then dance all over the room and then maybe marry her, but instead he just said: 'How would you like to be famous?'

The trick was getting just the right sound. Sometimes it was hard to get them to co-operate, but with Esther, the problem was something else. The girl wasn't living up to the potential of her vocal chords. It didn't seem to matter where Sarah stuck her needle, or how deep she cut, Esther couldn't hit the note.

The breakthrough came on the fourth night, just after Xander left. She had deprived Esther of water, hoping the roughness of her throat might add a husky quality to her cries, but when she tried to prompt her, the girl merely swore at her. 'I know you're not going to let me go, you bitch! I've seen your face!' She tried to spit in Sarah's face, but there was no moisture. Sarah crouched in front of her, absentmindedly bouncing the tip of her needle in the palm of her hand. At last, it clicked.

She fixed the microphone nearest Esther's face, angling it and clicking it to record. As long as the right note sounded, she could edit everything else out. That was the plan: to collect each note separately and then patch them all together to weave her masterpiece. She removed the black ribbon she'd been using to tie her hair back and secured it over Esther's eyes.

'What the hell are you doing? I've already seen you. I'm not an idiot!'

Sarah didn't respond. Her heart was beating quickly, a thrill she only ever got when she was really there, right on the brink of True Art. When it was done, she stepped back and then crouched down, holding her breath and remaining absolutely silent.

Esther pulled her knees up to her naked breast, half from the cold, half from fear. She knew what was coming, but now she didn't know from which direction. Her skin was covered in tiny red and black dots, dried blood droplets from Sarah's previous attempts to ellicit from her the perfect sound. 'What are you doing?' she said again, her voice trembling, the defiant strength wavering.

Sarah waited. An owl hooted from the pine just outside the basement. A gust of wind made the rafters groan. She needed silence, and a minute later she found it in between Esther's breaths. She lashed out like a rattlesnake, the needle piercing Esther in the soft part of her thigh, and there it was: a scream that carried just the right timbre, the perfect pitch.

Sarah lowered the needle and stood up with a satisfied sigh. 'Thank you,' she said, and she meant it. Esther didn't seem to notice—she was crying again, a low moan that wasn't without value; here and there Sarah heard something she might be able to use. She leaned forward and patted her on the head. 'There there,' she said. 'It's over, now.'

This time, the needle went through Esther's neck.

Xander booked her into a few underground Jazz clubs, late night spots at first, then the more prominent weekend nine o' clocks. He spared no expense: he put out posters and flyers, he got her a stylist and paid for clothes and jewelry. Not that he could afford it, but he wasn't an idiot—he knew what was coming.

Sarah, for her part, was completely indifferent. Most girls would have preened and posed in front of the mirror; Sarah merely stared while she got a makeover worthy of any supermodel, the stylist chatting away and complimenting her, oblivious. When she was done, Sarah said: 'Thanks Julia,' and then walked out on stage looking like a movie star from the twenties and singing like Billie Holiday. It was magic.

He tried to kiss her once, after a celebratory dinner of wine, oysters and rare steak, and she'd let him. It was like kissing a dead girl, her lips cold and soft, her tongue unresponsive. Somehow, it only made him want her more. *Give it time, my friend. It's all new to her.*

Later that same night, they walked along the beach in front of the row of nightclubs and casinos known to locals as 'Sinner's Strip'. She let him hold her hand, so delicate and smooth, with nails as long and filed as if they'd been designed to pluck strings. She'd sung one of her own songs that night, instead of covering an old hit, and the crowd had sucked in every word.

'You're gonna be big, you know,' he said. 'You're gonna be the next Lana Del Rey, or Amy Winehouse, or . . . Hell, better—you'll be your *own* thing.'

She nodded absently, as though this was something she already knew.

They turned down the pier at the end of the Strip, a shonky line of planks that ended in a viewing platform from which the whole bay and the rising hills beyond it were visible. She liked it there, she said. She was obsessed with great voids, and the bay at night was the only place you could see the emptiness of space and the vastness of the ocean at once.

They stopped at the end and he turned to face her. She ignored him, staring out over the blackness, hypnotised.

'You'll be famous,' he said.

'My music is too dark. I'll only ever be on the underground. I like it that way. I don't want to be famous. I don't want anyone to know who I am. I want to sing quietly in an empty stadium, and have no one hear my words but me. Then I'll die starving and alone, and only then they'll say I was good and give me awards.'

Every time he thought he her figured out, she found a new way to mystify him.

'That sounds . . . painful,' he said eventually.

'All art comes from pain,' she said.

He couldn't think of anything to say to that, so he looked out over the bay and said nothing.

Thirty seconds of sound, pieced together from countless snippets, some milliseconds and others several notes long, edited smoothly together by Sarah's deft touch and impeccable ear. Her working title was: an Ode to Misery. The sounds of suffering, she found, had a very distinct flavour and range—the same way you could always tell a blues song, regardless of what instruments were playing.

There was a long way to go, yet—she hadn't even begun to reach the climax of the piece—but she decided to let someone listen to it.

Not deliberately, however. This was too intense for the conscious mind. It worked best with a subtle approach; it was more a soundtrack than an epic solo, more a dream than a story, like a David Lynch movie.

So she asked Greg if she could play her own music as the bottle store's background noise instead of the usual pop songs and ads they usually played. 'Only on the late night shifts, when I close by myself,' she added quickly.

He squinted at her. 'What kinda music is it?'

'Alternative.'

'Any swearing in it?'

'None.'

'Sure. Knock yourself out. Not in busy hours, okay? The area manager's a tightass about having those damn jingles every twenty minutes. Makes me wanna neck myself.'

'No problem. Thanks, Greg.'

He left at five, and she waited until ten, the last hour of the shift, when only the occasional customer came strolling in. She put the volume down by half and, since she only had half a minute of music, stuck it on repeat. Then she stood behind the counter and pretended to read a copy of *Women's Lifestyle*, and watched.

No one commented on the track, or seemed aware of it at all. The music was a mosaic, each note distinct and separate from every other and yet each leading logically to the next, creating a strange patchwork of sound. It had a human quality so unusual in the modern world of autotune and DJ technology, and yet also superhuman—vocal chords stretching far beyond their normal range.

A young couple came in, smiling at first, then frowning and finally bickering over which wine to buy, their voices taking on a bitter, jarring quality that intrigued Sarah. They hardly acknowledged her at the counter, and by the time they left the girl had mascara streaming down her face and her boyfriend's face had turned to stone. Sarah wondered, for the first time, what heartbreak sounded like.

One of the regulars entered a few minutes later, a fat old man with yellow tinged eyes who bought exactly two cans of beer every day. He stood staring at the shelf for five or ten minutes, muttering to himself. He picked up a six-pack, then a case, and finally cursing, headed for the hard liquor section, where he picked up two bottles of bourbon, a hundred proof. At the front, he ordered a pack of cigarettes.

'Hey Jim. I though you quit,' she said. He scowled at her, and when she looked into his eyes she was sure she saw something working at him. The voices of his inner demons, roaring for a fresh piece of his soul and having it granted them.

'One of those nights,' he said, snatching the bag from her hand.

Sarah's bright gaze followed all who entered that night. She saw it happen again and again: customers came in and seemed to get lost somewhere between the entrance and the counter. Lost in time, lost in their thoughts, turning inward, bothered, irritated, disturbed. They were drowning and they didn't even know it.

At the end of the shift, Sarah knew she was on to something special. There was a real bite to that music, some vein of raw human power she was tapping in to . . . but there was a lot of work to do, yet. There was too much still missing.

She took her time walking home, playing the tune in her iPod and singing lyrics to herself, improvising as she went.

The clubs were getting bigger now, and soon Xander started to book her in theatres. Money came in, and she quit the bottle store. Xander couldn't sleep most nights. He was obsessed with her, and all the more because of her indifference to him, her casual brushing off of his advances, which he was compelled to keep making against his friends' advice and his own better judgment.

'She's an ice queen, buddy,' Jake said to him one night, patting him on the back while he nursed a beer. They were sitting out front of their favourite Hawaiian cocktail bar—Heart of

Honolulu—feet up on deckchairs while they watched the waves rolling in.

'I know,' he said. 'But the queen is worth the ice.'

The truth was, since he'd met her, everything in his life had become a kind of rocket, speeding up with engines roaring until it was threatening to blow through the stratosphere. Even Jake was in awe of the way she was snowballing toward stardom, but no one was surprised—no one who had heard her sing, anyway.

The turning point came when he booked her at the Kingdom Theatre, just a few blocks north of the Strip and one of the biggest venues outside of the City. At five thousand seats, the only place to go after that would be The Olympia, and if you were playing The Olympia, baby, you were Big Time.

He'd broken the news to her just the day before, deciding to surprise her with a bottle of wine. She'd been playing a violin, a hauntingly beautiful song she seemed to be improvising, and didn't even notice him come in. She swayed, her eyes closed, delicate fingers dancing along the frets with stunning agility, and he watched her for who knew how long before she saw him and jerked upright, the song coming to an abrupt end.

'What are you doing here?'

He held up the wine, a ten year old cellar release cabernet that would have emptied his bank account just a few months ago and was now barely a drop in the ocean. He smiled. 'Guess where I just got you a gig?'

'I don't care.'

And, to his amazement, she dropped the violin and came to him, enfolding him in her arms and kissing him like never before. She smelled like sweat and leather. She hadn't been cold *that* night, and he'd left the next morning feeling dazed and drunk on more than wine, his back covered in stinging scratches.

He raised his glass to Jake, smiling. 'Hey, here's to us.'

Jake smiled and raised his own glass. 'It's all you, buddy. The

Ravenites are great, but they're a Strip band at best. No way could I get them a gig at Kingdom. It's all up from here. I'm just saying though, you gotta be careful.'

And there it was, at last—that subtle note of jealousy that Xander had never believed he'd ever hear in Jake's voice. He almost felt bad for him. 'What, am I gonna get corrupted by success? Spiral downward in a haze of women and heroin like Jim Morrison and die young? Doesn't sound so bad to me.'

He was joking, of course, but Jake wasn't laughing. 'Oh you'll die young, alright,' he said, shaking his head. 'But it's that crazy singer of yours that's gonna kill you.'

It was late, but not too late, and a freak heat wave from the previous day hadn't quite surrendered to the rain and autumn cold. Steam rose from the asphalt carrying with it the smell of tar and gravel. Lana took turns at random, favouring narrow streets, and those with broken windows and graffiti. The sirens of the police and ambulance were frequent here, a kind of night music of their own. Sarah frowned as she ambled along, thinking of nothing in particular—until she heard an unfamiliar sound: The laughter of a small boy.

It seemed so out of place in this neighbourhood she had to follow it. She found the culprit soon enough, a youth of no more than six playing with a tennis ball in the road. His mother sat against a mouldy wall, sucking on a cigarette with sunken cheeks and rocking. She looked tired and worn out, like all junkies. The kid was having a blast, slapping his ball up against the factory wall and giggling when it bounced back at him at crazy angles. The old lady watched him with a sad smile on her face.

Then she caught sight of Sarah, watching her. She coughed out her last drag. 'Haggghh. H . . . Hey, this isn't any place for a . . . are you lost, honey?'

Sarah didn't answer immediately. She had her head cocked to

one side, the part of her brain that could tell pitch with perfect accuracy working, hearing the unique qualities in the two voices, mother and son, young and old. Another part of her mind, a more emotional part, was thinking about suffering, and about how physical suffering was only a part of it. A small part, really. Some people would prefer to be horribly tortured rather than suffer the agony of grief, or sorrow, and wasn't that interesting?

'Are you—Haaaggh. Are you okay?' The kid had stopped his game and was staring at Sarah now, meeting her curious gaze with one of his own. The mother stubbed out her cigarette and got to her feet, and Sarah snapped out of it at last. She put a hand to her chest. 'Oh, I'm so sorry I was just, I heard your son and I was worried he might be lost or . . .'

'Oh. Oh, no, he'd be right at home in a pigsty. Heh, isn't that right, Denny? Just as happy as a cow in a mud hole, ain't ya?'

Denny shrugged, suddenly shy. He went over to his mother and she patted his head. 'Nah, we're all right,' she went on. 'But you better get on, lady, this place can get dangerous after dark.'

'Isn't it dangerous for you, too? Don't you have a place to stay?' Her voice cracking with concern. She kept her eyes wide and unblinking, a naïve college girl in the big city.

The old lady shifted on her feet. 'Ah, we'll be fine. Wouldn't say no if you could pass a dollar or two our way though, would we, Denny?'

'No, no. Look, my house isn't far from here. Why don't' you stay one night? My good deed for the day, kinda thing.'

'Aw, honey, you don't—'

'It's fine. Really, it's not far. They said it was going to rain again, tonight.'

Something gave way in the old mother's shoulders and she let out a soft laugh. 'Well, isn't that something, eh Denny? There's good souls out in the world, aren't there?'

'Does the lady got balloons, mama?'

'Sure I do,' Sarah said. 'I got all the balloons you want.'

The gig at The Kingdom was like nothing she'd ever done before. When she walked out on stage they were screaming for her, their voices joining and rolling across the theatre like a wave. Staaaaaaar giiiiiirrrrrllll! Staaaaaaarrrrrr Giiiiiiirrrrrllll! It was a name she'd picked up as she was getting more popular in some of the bigger clubs. Stargirl. Xander said it was because of the blue flecks in her eyes, but she knew different. It was because they could see who she was.

They wanted her soul, and they were drinking it in with their open mouths. She stood up in the middle of the stage for a long time, motionless, watching them as though they were the ones performing for her, seeing their manic eyes and their desperate, thirsty need for her, for what was *inside* of her. They wanted her soul, and she was going to give it to them.

And so she sang.

Xander was out of his depth, and he was loving it. Out of his depth with the girl, with the music, with the business, with the money. He barely slept four hours a night, the phone rang night and day, and he felt himself being swallowed by the machine, swept along by her success. All that stuff he learned in business school about the networking and the advertising and the hustling fell by the wayside—they'd never prepared him for this, this mad hunger for Stargirl. It was all he could do to keep them from finding out where she lived, and thank god he had, because the kind of people that were so nuts for Stargirl were also the kind of people who would all but tear her to shreds if they could get their hands on her.

He rubbed his eyes and ran a hand through his thinning hair, thinking for the hundredth time that he was going to have to hire a whole crew of people just to keep him from having a heart attack. For now, though, as he came to her peeling front gate, pondering the thought of her slender cream-skinned body and how happy she was going to be when he told her the latest Big News, he had to admit he felt pretty good.

Until he came down the overgrown walkway leading to her front door and heard the music coming from inside her shaded house. Not that music was anything unusual—but this was something else, some awful new instrument or song that put his nerves on edge and dread in his heart. He pushed open the front door—it was never locked—and braced himself for whatever fresh madness she was concocting.

The music was not coming, as Xander had expected, from an instrument at all, but from top-of-the-line speakers that Sarah had arranged around the main room. For all his years in the music business, listening to the mixtapes of a million aspiring musicians, Xander had never heard anything so raw and unpleasant as this. He couldn't discern a single instrument in the strange, jarring melody. There were no lyrics, nor chorus, nor harmony—but there was a kind of pattern to it, a trance inducing fractal made of notes. Xander didn't just dislike it—he hated it with emotional force. It affronted every possible musical taste; it could appeal to nobody.

Sarah was in nothing but a black bra and leggings, her back to him and a half full bottle of Jack in one hand, dancing.

Xander couldn't help but stare. She was somehow—impossibly—moving in time with the music. Slow now, then faster, arms and legs twisting and waving like snakes, hips sliding, head thrown back as she took another swig, lost in the madness. She simultaneously attracted and repelled him, and at last he couldn't take it any more and he stepped over to the stereo and pulled the plug out at the wall.

As soon as the music stopped she spun around, eyes wild, a light film of sweat on her forehead. 'Oh! Hey.'

'What *was* that?'

'My backing track for the big song,' she said, catching her breath. Her starry eyes were bright, but his heart was sinking. *No one's gonna hear that*, he thought. *No one would* want *to hear that*.

'I've written the lyrics and everything. I'm going to blow them away, Xander.'

'Uh huh,' he said slowly, resisting the urge to roll his eyes. 'You'd better save it for after . . . you . . . play . . . the . . . Olympia!' He stepped closer to her with each word, and just before he said *Olympia* he put his hands on her shoulders and flashed a smile. He was expecting *something*, a raised eyebrow or a disbelieving gasp or a kiss, even. But the name of the Theatre hardly seemed to register. She stared at him—with surprising clarity given the amount of liquor she'd just consumed.

Silence.

'Hello? Did you hear what I said?' Still smiling.

'I'm playing my song, Xander.'

He took a deep breath. 'Sarah. Once we get it all polished up and edited and all that, sure. But the Olympia is at the end of the month and the fans want to see Stargirl, not . . .' *Whatever the fuck that was just now*. His inner voice finished for him. Even though he'd only heard twenty or so seconds of the strange music, it seemed to echo in the room, infusing the very air with menace. He wanted to shake her. *No one wants to feel like that, don't you understand? No one wants to hear music that makes them want to fucking kill themselves!*

But the fact that the words did not leave his mouth made no difference: Sarah heard them all the same. She heard them in subtitles in his tone, the way she could always tell when people were lying, or fake, or sad.

'That music is my soul, Xander,' she said, and he heard real emotion in her voice then, real hurt. 'Don't you understand that?

I just want them to hear my *soul*.'

His mind was racing, torn between the desire to keep her happy and the sure and certain knowledge that if he agreed both of their careers were going to take a nose-dive straight into the asphalt. *It's for her own good.* 'Sorry, I can't let you do that,' he said.

She stepped away from him, a wall dropping down in front of those exquisite eyes, shutting him out forever. He felt it like a physical thing, a blade of ice piercing his heart even before her next words left her lips.

'Goodbye, Xander.'

'Are you . . . are you firing me?'

'No,' she said. 'I'm breaking up with you.

JAZZ CITY MAGAZINE

October 25th 2018

Ella Shwartz

Rising force of nature Sarah Wilson, known to her adoring fans as 'Stargirl' makes her debut at The Olympia this weekend, and tickets are selling like ice creams in the Sahara. Any other musician would be in their element, making the most of their newfound fame, but as Stargirl has shown us time and again, she is not like any other musician.

For one thing, no one really knows what she looks like. We have a version of her, a dark beauty on stage who can bring tears to your eyes with lyrics (all her own) or voice equally. She is, in a word— haunting, and her life outside the limelight is certainly ghostlike. She vanishes after shows, refuses interviews, and even her most dedicated fans (and there are many) know only the most on-the-surface details about her, and much of that is speculation.

Perhaps she is merely acting the part of the enigmatic artist? I, for one, doubt it. Her lyrics speak honestly of deep pain, grief, and heartbreak and ring with truth that can only be gained by experience. Her skill with the various instruments she uses to accompany her singing is unparalleled by any other working artist. During her last show at The Kingdom Theatre, I personally witnessed her perform with a guitar, a violin, a cello and a saxophone on four separate songs, and in each case she could have qualified as a virtuoso.

The only valid criticism of Stargirl would concern the fans she seems to attract. Perhaps it is the inherently bleak subject matter of her songs, or perhaps the deep melancholy her music inspires. Whatever the reason, each successive concert has stretched the growing numbers of security personnel to their limits. Fights, vandalism, drugs, alcohol, tattoos, motorbikes, knives, long painted nails, piercings in every conceivable body part, and all around recklessness: if these things are to your liking, you will fit in very well at a typical Stargirl concert.

If not, no worries: hang back and enjoy the show: I guarantee you'll see something special. Mark my words—Stargirl is no less than a legend in the making, this generation's answer to Jim Morrison, and I would bet my life she won't disappoint at the Olympia this weekend. See you there!

He stopped by the bottle store she used to work at. Her boss, Greg whoever, didn't recognize him, and didn't comment on his purchase of a half-litre of Polish spirits, the strongest stuff they had. Perhaps he thought Xander was going to use it as a disinfectant.

In a way, he thought as he slid into the front seat of his car and took a tentative sip, he was. It was just that the wound he wanted to disinfect was in his heart. He kicked the car into gear and pulled onto the highway. He had nowhere in particular to go; just one he had no intention of getting anywhere near: The Olympia.

Sometimes it was just nice to drive.

This time, though, the miles of city road started to get to him. He drove in silence, staring straight ahead, hands tight on the wheel. Normally he had something playing in the car, but there was only one CD in the drive right now—a new pop rock band—and the thought of listening to their sickly sweet upbeat jams made him want to vomit.

He turned onto the Strip and accelerated, winding down the window so the salty ocean air flew in his face and kept him sober. The billboards shot by the opposite window in a fluorescent blur, each one seeming to bring another memory of Sarah bubbling to the surface. Ever unsmiling, dancing with her hands over the head, too drunk on tequila. Walking the pier late at night and seeing the stars. On stage for the first time, killing it like no one ever before and then asking him afterwards, *was I okay?*

He rolled down familiar streets, where he could cruise the back roads for as long as he wanted, without worrying or thinking too much.

Thoughts found their way into his mind, all the same.

Despite the stern voice—Jake's voice—telling him it was alright, that she'd been poison from the beginning, he couldn't let go of that empty look in her eyes at the very end, when she'd . . .

The memory triggered another: him shutting off the CD player and popping the disc out. He hadn't meant to take it away—he'd just wanted to make sure she didn't play it again, that awful nerve-torturing yowl. But just then, he realised he had—in fact he was wearing the same jacket. Sure enough, when he reached into the inside pocket, it was still there.

He tossed it onto the seat beside him. *She's ruining herself tonight*, he thought. *She'll get laughed off stage.* Every minute or so, his eyes darted to the seat. The disc was plain silver, with block letters written in permanent marker across the face:

ODE TO MISERY
DEMO

He ejected the mixtape belonging to the High Street Wranglers and put it in.

Sarah had put the finishing touches at last. For days she'd pursued those elusive notes, the missing pieces she'd needed to string everything together and make it just right, but after some trial and error, she pulled it together.

There were nineteen bodies buried in the back garden to prove it. Some had died more painfully than others, or more terrified, or more broken. But they'd all given her their precious sound, in the end, not knowing that they were giving her a piece of their soul along with their utterances. It was the most ambitious thing she'd ever done, the most impossible—and yet, she'd *done* it. Every note in the right place; the melody tight, the pacing on point, the tone . . . sublime.

It was the greatest thing, she thought, that she would ever do.

After a couple of swigs, he stopped coughing. A couple more and his throat was numb. Another, and his heart and mind were numb, too. He drove faster and put the music up. It was a beautiful thing, this car—he'd bought it after her first really big gig. He remembered the way she'd looked at him after he'd given her the news: her eyes seemed so deep to him, then. So full of meaning and feeling.

He took another long slug—almost finished now—and despite his nerveless tongue he detected a certain bitterness. Everything tasted bitter, now.

The music played in a loop. This version was unfinished, of course, and only three minutes long. Every time the loop came to an end he urged himself to slam the eject and throw the thing out the window. He was grinding his teeth like a crack addict, knuckles white on the wheel. But then the track would start again and he'd hear a strange kind of *whoop!* Like someone surprised, but not in a good way—the kind of surprised you might get if someone curled a knife around your throat from behind—and that was the hook; every note that followed was like someone working under his fingernails with a screwdriver. Like scratching his retinas out, making him see black: death and despair in a dark cocktail.

At the end of the Strip, he skidded the car around a tight corner, ran a red light, and headed for the city limits.

Sarah always zoned out in the dressing room. The stylists were chatty, so she let them monologue about celebrities and *oh my god have you seen that show it's amazing and . . .* and she would glaze over and think of the music.

Another band was out there opening for her, and she could hear the heavy thump of drums and a good bass player making the building vibrate rhythmically. The crowd was loving it, the cheers and shouts of fifty thousand people rocking the building. But Sarah was late, as usual, and it wasn't long before the chaotic ruckus solidified into a steady chant. *Starrrrrrr Giiiiiiiiiiiiiirl! Starrrrrrrr Giiiiiiiiiiiiiirl!*

At last her makeup was done and the stylist, a twenty something with pigtails and a brilliant smile, stood back and made a ta-da motion. 'All ready, Stargirl! Go get 'em, baby, I believe in you!'

Sarah poured herself a fresh scotch on the rocks and the lit a cigarette. She took a drag and faced her reflection. The thing in the mirror wasn't really her. A made-up queen, a superstar, a smoky-eyed crooner. It wasn't the real Stargirl.

'That's okay. They'll all see Stargirl, soon enough,' she said.

'Huh? Better get moving, girl! They're calling for you!'

Starrrrrrr giiiiiiiiiiiiiirl! Starrrrrrrr giiiiiiiiiiiiiirl!

Sarah stood up, glass in one hand and cigarette in the other, and spread her arms. 'How do I look?'

The pretty pigtail girl clapped her hands. 'You look like a

Star, baby!'

'Thanks.' And she pushed the other girl backward, the comical shock registering on her face as she half landed on the dressing table, cracking the mirror behind her.

Tina, the other publicist, let out a tiny scream and put both hands up to her mouth, but by then Sarah was already heading through the doubled doors for Stage Left.

Xander didn't look back: he just kicked into high gear and drove, and thumbed the dial on his radio all the way up to ten. Why, he'd push it to eleven if he could—he'd push it all the way to hell!

That was where he was going, after all. He knew that, now. It wasn't that he was heading away from the city—no, it wasn't that at all. He was heading where the music told him to go. And it had a lot to say, once you really listened. That was what he found, driving for an hour and then two, and three.

It hurt—there was no mistake about that. The chords and half-screamed moans twanged around in his head like steel wool on a burn . . . but it was a good kind of pain, and it spoke to him of the future, a future full of blood and rage, and Xander was all too happy to listen.

It was Xander's future, and as the road thundered under his wheels and the air blew in through the open window, hot summer air, he found he couldn't wait to get there.

As she stepped out, the crowds chanting erupted into an ocean of screams and applause, thousands surging toward the line of security at the front. A forest of arms reached out for her, many of them holding bright phones with the camera lights on. Sarah wondered what the sound quality was like on those. Never mind, the show would be broadcast through the best media available all over the country.

She didn't so much as glance at the roaring crowd as she

walked on stage, just headed over to the stool near the front. It wasn't meant for sitting, but for holding her glass. She took a long swallow and they loved that, too, hundreds lifting their own drinks in toast.

Stargirl didn't care for any of it. There was no *How is everybody doing today?* Or *Hey, what a crowd, you look great.* There was no *Thank you for coming out!* There were only the three even steps to front and centre, the raising of the microphone to her lips, and the short intake of breath. This was enough to make the whole theatre silent.

In that brief instant before she began to sing, someone in the Tech room flipped a switch, kicking off the first notes of backing music.

Sarah saw the expressions change on a ten thousand faces all at once, saw the humanity vanish from their eyes in an instant, and she knew this would be a night to remember.

AUTHOR'S STORY NOTE

The seed for this story came from the work of one of my favourite horror writers: John Adjvide Lindqvist. For the life of me I can't recall the title of the short story I read, but it involved a scene in which a man uses a child's screams to make music. [*Little Star: A Novel*) Now and then I come across a concept that takes root in my mind and refuses to leave it until I write it, like some kind of parasitic muse. I'd been wanting to write dark noir story with a singer/musician in it for a while, too. There was a Lana Del Rey song I kept listening to called 'Heroin', which gave me the image of the disconnected psychopath that became Stargirl. It all seemed to fit together pretty nicely, and I'm happy to say the parasite has left my mind for the page. It was also, for what it's worth, a lot of fun to write.

QUEER
WEATHER

SCÁTH BEORH

From *Queer Weather: A Poetic Tablua Rasa*
Barnes & Noble Press

Strange outposts.

Voices undulating.

Lamps like suns against
the darkness of God.

Silent rush of wings.

Prey down and dreaming
no more.

Forgiveness in sweet tones.

Inner hallelujahs, knowing the Bible-worshipers
and the idol-kneelers both hate the free soul intwined
with Christ.

Whispers amongst true Believers.

There is a God—
a God of war
and love.

I was the one who inspired you
to sacrifice your children
to Moloch.

So that you would be horrified,
and turn back to my love.

The enemy seethes and creeps,
long grasses, yellow eyes, breathing acrid,
burns nostrils, burns brain and heart and soul

like hellfire they have but heard about,
yet one day know like nauseated lovers
burning with horrid perversion,
spines broken, pulled from their backs,
trailing behind like reptile tails.

Thus the unworthy, the God-haters,
shall live eternally, gnawing,
squeezing their hands now twisted twigs,
old trees ready for the fire.

More voices, dulcet song, music on the night air—
strings, winds, tap-tap; tap-tip-tap—duerrr!
People whispered
that God
lived
in the old house.

Sometimes we believed that
when we heard it
after we read a few scriptures,
got our souls realigned
for another day.

Others screamed
that God placed in their hearts
to kill their own children,
sacrifice them all to gods
of their own design.

At first we were scared to hear that,
but then the people said
God did it to horrify us all
so we would turn back to him,
away from Gehenna

away from the cries
the anguished cries
of mother and burning child
weep mother for your burning child!

That we would turn from the words we idolize
and seek God in those selfsame words—

that we would turn and run from this biblical haze
and use the Sword to cut our own hearts out—

use the Word to chop chop chop chop—

We know you fear us
We know you hate the us in you,
the light-bearers you see that blind you,
our salt rubbed into your wounds—
we, another race among you

aliens among you

the true aliens

you speak of us
sometimes in your dreams

drawn to us
like moths to candle blossoms

but then, when you run,
when you vie against the Holy One
your blood licked up by the hounds
your head, hands, and feet
run from because of your nasty meat—
all that was left of you

after soul died,

queer weather
coming

after your pride overtook you and cried
a fleeting cry of victory
in the Valley of Hinnom.

This looks like mud;
like my sad mouth before the Flood

I drink your Blood
I drink your Life
You said I should
You laid my food

O God!

You stayed the rude,
  halted the horde
polished my wet red shiny sword

I eat your Flesh
in quiet now, and Gilgamesh
stands at my side . . .

I put my fingers out in pride
and touch your Wounds.

man said not true,
but came the Hounds
of Death for him

just like for each savant . . . came grim

and licked his blood like Jezebel

I drink your Blood
I am your special Hound of Hell

I eat your Heart
  your Sacred Burning Heart for me

I eat and drink
I drink and eat your bloodied Tree

I kiss your Feet and majesty—

Tetragrammaton has won
over all other sigils now
and Symeon shall say a sign
before Day of the Lord;
'fore ADONAI and Hittite line
and coming horde.

More flight downward
to mice, men

more voices of our kith and kin

we, the rebel race so loved

by hungry childlike souls
by goodly childlike souls

Too disturbing!
What are all these disjointed words?
Horror. You speak horror. Why?

Indoctrination calls forth the dark prophet

to slay the soothsayers
on the mountain before God

—God Almighty.

That is why we remain
after we drown to death
in Blood and Water—

we remain for you

light-bringers

salt cellars
not cast out and trampled by men

Race of Light.

You are also called in.

Come home.

Within.

swiftly run

for what could be more glorious
than creating for God,
in God,
his signet ring upon your hand
your imagination wild
free, so free!
Outlanders have come,
cloaked in shadows, billows,
scythes in hand like Azrael,

and like Azrael they come
to bring the word of death

run, run!

embrace these misty monsters now
they are your brothers, sisters
bringers of the Light

There comes a time soon
when the Spirit of God
will remove Itself from the land
and the voice of the Lord
will no longer be heard,
  felt,
    seen

and the liars shall stand agape,
silent, hearts liquid and burning
like an oil spill aflame

then shall come the fire

no heavens

no more Earth

you look for a God too small,
as small as you

this is the reason
you fail to find him

O Lord, let nothing remain

Under a bed there runs a flood:

(The bells of Paradise,
I heard them ring)

one half runs Water,
the other runs Blood:

And I love my Lord Jesus above anything.

and I love my Lord Jesus
above anything

AUTHOR BIOS

SCÁTH BEORH writes stories permeated with themes of violence, brutality, anguish, punishment, magical realism, and blurred lines between this and the afterlife. Sometimes veiled and at times more overt sarcasm about Christian values and moral inconsistencies underline an ingenious design behind the entertaining tales.

DUANE BRADLEY is the author of the novellas *Sick In The Head* and *Second Coming* (published by Comet Press) as well as the non-fiction collections *Midnight Spookshow* and *Schlock Theater*. His short fiction and articles have appeared in *Red Room Magazine* and *Unnerving* as well as the anthologies *Dig Two Graves* and *What Monsters Do For Love*.

MATTHEW V. BROCKMEYER lives deep in the forest in Northern California with his wife and two children. He is the author of the critically-acclaimed novel *Kind Nepenthe* and the short-story collection *Under Rotting Sky*. When not writing he enjoys howling at the moon and bathing his fangs in human blood.

SYON DAS is 23 years old and lives in Queens, New York. He loves writing about himself in the 3rd person like a self-absorbed psychopath. His other hobbies include watching horror movies, listening to true crime podcasts, playing heavy metal, fusion, and classical guitar, reading novels, listing things, and surfing through HBO documentaries. When he's not thinking of twisted shit to write about, Syon loves working on poetry and songwriting. You can contact him at syondas1996@gmail.com with business inquiries or any comments regarding his work.

MICHAEL PAUL GONZALEZ is the author of the novels *Angel Falls* and *Miss Massacre's Guide To Murder And Vengeance* and the creator and producer of the serial horror audio drama *Larkspur Underground*, available for free on iTunes and all major podcast directories. His short stories have appeared in print and online, including *HeavyMetal. com*, *Lost Signals*, *Gothic Fantasy: Chilling Horror Stories*, *Seven Scribes*, *Great Jones Street*, *the Booked. Podcast Anthology*, and *Where Nightmares Come From: The Art of Storytelling in the Horror Genre*. He resides in Los Angeles, a place full of wonders and monsters far stranger than any that live in the imagination. You can visit him online at Michael-PaulGonzalez.com

SEAN PATRICK HAZLETT is an Army veteran, speculative fiction writer and editor, and finance executive living in the San Francisco Bay area, where he considers writing fiction as therapy that pays for itself. Over forty of his short stories have appeared in publications such as *The Year's Best Military and Adventure SF*, *Year's Best Hardcore Horror*, *Terraform*, *Galaxy's Edge*, *Writers of the Future*, *Grimdark Magazine*, *Vastarien*, and *Abyss & Apex*, among others. He is an active member of the Horror Writers Association and Codex Writers' Group. His first anthology as an editor, *Weird World War III*, is expected to be released by Baen in the fall of 2020.

ALICIA HILTON is an author, law professor, actress, and former FBI Special Agent. She received her BA in Sociology from the University of California, Berkeley, and her JD and MA from the University of Chicago. Her recent work has appeared or is forthcoming in *Akashic Books*, *Bronzeville Books*, *ChiZine Publications*, *Daily Science Fiction*, *Demain Publishing UK*, *Dreams & Nightmares*, *Vastarien*, *Year's Best Hardcore Horror 4*, and elsewhere. Her website is http://www.aliciahilton.com Follow her on Twitter @aliciahilton01.

GWENDOLYN KISTE is the Bram Stoker Award-winning author of *The Rust Maidens*, from Trepidatio Publishing; *And Her Smile Will Untether the Universe*, from JournalStone; and the dark fantasy novella, *Pretty Marys All in a Row*, from Broken Eye Books. Her short fiction has appeared in Nightmare Magazine, Black Static, Daily Science Fiction,

Shimmer, Interzone, and LampLight, among others. Originally from Ohio, she now resides on an abandoned horse farm outside of Pittsburgh with her husband, two cats, and not nearly enough ghosts. Find her online at gwendolynkiste.com

JOANNA KOCH writes literary horror and surrealist trash. Author of the novella *The Couvade*, their work has been published in journals and anthologies including *Synth*, *The Big Book of Blasphemy*, and *In Darkness Delight: Masters of Midnight*. Follow Joanna at horrorsong. blog and on Twitter @horrorsong.

ALESSANDRO MANZETTI is a Bram Stoker Award-winning (and 7-time nominee) author of horror fiction and dark poetry. Furthermore, he has been nominated two times for the Splatterpunk Awards and many other literary awards. Among his English publications: the novels *Shanti* (2019), *Naraka* (2018), the novella *The Keeper of Chernobyl* (2019) and the story collections *The Radioactive Bride* (2020) and *The Garden of Delight* (2017). He lives in Trieste, Italy. Website: www.battiago.com

RAJIV MOTE is a writer living in Chicago with his wife, daughter, and puppy. His stories make appearances in *Cast of Wonders*, *Diabolical Plots*, *Factor Four*, *Metaphorosis*, *McSweeney's Internet Tendency*, *Truancy*, and others, and he has served as a slush-reading Badger for Shimmer. During the day, he gathers source material by masquerading as a software engineering manager. He scrapes off excess words on Twitter at @RajivMote, and occasionally realizes he should put some effort into rajivmote.co

ANNIE NEUGEBAUER is a two-time Bram Stoker Award-nominated author with work appearing in more than a hundred publications, such as *Cemetery Dance*, *Apex*, *Black Static,* and *Year's Best Hardcore Horror* Volumes 3 and 4. She's a columnist for Writer Unboxed and LitReactor. You can visit her at www.AnnieNeugebauer.com.

BEN PIENAAR was born in South Africa and moved to Melbourne, Australia in 1999. He works in a coffee shop to finance and enable his crippling caffeine addiction, and spends his free time surfing, reading, and training Jiu Jitsu. He has published stories in several anthologies and magazines, and his unpublished work can be found on www.freenightmares.wordpress.com and he's currently working on a horror novel.

HAILEY PIPER is the author of novellas *Benny Rose, the Cannibal King* and *The Possession of Natalie Glasgow*. She is an active member of the HWA, and has contributed short fiction to *Daily Science Fiction*, *The Arcanist*, *Tales to Terrify*, and more. Her debut novel, *The Verses of Aeg*, will be published by Bronzeville Books in late 2020. Find her at www. haileypiper.com or on Twitter via @HaileyPiperSays.

LEO X. ROBERTSON is a Scottish process engineer, writer and film-maker, currently living in Stavanger, Norway. He has work published in *FlameTree Publishing's Urban Crime* anthology, *Pulp Literature* and *Unnerving Magazine*, among others. Find him on Twitter @Leoxwrite or check out his website for more details: leoxrobertson.wordpress.com

DEBORAH SHELDON "I'm an award-winning author from Melbourne, Australia. I write short stories, novellas and novels across the darker spectrum. My titles include the horror novels *Body Farm Z*, *Contrition*, and *Devil Dragon*; the horror novella *Thylacines*; and the collections *Figments and Fragments: Dark Stories*, and the award-winning *Perfect Little Stitches and Other Stories* (Australian Shadows "Best Collected Work 2017"). My short fiction has appeared in *Quadrant*, *Island*, *Aurealis*, *Midnight Echo* and many other well-respected magazines. I'm also the guest editor of this year's edition of *Midnight Echo*. My fiction has been shortlisted for numerous Australian Shadows Awards and Aurealis Awards, long-listed for a Bram Stoker Award, and included in various "best of" anthologies. Other credits include TV scripts, feature articles, non-fiction books, stage plays, and award-winning medical writing."

D.A. XIAOLIN SPIRES steps into portals and reappears in sites such as Hawai'i, NY, various parts of Asia and elsewhere, with her keyboard appendage attached. Her work appears or is forthcoming in publications such as *Clarkesworld*, *Analog*, *Nature*, *Terraform*, *Grievous Angel*, *Fireside*, *Galaxy's Edge*, *StarShipSofa*, *Andromeda Spaceways (Year's*

Best Issue), *Diabolical Plots, Factor Four, Pantheon, Outlook Springs, Robot Dinosaurs, Mithila Review, Lontar, Reckoning, Issues in Earth Science, Liminality, Star*Line, Polu Texni, Argot, Eye to the Telescope, Liquid Imagination, Gathering Storm Magazine, Little Blue Marble, Story Seed Vault,* and anthologies of the strange and beautiful: *Ride the Star Wind, Sharp and Sugar Tooth, Future Visions, Deep Signal, Battling in All Her Finery,* and *Broad Knowledge.* She can be found on Twitter @spireswriter and on her website at daxiaolinspires.wordpress.com.

DAVID L. TAMARIN is an extreme and bizarre horror writer and screenwriter whose debut novel *Hurting My Toys* was published by Red Room Press. His subversive stories may be hazardous to your mental health. His story is an homage to legendary writer William S Burroughs, author of transgressive and extreme fiction that has shocked multiple generations of writers, film-makers and other artists.

KRISTOPHER TRIANA is the Splatterpunk Award-winning author of *Full Brutal, Shepherd of the Black Sheep, Body Art, The Ruin Season, Toxic Love* and more. His fiction has appeared in countless magazines and anthologies and has been translated into multiple languages, drawing praise from Publisher's Weekly, Cemetery Dance, Rue Morgue Magazine, Scream Magazine, The Ginger Nuts of Horror and others.

TIM WAGGONER has published nearly fifty novels and seven collections of short stories. He writes original dark fantasy and horror, as well as media tie-ins, and his articles on writing have appeared in numerous publications. He's won the Bram Stoker Award, the HWA's Mentor of the Year Award, been a multiple finalist for the Shirley Jackson Award and the Scribe Award, his fiction has received numerous Honorable Mentions in volumes of *Best Horror of the Year,* and he's had several stories selected for inclusion in volumes of *Year's Best Hardcore Horror.* He's also a full-time tenured professor who teaches creative writing and composition at Sinclair College in Dayton, Ohio.

ACKNOWLEDGEMENTS

"Feast for Small Pieces" © Hailey Piper, from *The Bronzeville Bee* (June 2019), Editor: Sandra Ruttan

"Goddess of Gallows" © Kristopher Triana, from *The Big Book of Blasphemy*, Publisher: Necro Publications (November 2019), Editors: Regina Garza Mitchell & David G. Barnett

"Late Night Incident At The White Trash Motel" © Duane Bradley, from *Deep Fried Horror,* Publisher: Deadman's Tome (August 2019), Editor: Becky Narron

"A New Mother's Guide To Raising An Abomination" © Gwendolyn Kiste, from *The New Flesh: A Literary Tribute to David Cronenberg,* Publisher: Weirdpunk Books (November 2019), Editors: Sam Richard & Brendan Vidito

"Upper Crust" © Michael Paul Gonzalez, from *Tales From The Crust*, Publisher: Perpetual Motion Publishing (August 2019), Editors: David James Keaton & Max Booth III

"Redless" © Annie Neugebauer, from *The Binge-Watching Cure II: An Anthology of Horror Stories,* Publisher: Claren Books (December 2019), Editors: Bill Adler & Sarah Doebereiner

"A Touch of Madness" © Tim Waggoner, from *The Pulp Horror Book of Phobias,* Publisher: Lycan Valley Press (November 2019), Editor: MJ Sydney

"Paradisum Voluptatis" © Joanna Koch, from *Honey & Sulphur,* Publisher: Carrion Blue 555 (November 2019), Editor: Joseph Bouthiette Jr.

"Radix Malorum" © Sean Patrick Hazlett, from *Vastarien,* Volume 2, Issue 3, Publisher: Grimscribe Press (December 2019), Editors: Jon Padgett & Matt Cardin

"Lackers" © Leo X. Robertson, from *The New Flesh: A Literary Tribute to David Cronenberg,* Publisher: Weirdpunk Books (November 2019), Editors: Sam Richard & Brendan Vidito